Earthbound Creatures

Jennifer Olmstead

VOLUME III
THE VIRGINIA SOUTHERN POINT COLLECTION

ABOUT JENNIFER OLMSTEAD

Jennifer Olmstead is the creator and author of THE VIRGINIA SOUTHERN POINT COLLECTION, featuring contemporary stories as unique as their setting in the beautiful southernmost region of Virginia, where the pastoral farms of Back Bay meet the beaches of the Atlantic Ocean. MEN AMONG SIRENS and THE STRAY are Volumes I and II in the collection.

WWW.JENNIFEROLMSTEAD.NET
FACEBOOK: JENNIFER OLMSTEAD, AUTHOR
Twitter: @jolmsteadwrites
Instagram: jenniferolmsteadauthor

Copyright © 2019 by Jennifer Olmstead and Titian Press
All rights reserved worldwide.

This is a work of fiction. Names, characters, businesses, places, events, locales, and incidents are either the products of the author's imagination or used in a fictitious manner. Any resemblance to actual persons, living or dead, or actual events is purely coincidental.

ISBN: 9781727389869

ACKNOWLEDGMENTS

Many thanks to my family: David, Patrick, and Mary Ann (who always liked this story the best); my readers: Susie, Sharon, Carrie, Robyn, and Dr. Michael Hall; Kaitlin Severini, for your editing skills and so much more; R.P., for the lifelong inspiration; Patty; Dr. Cummings, my freshman English professor at Chatham College, and Elaine Spencer of The Knight Agency, who inspired me to think before I write.

For Mary Ann

PROLOGUE

September 9, 1981. Three in the afternoon and a gulping-thick, ninety-four-degree incarnation of a Thursday. No chance for rain, shade, or any other environmental reprieve until well after sundown.

A Southern Point school bus, its yellow paint granulating and flaking in revolt against the brackish assault it cut through every day, hissed to a stop, depositing two middle-schoolers at the edge of Goose Pond Road. After the bus had swung around the bend—all the way around the bend—KM's Algebra I workbook skated down the center aisle and skidded to a dead stop next to the bus driver's door lever. By then, its rightful owner, Kerry McCullough, had sprinted from her side of the gravel lane that separated Jimmy Whistler's sprawling farm from her family's 25-acre homestead and caught his stride.

"You get hot in that shirt?" she asked. They walked side by side. "I surely would."

"Nah, it's okay," he answered, trying his best to sound nonchalant as his neck and forehead slicked up with a salty mix primed for a crawling descent onto his cheeks. His striped shirt was darker in several spots where a full sweat had already broken out, and the pale skin on his neck was beginning to flush from the trapped heat.

"Maybe—um—are you just cold all the time?" Kerry's slender arms flowed out of her sleeveless white blouse, toned and tight like a dancer's. She was strong for a girl of twelve, accustomed to helping her grandmother in the family garden and with daily housekeeping, since her own mother had died years before. Long legs, flawless and perfectly proportioned, separated her blue skirt and white sneakers. A straight ponytail sat at the nape of her neck. Each morning, Grandma Sally ironed Kerry's dark hair before fastening it at the nape of her neck with a small bow, reasoning that if she looked a little more like the white children at school, they might accept her better, if only in the smallest of ways. There were mornings that the hot iron burned a spot of skin on Kerry's neck. "Sorry, honey, but I do this for your own good," Grandma Sally explained. "I'm hopin' it'll help make things a little more . . . fair for you."

Jimmy's chestnut hair was now saturated, stuck to the contours of his face. He fumbled with his shirt sleeves a little, trying to cool his arms. The button on his left sleeve popped off, exposing his forearm.

Kerry stopped in her tracks. "Let me see that!"

Jimmy jerked down the shirt sleeve. "No!"

"Come on!" She folded one arm over her chest and played with her short ponytail, waiting for him to give in. He always gave in when she did that.

He hiked his left sleeve back up to the elbow.

"Eeeew." She curled her upper lip, then caught herself and remembered her manners. "I—sorry—I mean—what is that, Jimmy?"

"Just a cut." He tried to pull down his sleeve again, but she grabbed his arm, staring at the blistered wound, a dark red bullseye crowning translucent white skin.

She frowned. "That doesn't look like any kind of cut to me. Are you sick?" Her brown eyes held his, stubborn and unblinking. "Jimmy, what's wrong with you? Do you have chicken pox or somethin'?"

"No!" he said as indignantly as a fourteen-year-old could.

"Come on, Jimmy. Where'd you get that?"

They stared at each other for what seemed like forever. She won the contest.

"My . . . dad," Jimmy mumbled, looking at the ground.

She was bewildered. "Your dad? What do you mean? Did he give you something—is he sick too?"

Shame passed over his face. "No. It's—well—when I do something stupid, he—he—punishes me."

"But how'd you get that kinda mark?" she asked.

"Cigarettes."

"You mean a lit one?" She tried to make sense of what he'd said. She had known no significant punishment in her short life save a harsh word or two, or an hour's restriction to her bedroom, and those meager sentences were reserved for the rare instances in which she talked back to her grandmother or was lazy with her chores. Her small family was a solid, loving unit. She stared at the ground, calculating the sum of the last three exchanges. "Wait, now. Your dad—he *burned* you?"

"Yeah, but I reckon I deserved it," Jimmy replied.

"How come? What did you do that was so bad to get burned like that?"

"We get on his nerves—me and my mom. I'm worse than she is though." He spoke the words as if he believed they were true.

Kerry reexamined his scabbed arm. "I don't think that's right, Jimmy. I mean, on some days, my grandma burns my hair—in the back—by mistake. But she doesn't mean to—and she's real sorry! I know she is. She hugs me. And, my daddy says nobody should hurt anybody else unless the other person's tryin' to hurt you or your family. He says that's why the war back then was wrong."

"What do you mean 'wrong'?"

"Daddy says we shouldn't have ever been over in Vee-et-nam, killing all of those people. He said some papers about the president prove it was wrong to make my daddy be in the war, too. He heard all about it in a book when he was up north in Washington—on a hauling job."

"Well, I don't care what y'all think. I hope they start a new war—an even worse one—'cause I'm gonna run away from here and fight in it, soon as I can."

"No! You shouldn't go fight!" She stomped the ground with one foot. "And your daddy shouldn't be doin' that to you! Oh, anyhow, my grandma's got special cream that'll work for that cut. She makes it herself. I'll be sure and bring it with me tomorrow."

They reached the split in the road: a dirt lane taking Kerry home to her doting grandmother and overprotective father; a gravel road to Jimmy's house leading in another, darker direction.

He stopped and turned back to Kerry. "Kerry, promise ya won't tell, please," he pleaded, his eyes searching hers for reassurance. "Promise—or I'll get in worse trouble with my dad. *Please.*"

Kerry put one hand over her heart. "I won't tell anyone, no matter what they do to me. Not ever." She kept her promise.

∽

CHAPTER ONE

Hazel eyes, more gold than green, burned a reflected glance back at Rory Fielding from the rearview mirror of her black 2016 pickup as she cruised at a fast clip along Southern Point, Virginia's lone main road. Too fast. It was early December, but unseasonable temperatures and the intense southern Virginia sun made the cab's dark interior stifling. Rory almost nodded off—until a sharp turn in the road brought her within yards of a head-on collision with a 25 MPH speed limit sign. She cranked the steering wheel hard left, ducking both the sign and a short skate across the road's slim gravel shoulder, which would have led to an even shorter nosedive into a yawning drainage ditch, bubbling with runoff from the last night's rain. Her violent steering maneuver jostled a thick stack of collapsed cardboard moving boxes—boxes that had been riding quietly in the truck's bed for the past hour—out of their twine tethers.

The box flaps began a loud, frenetic dance against opposing sides of the slick bed, threatening to take flight and scatter across the road. A large digital camera, Rory's constant companion, flew off the front passenger seat and slammed against the glove box before bouncing onto the floor.

"Damn it!" she cried, jamming down the brake pedal until the truck slowed to a crawl and the boxes settled back inside the bed. She strained to reach for the camera and scrutinized its latest damage before returning it to its open case on the seat. Accelerating again, to just below the speed limit this time, she counted each mile that hummed underneath the truck's tires, ticking each of them off like a small weight shed from her shoulders and cast off through the truck's windows, all four of which were now wide open.

Amber tendrils, caught up in the wind, competed with every feature of her face, except for what she had spent four decades convincing herself was an overly generous lower lip, slicked over with a glaring shade of red lipstick that a Macy's saleswoman had insisted was a spring gotta-have. It had been a bad day when the woman—who couldn't have been more than twenty years old—stalked and then pounced on Rory in the store's cosmetic department. To Rory, the lipstick sounded frivolous enough to evoke a positive change, yet despite a generous application of *Crimson Gala Rouge*, no such transformation occurred. She scrubbed the lipstick from her lips with a fraying gray linen handkerchief that she'd dug out of the center console, tugged off her suit jacket, and turned up the volume on Finis Tasby asking for a kiss once in a while. Like most days, Rory was leaving behind meetings, pollution, and a grinding twelve-hour stretch in Norfolk to head home to rural Southern Point. Today was different, though. The start of a new life, pitching out the past and its collection of disappointments for an uncharted mix of equal parts fresh possibility and potential catastrophe. That trade—those blind prospects—sent a rush of excitement through her. Excitement tempered only by a more familiar emotion. Fear.

CHAPTER TWO

"Where are you?" Rory's voice rose above a pyramid of moving boxes and echoed through the empty rooms of her old farmhouse. The elusive phone rang again, its synthesized horse whinny too faint for her to track to its precise location. Who was calling, however, was clear from the phone's virtual assistant: "Tom is calling. Tom is calling." She strained her ears and hoped for one more ring to serve as a homing device. If she missed this call, a dozen more would follow—rapid fire—until she picked up. *The hall table*, she guessed, leaping over a box to retrieve the phone before the call went to voicemail.

A deep breath in. "Hey there, Tom."

"Rory, have you actually reasoned this thing out?" Tom Fielding pressed, dodging niceties in exchange for a straight shot to his agenda. "Are you serious about throwing away your money on this silly gamble? How do you see your non-master plan reaching fruition?"

She clenched her jaw hard before answering him, knowing her response would abruptly end what had been a peaceful, if somewhat somber, morning. "What do you mean by 'silly,' Tom?"

"First, you throw away twenty-five grand on that overpriced nag of yours. Now you want to turn him into a business? Seriously, is that a good example to set for Ian?"

Her frustration melded with hurt. And he knew just how to hurt her. "Nice one, Tom," she said, as even voiced as she could. "We've discussed this many, many times. And you know that my grandmother specified in her will to 'use the money to fulfill one crazy dream.' Not everybody's dreams involve turning a massive profit, Tom. What's wrong with loving your work and having enough?"

"Fine. You got that 'crazy dream' of a horse on your grandmother's dime a few years ago. But let's live in the present. How long is enough going to be enough? Everyone wants more. You should have let me invest your half of our profit from the agency sale. You could have lived out the rest of your life on the interest. You're pushing forty-eight, so living conservatively, figuring another thirty, forty years—"

"Tom," she interrupted, "it's my money. I did earn it, and I've done a lot of planning—research—on this." She switched her phone to speaker mode, sorting through the desk drawers of her mirrored secretary while she talked. It had taken an hour-long struggle involving three people to move the towering desk into what was supposed to be its final resting place five years earlier. Now, here she was, readying the fragile antique for another precarious journey. The phone slipped from the secretary and dropped to the floor. She seriously weighed the option of stomping on the thing, but then relented and retrieved it.

"Hello? What was that?" Tom demanded. "What the hell is going on over there? I'm on speaker! Who are you with?"

"Nothing—no one. Just trying to make some progress with packing my things for the movers next week. What were you saying?"

"I was saying, it's a total lifestyle change," Tom continued. "You're trading those designer pumps of yours for—for horseshit. Or, maybe for bullshit."

"Thanks for that analogy," she said, "I've actually been shoveling crap for years—here and at work. There's more to this—you know it. I'll be home based, Tom, and right now Ian needs at least one of us around more. Besides, at our age, change is good." As soon as the words passed her lips, instant regret. It was all the fuel Tom needed.

"Right," he answered back, his delivery scorching. "And you know all about that, don't you?"

With that exchange, their conversation had officially turned the corner on ugly, but she reasoned he had the right to say it. A few months earlier, after two decades of marriage, she had shocked him, their fourteen-year-old son, Ian, and even herself, by asking for a divorce.

If Rory had planned things out—which she always tried to do—she would never have picked the hottest Sunday in August to break the news to Tom. It just happened that way. Ian was at a friend's house for the weekend. She had run through every possible rationalization and trick to play on herself. Honored the final this-really-is-the-last-time bargain with her soul to forfeit her own happiness in favor of stability for Ian. Still, as often as she rehearsed the words, uttering them was the hardest thing she'd ever done. A half dozen times that afternoon, as she and Tom sat at opposite ends of their sunporch, wading through familiar silence, Rory opened her mouth to speak, but no words came out. She pretended to read *The Beautiful and the Damned*, tilting her head and then staring blankly at each page for a minute for two before turning to a new page and repeating the ruse. She had read the novel a dozen times over the years and knew the story and all of its characters by heart. Each time she reached the end and closed the cover, she came away with something she'd missed in the previous read. She wondered if Tom, a self-proclaimed non-consumer of anything that wasn't business-related, knew that about her. It seemed irrelevant now.

An hour later found the two of them still a yard away from each other on the sunporch, the space of time hanging heavy between them, heavy as the sticky, midday humidity that clung to the sunporch's walls and windows. The cloying air hit the windows and quickly softened, forming thin teardrops that ran down the glass panes. But the silence between Tom and Rory only hardened—until it grew into a stony, unbearable wall. Rory didn't know if she was beautiful, and she accepted the mantle of being damned for what she was going to do next.

"Tom," she bowed her head toward her lap, staring at the worn grain on the cover of her book. "We have to talk. You know that we have problems."

"Huh?" he answered distractedly from behind the *Wall Street Journal*. "What problems? What is it now, Rory?"

She was nauseated from anticipation. "Tom, we both know we're not happy. We haven't been."

"Happy?" he huffed. "*Happiness.* That's such a relative term."

"Tom, please, put down that paper and listen to yourself," she said, short of breath from raw nervousness. She hated confrontation and conflict and usually worked as hard as necessary to avoid it. "A relative term . . . relative to—what? Happiness is an absolute." She surprised herself by breaking into a shout. "You either are—or you are not! We are not happy!"

"What is this? What is wrong with you?" He stood and hurled the newspaper at her feet. "If you're not happy—leave!" he yelled. "Go! Get the fuck out! Just don't change your mind and try to come back. That's not part of the deal."

"Deal? Is that what our marriage is? A deal?"

Without a reply, he stomped off the sunporch. As she collapsed onto the cushioned window seat, her body shaking uncontrollably, she heard him through the porch wall, moving in the kitchen, filling a glass with ice from the refrigerator, step one of his daily gin-and-tonic mixing ritual, a little earlier than usual today. Minutes later he drove off in his Suburban. They never slept in the same bed again.

Rory kicked an empty moving box across the farmhouse's pine floor and made an angry face into her phone. "Tom, it's been months since we agreed to separate. We should be past this."

"Okay, fine. Sure. But this horse hotel idea of yours . . ."

"It's horse-boarding barn, not a horse hotel."

"Whatever you call it."

"I'll be doing something I know—that I do now—but on a larger scale," she said, pushing past his resentment. "Horse boarding is a solid business out here and the three biggest barns in Southern Point are closing within the next year. I already have six horses waiting to transfer over to my new place next September. Filling the other ten stalls should be easy as long as I get the land cleared, seeded, and fenced by spring. The rest is manual labor and some office work. And . . . I want to help out a rescue horse or two, on the side."

"Your place. Listen to you. I think you're forgetting that Mac Daddy barn," he scoffed. "Construction projects are notorious for not finishing on time, and it's almost January. And out here in Podunk central, who knows what timetable contractors operate on?"

"It's a prefab, Tom. They go up in six to eight weeks, and I've got five months. If I stay on schedule, I'll be okay." As she talked, she crouched her six-foot frame down to the desk mirror again and tried to smooth her hair into a braid. It wouldn't obey, instead producing a halo of small ringlets. She gave up.

"I don't know how someone like you expects to run a horse farm alone."

"I won't be doing it alone," she started, "I'll hire some help. I'll find my way through it—"

"Find your way?" He cut her off. "Oh, please! What'll you do when you have one of those heart things of yours? I'm not gonna be there to help you out. You're on your own now."

The heart thing. Random, terrifying episodes when Rory's heart took a crazy arrhythmic ride, lasting anywhere from a few minutes to an hour. Minutes that began with the sensation of being thumped on the back, immediately leading to breathlessness, her chest like a sponge being squeezed tight by massive, crushing hands, accompanied by the fear that this time might be the time she would lose consciousness, or her angry heart would transition from tachycardia to fibrillation, requiring hospitalization, maybe a pacemaker. Or, it could get stuck out of rhythm and just stop beating. Slam into blackness. The end. It was in those minutes that she ran through a series of embarrassing, often futile maneuvers her doctor had taught her, regardless of where she was or who was watching: pressing her fingers against her eyeballs, holding her nose and holding her breath, squatting down and coughing. And then there was the spontaneous anxiety and shaking, brought on by an overload of adrenaline coursing through her system, which was induced by a heart rate of more than two hundred beats a minute. Unpredictable episodes resulting from both known and unknown triggers, keeping her perpetually one step short of ever feeling complete relaxation.

"Is that fair?" she asked him, exhausted from their sparring. "That new medication they've got me on has made a huge difference. I've gone weeks between episodes, and the last one wasn't too bad." Although Rory's daily beta-blocker couldn't prevent the episodes from occurring, it did manage to restrict her heart rate to the mid one-hundreds when an episode struck, providing her with a small degree of comfort in knowing that her arteries wouldn't explode and her blood pressure wouldn't escalate to stroke-inducing levels. "Besides, I don't know that I equate you threatening to call 9-1-1 every time I have one with 'being there.' You know that if those episodes show up on my medical records, I could lose my driver's license."

"Just forget it. It's obvious that you've already made up your mind," Tom snapped, then fell silent for a few seconds. "I should have your first settlement check when I get back from DC next week . . . unless you need me to loan you some cash to close on the new place." The mere mention of money produced a calming effect on Tom.

"No, I don't need a loan. Thanks." She tried to steer the conversation in a positive direction. "So . . . I'll tell Ian you'll call him tonight?"

"Yeah. Tell him that for me. I'll see you. . . ." His words trailed off as he hung up the phone.

"Bye to you, too," she half-whispered, concluding another passage into the world of ex-spouses. The call was over. She sat in the silent house and let herself cry.

They met in 1998 at the Blackman Agency, a firm specializing in executive recruitment throughout Virginia and North Carolina. Tom Fielding, MBA, had left a Fortune 500 company, opting out of a career laced with high-level, down-on-your-knees groveling for performance bonuses, private air travel, and related swag, for a path to small-business ownership, and he decided joining the agency as a recruiter would provide an ideal training ground for this eventual transition. Aurora Tryon joined the firm a year earlier as its marketing director.

After sharing some after-work bitch sessions, Tom and Rory went on a picnic. Then to dinner. Then to a concert in Washington, DC. As their dates evolved into successive and longer weekends together, Ed and his partner, Katie Clark, took notice. Both Ed and Katie were old-school salespeople, who worked hard, played hard, and drank harder. Between them, they had chalked up five marriages and countless affairs. Neither objected to Tom and Rory's relationship, but one afternoon Katie warned Rory against interference with work or the firm's profits. "I don't care who you fuck, but don't fuck up." Katie pulled two mini wine bottles from her desk-side fridge and twisted off the tops. "Don't get me wrong," she squawked. "You two are cute together. Super cute. Tom and Rory—nice ring to it. Kinda makes me wanna puke—it's so cute." A few gulps of wine later she added: "There's a lot of money at stake here. Lots and lots. Either make it work with Tom—or knock it off."

Rory convinced herself she and Tom were in love. They spent most of their time together. They never argued. She felt safe with him. A yearlong engagement preceded a glitch-free, beautiful wedding, the meticulous planning of which Rory had approached as if it were a second job. Tom was thirty and she was twenty-eight on the day they formally committed themselves to facing the future together. It all made sense.

When Katie Clark was injured in a car accident four years later and left with permanent disabilities, the entire Blackman Agency was thrown into a state of shock. Ed nixed the idea of bringing on a new partner who might not share his joie de vivre and penchant for pre-lunch cocktails, opting instead to turn over the agency's reins to new owners and retire. His search for a buyer was brief. Expectant parents Tom and Rory took the well-calculated risk of buying the agency.

"I've run all the numbers and projections. It fits right into our plan," Tom decided. Rory didn't know that they had a plan, but she trusted Tom and went along with him on making the offer to Ed.

Ownership earned them gut-churning financial uncertainty, along with newfound flexibility and autonomy. Some days, Rory brought their son, Ian, to work. Others, she left early if necessary, no questions asked. As business partners, she and Tom imbued the agency with professionalism, earning heightened credibility and unprecedented profits. As parents, they worked to balance the agency's responsibilities with parenting the son they both loved. As a couple, they clicked along side by side for years. Respectful. Secure. Partners.

Moving away from the beach and into the country had been Rory's idea. Tom found no fault with their crowded, beachside town house. He had spent his childhood in a busy suburban duplex community in northern Virginia, where driveways were bigger than yards. It was what he knew. Rory was beyond tired of looking out her kitchen window directly into the living room of their neighbor, Jim, or listening to him belch with his buddies on the back patio during his frequent cookouts, which involved more keg pumping than burger flipping. Jim's infrequent sexual conquests, involving women clearly heard but rarely seen, meant one-night marathons of rhythmic headboard banging on the other side of Ian's bedroom wall.

"Mom, what's that noise?" Ian would ask Rory when the banging on his wall woke him up in the middle of the night.

"Uh, Jim must be hanging pictures again," she would reply.

"Why does he have so many pictures?"

She could no longer, in good conscience, argue against nine-year-old Ian's complaints about having no room to play soccer and having to ride his dirt bike at crowded commercial tracks, and wanted to pass down to him the freedom she had experienced growing up on a twenty-acre farm in Pennsylvania with horses, dogs, cats, and the occasional wounded wild animal she and her older sister, Madelyn, nicknamed Mad, had tried to rehabilitate.

"Hey, I think I have something for you," Rory's friend Liz announced over the phone one morning. Semi-retired after earning millions in real estate, Liz had been scouting for a rural property for months, in between wine tastings and Ladies' League golf games at her country club. Until now, everything she had found was either too far from the coast or too small. What she'd pulled from her MLS listing this time was a well-maintained, renovated farmhouse and barn on six acres on Rock Creek Road in Southern Point. "You'll be twenty minutes from the beachfront, but it's got a swimming pool—and a four-stall barn. You can keep a closer eye on that pricey horse of yours—keep him on your own property."

"What's wrong with it, Liz?" Rory asked, skeptical. "There must be something. . . ."

"Not a thing," Liz answered. "The owners live on Long Island and were planning an early retirement here, but they've decided to stay put and keep their retail business going. A broker from my agency sold it to them four years ago. It's prime. Speak now or forever hold your peace."

Ian loved the farmhouse's swimming pool and the possibility of creating his own mini motocross course on the property's back acreage. His enthusiasm and Rory's combined with miles of quiet country roads offering limitless running circuits and record low-interest rates pushed Tom off the fence about making the move. Even with their commuting time doubled, the change seemed manageable, especially when Rory found a contract bus company that provided Ian with door-to-door service to and from his private school every day. She brought her nine-year-old Appendix Quarter Horse gelding, Titian, home to live. She adopted Olga, a rescued thoroughbred show jumper whose owners wanted to sell her for dog food when she came up lame before a regional horse show. Rory also took on a boarder horse whose owner was referred to her by the manager of Titian's old boarding barn. The boarder was Mystic and her owner was Diane Davis, a divorced veterinary technician born and raised in Southern Point. Diane introduced Rory to her widowed older sister, Sandy Cross, who needed a job to make ends meet where her monthly social security income couldn't.

Sandy had a brightly patterned housekeeping smock for every day of the week, which she wore with ironed, creased blue jeans and spotless white tennis shoes, replaced regularly during trips to the local Walmart's shoe department. Unless she was called to officiate an unexpected bingo game at her church, or recruited to substitute-teach line dancing at the Southern Point Senior Center, Sandy never asked for days off, relishing her time immersed in the Fielding's hectic household—meeting Ian's school bus, grocery shopping, managing laundry and daily errands—helping to pull together all of the strings of family life. Sandy loved to talk, and when she discovered that both Tom's and Rory's parents were dead, she took pride in imparting to the couple her own brand of elder wisdom regarding parenting and rural neighborly relations. She cast herself as an informal Southern Point historian and free-flowing source of local trivia, some of which sounded so outlandish, Rory suspected Sandy had created it herself.

Rory's assessment of year one in Southern Point left little time for introspection. She and Tom were living as they always had, side by side, focused on common goals. They worked together, ate together, shopped together—no distance between them. There were hours, days, weeks, when Rory felt as though there wasn't enough room for her to take a separate breath of air. But overwhelming closeness didn't translate into intimacy, and with their business and financial goals attained, she finally had a chance to slow down and examine their relationship exclusively. Taking Ian and the agency out of the equation left her with little else. She realized that if she and Tom were alone together for a few days—which they never seemed to be—they would probably have nothing to talk about.

They'd hit the three-year mark in Southern Point when Rory first confronted the situation.

"Tom," she said, loading the dishwasher while he sat at the dining room table, nursing his third gin and tonic of the night—scant measure of tonic, mostly gin. "I think we should try counseling or talking to Father Chris at church." It wasn't what she'd planned to say and labeling it—making it tangible—terrified her.

Tom surveyed her over his half-specs, dumbfounded.

She spoke again, unsure where the words were coming from. "I think we both know things aren't . . . quite right. And I'm not sure what to do about it."

"No priest or counselor is going to tell us anything about our relationship that I don't already know." His dismissal intensified. "Accept it. This is what marriage is like at, what, thirteen years, Rory. Some of the shine wears off. You don't cash in prematurely. You don't dissolve the corporation just because the stock takes a dive." He pushed his glasses up onto his head until the frames vanished into a bush of wavy roan-brown hair. "What's so bad? We get along fine. Always have. You expect too much. If you want to go 'find yourself' through counseling, have at it. I don't need any help. I'm satisfied with my investment, with things as they are." He took a gulp from his glass, spit back an ice cube, and resumed reading the latest issue of *The Economist*.

"So that's it?" she asked. "You won't even consider going with me to get help?"

"Christ, Rory," he groaned. "Time will take care of these things. It always does."

Time couldn't. Time didn't. Rory hobbled through the "LLC" of her marriage for just short of two more years until quiet misery and flashbacks of the downward spiral of her parents' volatile union consumed her. She and her older sister, Mad had spent their childhood bandied between their parents in a near-miss divorce war, witness to the metamorphosis from avoidance to innuendo to hostility and rage. She and Mad had lived in a near-constant state of anxiety as they waited for days of icy silence between their parents to give way to a new round of vicious arguments, slamming doors, and cars driving off into the night. Some nights, both cars drove off, leaving the girls alone at the house until morning. Rory couldn't go through it again—or chance subjecting Ian to it, either. She wanted to set a new example—a good one. To teach him to be true and fair to himself and others. And to do that, she had to first be honest with herself—no matter how difficult and wrenching the journey.

That sweltering August day when Tom drove off and left her alone in the house, Rory tried several times to put her thoughts about him, and their marriage, on paper, but as soon as she began writing the letter, she started to cry. The flow of tears shocked her. Crying was something she just didn't do. She'd trained herself out of that response during childhood, with her parents hurling insults and unseen objects at each other from various rooms in the house. On the worst nights, Rory and Mad would huddle together under a blanket in Mad's room, holding their breaths until the turbulence, and their tears, stopped. "Ready, set, go," Mad would whisper, as they sniffled and wiped their faces on their nightgowns. Whoever stopped crying first was the winner for that night, and awarded a linty stick of gum, a half-wrapped sourball, or whatever Mad could dig out of her school bag. Rory hated the game, but she loved her sister until it hurt, for inventing it.

Tom came through the front door hours later, at dinnertime. "Ian still gone?" he asked Rory, not speck of emotion in his voice as he began rooting through the refrigerator shelves.

Rory forced herself off the living room's fireplace hearth and into the kitchen. "Tom, we both know that we haven't been happy," she said, her voice edged with sadness. "This isn't all about me . . . just because I'm the one who brought it up."

Tom ignored her puffy eyes and red nose. "The marriage suits me fine," he said flatly, closing the refrigerator door empty-handed.

"I thought our marriage was about us," she said softly. "Are you're saying it's up to me to initiate . . . changes?"

"Rory, I don't know where this stuff you get into your head comes from, but if you're changing the plan, if this marriage is going to end, you're going to be the one to do the dirty work," he said. "And you can go ahead and move into the guest room."

CHAPTER THREE

By mid-September, the Fielding's preliminary settlement agreement had been drafted, and while they were at odds over most issues about marriage, they agreed on the most important one. They both loved Ian and wanted a good life for him. His laundry list of teenage growing pains included periods of moroseness: "I don't want to go to college and be like you and Dad. And I hate living here now—there's nothing to do." His objections alternated with excited obsession over rediscovered music and musicians from the classic rock era: "Mom, we're starting a garage band." "Can I get a guitar?" "Where can I get boots like Bob Dylan's?" "Do you know anyone who went to a Zeppelin concert?"

Ian's rapid physical development and striking appearance presented its own set of challenges. Shoulder-length yellow ringlets, slate-blue eyes, and a precociously developed, statuesque physique lent him a distracting appeal to female parishioners at the Fielding's church—young and old alike. Even a full set of braces failed to lessen the visual impact.

"Can I please drop out of the acolyte program?" he begged Tom and Rory a few weeks before he turned thirteen. "Everyone always stares at me. It's so embarrassing."

"Ian, I think you're imagining things," Tom said in disbelief. "You're a kid. No one's staring at you. Except maybe God. It's church. People are looking at the cross—the altar."

The next week, Tom and Rory witnessed prurient stares from teenage girls—and their mothers—as Ian bore the cross up the aisle at the start of his assigned church service.

"I guess you can help serve at the food pantry on Sunday instead of acolyting," Rory told him. "Sorry we didn't believe you."

"No prob. I like doing that better anyway," he answered, closing the exchange amenably, a rare and astonishing exception to his usual "Ian vs. the world" mindset.

As the raging of Ian's hormones became deafening, his responsiveness to, and communication with, his parents waned. He hid things from them. He flagrantly disobeyed. He lied. Tom questioned what kind of person Ian would eventually become—if he would ever "snap out of it." For her part, Rory vacillated between hopelessness and faith—that if she could stay the course, his newly fractured personalities would somehow, someday, converge, enabling her to resume the relationship she'd shared with him from infancy to puberty. In the meantime, she resigned herself to working sometimes alongside—but mostly around—Tom on the thankless task of imposing the boundaries of acceptable behavior upon their unreceptive son.

After deciding to formally separate, Rory and Tom made every effort to conduct the bulk of their negotiating in the neutral surroundings of their agency, and out of Ian's earshot. They nearly succeeded—until he walked in on them discussing probable dates to sell the agency as they locked up the house for the night, a ritual carried over from their beach neighborhood days, and one that was entirely unnecessary in crime-free Southern Point.

"You guys are selling the company?" he asked, dropping onto the living room sofa. "And Dad's gonna stay here?" He glared at Rory as he talked. "What about me? Are we moving away after you leave Dad?"

Tom was silent, leaving her to answer.

"No, we're not," she reassured Ian. "And your dad and I are trying to keep everything that we can the way it's always been. Right, Tom?"

Tom headed toward the kitchen, where he began mixing a drink for himself.

"You're gonna just split up?" Ian asked. "When, Dad?"

"Your mother will explain it," Tom answered, still unwilling to back Rory up.

Rory took a breath and held it for a moment. "We'll probably have things sorted out around Christmastime, or by the first of the year. We wanted to be certain about separating before we talked to you."

Tom watched from the open kitchen as she stumbled through an explanation of the separation timeline and visitation options. As Ian listened, his sharp queries melted into cool silence.

It was the setting October sun, casting a dim light into the kitchen, that first drew Rory's attention to the bright white notebook paper. She removed her shoes and set down her keys on the counter as she reached for it, handwritten in purple marker, looking at first glance like one of Ian's music doodles. She leaned on the counter and began reading, suddenly conscious of the stillness of the room: her two dogs sitting nearly motionless, shifting their weight from one haunch to the other, their nails clicking against the wood floor as they watched her, sensing her anxiety; the emptiness of each vacant second between hollow ticks of the old wall clock. She dropped the note from shaking hands and frantically searched for her phone to call Tom, who had stayed behind to close the office.

"Ian's run away," she started, erupting into choking tears. "He's—he's gone. . . ."

"Wha-what?" Tom stammered.

She could count on one hand the number of times in their two decades together that she had heard fear in Tom's voice.

"Tom, there's a note—on the counter—it's from Ian—he's saying he's left for a while. It's because we didn't trust him enough to tell him about the divorce sooner!" She panted from terror, her imagination, her heart beginning to race. "Oh God, he's gone . . . with Noah. . . ." She yanked opened doors and searched through rooms as she talked.

"I'm leaving right now!" Tom shouted into the phone. "Wait! Are you sure he's not in the back or out in the barn? Where's his dirt bike?"

"I'm outside now," she said as she closed the garage door behind her. "I've checked the whole house. I'm going to call Sandy and the police."

"Keep looking," he ordered. "I'm on my way. I'll be there in forty-five minutes."

Rory called the police and relayed the necessary information, trying to remain calm as she stood in Titian's paddock and tracked the sun's rapid disappearance into the horizon. She fought a losing battle against panic as it grew dark and cold outside, a familiar sick feeling radiating from her core in churning waves. She remembered it from years earlier when Ian had vanished while with her in a department store. That day she had turned for only seconds to read the store directory, and in those moments he'd disappeared. Until he was found minutes later under a display rack of blouses, Rory had felt breathless, helpless, disoriented, split in two—as though someone had ripped part of her away. It was like a deep, violent wound with no way to stop the bleeding. The wound felt much deeper this time.

She thought of her son out there somewhere, his fourteen-year-old bravado no match for an opportunistic predator or even a distracted or drunk driver. Her heart started to race; she staved off a cardiac episode by snapping a beta-blocker in two and swallowing it in broken pieces. She held her breath for a solid minute, crossed her arms over her heart and breathed the 4-7-8 rhythm—4 second inhale, 7 second hold, and 8 second exhale. Then, after sobbing uncontrollably for a minute or two—a reprise of the crying jag she had had after she'd told Tom she wanted a divorce—she cursed herself for wasting time and started a phone chain while she waited for the police to arrive. Reaction was quick; several friends and neighbors put their evening on hold to help in the search for Ian.

Having been at the house when Ian got home from school, Sandy reported that he'd seemed fine. "When I left at five, he was on his schoolwork—writing away—and eating a sandwich, so I locked up behind myself, like always," she said. "The doggies were good. I told Ian to call me if he needed anything before you got home. He was a little quiet, but he seemed okay." A loud gasp led to a pause. "Oh, good Lord! He was probably writing that note to you then—not homework. Oh, my goodness!" Sandy apologized multiple times and then volunteered to cover the fifteen-minute route north of Southern Point to the shopping centers and bank branches frequented by skateboarders and amateur stunt cyclists.

By the time Tom got home, Rory had ascertained that one of their bicycles was missing, but the swirl of clothes and clutter on Ian's bedroom floor made inventorying for additional missing items impossible. Noah's mother showed up, hysterical, at the front door, having received a similar note from Noah. "He took eight dollars from the cookie jar. Only eight dollars! What—what can he do with that?" she sputtered out before bursting into tears.

Tom and Rory's next-door neighbor, Mike Rawlins, born and raised in Southern Point, stopped by their house before making the rounds of public boat ramps and abandoned farmhouses, both of which were popular gathering places for local teenagers. "There's not a hangout in Southern Point that I don't know about. I promise you, if they're out here, I will bring 'em home."

The entire ordeal lasted under three hours. Three hours that dragged like days. Mike was true to his word. He found Ian and Noah, huddled, jacketless and scared, on an abandoned boat at the old Southern Point Marina. Aiming a Marine-grade flashlight in their faces, he bellowed out, "Get your asses off that boat and over here—now!" They immediately obeyed, sheepishly scrambling into the bed of Mike's truck for the ten-minute drive home.

Sergeant John Adderson of the Southern Point Police Department was waiting at the Fielding's house when Mike returned with the boys, and quietly instructed both sets of parents not to talk to them before he did. "In these situations, it's best to make the kids responsible for their actions, just like they'd be if they were adults. We don't want to give 'em the benefit of runnin' straight back to their parents' protection after pullin' a stunt like this."

One at a time, he sat the boys down and quizzed them about what could have happened to them if they had encountered a bear, a poisonous snake, a stranger, gotten lost in the woods, or were hit by a car. Noah broke into loud sobs and ran to his mother. Ian sat, emotionless, through the entire interrogation. Rory knew that his face-value acceptance when she and Tom had told him about the divorce had landed the three of them around the table with Sergeant Adderson that night. It was a mistake she and Tom could not afford to repeat.

CHAPTER FOUR

Two months following Ian's runaway misadventure, the Fielding's divorce settlement terms, which they had first discussed with him, and which they designed specifically to minimize the scars caused by the termination of their marriage, were set. In an act of unexpected sensitivity, Tom awarded Rory custody of Rocket, his eight-month-old black Lab puppy.

"Look, Ian, I'm out of town too much to care for her in the right way," Tom said, spreading his manufactured concern a bit thick. "Would you help your mother watch over her for the time being?"

"I guess," Ian said, puzzled. "Are you sure . . . that you don't want her anymore, Dad?"

Tom sighed. "It's not that I don't want her, Ian."

"I know Al would miss her too," Rory chimed in. "It might be best to separate—wean them from each other—gradually."

In truth, Rory's German shepherd, Al, barely tolerated the puppy's constant badgering and barking. If not for her obedience training, she would have dispatched the annoying interloper months before. Tom had forfeited guardianship of Rocket because Ian was attached to her; it was one less loss for the boy to absorb.

Living arrangements involved another, less conventional decision. Rory and Tom agreed to live in the same rural neighborhood for a minimum of one year—houses less than two miles apart—to maintain continuity in Ian's school, music, and sports activities.

Selling the agency had provided ample capital for a comfortable co-settlement, and when Rory saw a FOR SALE sign at a house on some substantial acreage nearby, she opted to invest her half in a home-based business allowing her more involvement in Ian's routine. She would earn her daily bread from hard physical labor and catering to unpredictable equines their equally unpredictable owners. On the plus side, it was a return to the environment where she'd always been happiest: outside and surrounded by horses.

In conversations with Tom, she downplayed her excitement about the property she was buying. "The house is okay. The real value is in the land—for pasture, for the boarding barn business," she told him. It was strange not disclosing more significant information about the house to him, asking for his advice on the financial aspects of her plan, but she was learning where to draw the line. Ian could answer any of Tom's general questions about the house later on, once they'd moved in. Until then he wouldn't be privy to the details.

Driving by the farm on Whistler Ridge Road for the first time, Rory knew she could live there until the day she died. It was the land. The view from the road was both unostentatious and extraordinary. A gravel drive, a thousand feet long and lined with dozens of river birches, split the front of the property in half. Now, each time Rory drove up that drive, she felt like she had taken a deep breath of pristine air that wiped clean whatever was weighing on her mind when she turned onto it from the road. To the right of the private lane, four acres of groomed green turf, dotted with saplings, rolled out to a parking circle and a white-columned house with black shutters and a full-length front porch. Its traditional exterior belied the simple, clean spaces within. A fifty-foot central gallery spanned the length of the house from the front porch, which faced east, all the way to the living room's French doors. The kitchen, dining room, and living room all branched off the gallery. Light streamed into the house through large windows and bounced between thirteen-foot cathedral ceilings and immaculate white oak floors. The north wing housed the den and two bedrooms. The master suite, laundry room, and a family room over the garage were on the south wing, facing a three-car garage and barns. Oak-board fencing traced the land's left frontage and continued around and behind the garage. Beyond that were two shed-row stables totaling five stalls. Thirty more acres of overgrown fields and woods stretched out behind the house and outbuildings, framed by a lattice of dirt farm lanes and crop fields. It had all the elements Rory required for her new business—and the next however many phases of her life that lay ahead. But she wasn't alone. The Barnetts were juggling several prequalified offers from potential buyers who had fallen in love with the place. She had no choice but to deploy the one weapon she had—one that could turn on her and wipe out her future security. In direct contradiction to her original plan to finance her house and property, and use cash to build the barn and pastures, she offered the Barnetts five percent above their asking price in cash. They accepted immediately.

Rory's future home was originally part of Whistler Crop Farm, purchased from the Whistler family's estate in the early nineties by the Stark Grain Company. Fred Stark had bought out several other small- to medium-sized family farms in Southern Point and merged them with his existing inventory of agricultural properties. He sold off those he deemed too small to earn him significant agricultural income to a local builder for residential development. Rory's property was subdivided from the prime Whistler Farm parcel and sold to a private buyer two years before. High and dry on the front end, and lower and marshy in the back, most of the acreage was cultivated through the 1980s and then ignored for subsequent decades. In their short time as owners of the property, Pat and Candy Barnett had made use of less than five acres of land surrounding their custom-built home and never even walked the entire property line.

They listed the house themselves and weren't greedy about the asking price. Eighteen months earlier they had moved from the suburbs with their daughter, Kimberly, envisioning several pre-college years filled with pony clubbing and 4-H shows.

In the end, Kimberly proved incapable of reconciling herself to the final, inevitable fate of her lamb and piglet livestock "projects," and after two winters of the home's attic playing host to rodents, raccoons, and starlings, Candy and Pat, self-proclaimed "indoorsy" types, convinced themselves that it was best to head back to "suburb-ilization." Pat threw a decent tractor and matching implements into the farm's purchase price and assured Rory that they would leave the house move-in ready well before closing.

Rory hadn't taken much note of the two masonry pillars on either side of the driveway entrance the first couple of times she'd visited the property. The security gate struck her as overkill, as did the satellite backup alarm and whole-house integrated sound system. It was clear—the Barnetts loved their toys.

"If y'all need any other work done, our contractor guy is really good," Candy said. "His name's Scott Smith and he built our little stables, put up the fencing, and added our back deck. He's close by and reliable."

"Great," Rory responded, glad for a lead on a local construction resource.

"Oh, and there's a ten-foot Christmas tree in the attic," Candy added. "We'll leave that for you. It's pre-lit, too. Beautiful. Even smells real. And there's an extra can of pine scent spray under the kitchen sink so you can freshen it up. So much better than a real tree."

"Thanks a lot," Rory forced herself to sound genuine. "I never would have thought of that."

CHAPTER FIVE

Agreed: cohabitating and decorating a Christmas tree together would be disingenuous and awkward in the wake of Rory and Tom's separation. Solution: Tom purposely scheduled a trip to Washington for the second week of December to finalize the agency's sale, allowing Rory to vacate the Rock Creek Road house on her own. The Barnetts settled on renting Rory the Whistler Ridge house until her New Year's week closing, which meant she and Ian could spend their first Christmas there.

Control yielded comfort. Rory's solace in the process of sorting and organizing objects and spaces reached back to the period when her parents' marriage was at its most fractured—which in her recollection was more often than not. She would retreat, unnoticed, to her bedroom, and lock herself in. Then she would close the curtains and organize her books and toys and hang her clothes by type and color. It helped to block out the chaos just outside her door. As an adult, she obsessively reverted to the behavior whenever she was anxious or confused. Alone in the farmhouse during the week Tom was in Washington, she succeeded in splitting twenty years of a life together into two fairly equal pieces, reminiscing and grieving in silence as she went along. She left behind her a model home for Tom's new solo existence, every piece of furniture and accessory immaculate and strategically arranged. A local moving company then transported her furniture, artwork, and barn equipment to the new farm. After helping Ian set up a bedroom in each house, one last step in the transition remained for Rory—leading her horses on their two-mile trek to Whistler Ridge.

Twelve hooves rhythmically clipped the ashen pavement on Rock Creek Road, leaving a hollow thud of emptiness behind each step. The short trek to the new farm resembled more funereal caisson than hopeful new start. Rory walked between Titian and Olga, a halter lead rope in each hand. Behind her, Ian silently led Diane's horse, Mystic. Not one car passed them in the thirty-minute journey to Whistler Ridge Road. The horses' pace remained consistent, on beat, until the procession ended at the new farm's gravel drive. Rory opened the pasture gate and led the horses out into the expansive front field. "Watch this, Ian!" she called, running back to the gate after she'd released their lead lines. She loved the moment horses entered a new pasture—a thousand pounds of muscle and bone pounding and snorting across the earth as they explored new territory. She swung the gate closed and stood back waiting for the stampede. The three horses plodded to the center of the pasture and formed a loose huddle, heads down. And, they stayed there.
Ian shrugged. "What are we waiting for?"

"Nothing. We're waiting for nothing," she said, shrugging back. "Come on. Let's go inside."

"Rory, why don't you sell some of these—on eBay or at some local gallery?" Mad asked as the two sisters waded through clusters of newspaper and Styrofoam peanuts, unwrapping and hanging some of Rory's framed photographs in the living room of the new house. "They're good enough—they are." A few days before, Mad had abandoned her husband and their three rescued cats in Malibu, so she could spend the Christmas holiday at Rory's farm, helping with odd jobs and arranging furniture.

"Oh, I don't know about that, Mad," Rory answered. "I just like capturing that split second that I see every once in a while—recording the wildlife and the landscape out here."

"I really think you should check into it—putting them up for sale," Mad insisted. "I'd buy one. No, I'm going to buy one and give it to Will as a Christmas present."

"I doubt he'll speak to you when you get home, after you left him there all alone."

Mad laughed. "Will knows the deal. He's fine with it. He knows you'll always come first—that it's just the two of us. He gets plenty of seconds—got nothing to complain about. That massive family out there. It's like the bloody Waltons or something. It really freaks me out at times. Too much warm and fuzzy togetherness. They all *like* each other! Too damned perfect. I need to get away—get my fix of the old Tryon dysfunction." She laughed again. "Come on, Rory, you needed my help."

"I could have managed," Rory said, trying to sound nonchalant.

"God, what can't you ever admit you need help? I'm helping you until the work is done. Period!"

Living in California, Mad only saw Ian once a year, and this year's live performance of his bratty behavior was a disappointment. He barely managed a thank-you when Mad handed him a vintage Woodstock T-shirt she had found for him in an LA boutique.

"I tried to warn you," Rory said. "I love him, but I'm having a tough time liking him right now."

"Boy, are you jaded!" Mad smirked. "I was going to ask Ian, 'Where did you hide my sweet little nephew?' Rory, try not to let it get to you. I'm sure some of it's the shock of the divorce. Remember us?"

"Of course, I remember," Rory snapped, "no matter how much I want to forget." She remembered most of it—when anxiety triggered the flashbacks she had tried blocking out, or when Mad felt the need to rehash scenes Rory wanted to delete from their painful childhood. "Mad, don't even think about making a comparison," she said defensively. "Unlike Mom, I'm putting Ian first in all of this. I don't deserve his resentment. There's no similarity. I have always been there for him." She fought back tears. "Let's consider the subject closed, okay?"

"You never cry, Rory." Mad put down the bubble-wrapped framed photo she was holding and gave Rory a sideways hug. "Don't pick up the habit over this. Come on, brat. Let's go play with the horses for a while. This stuff can wait."

Ian and Rocket stayed with Tom at the house on Rock Creek Road from the day after Christmas through the end of the holiday break, freeing Rory to putter around the farm and concentrate on household projects after seeing Mad off at the airport. With a large attached garage, and only one vehicle to house, she decided to convert the end bay of the garage into her barn office, and the middle bay into temporary hay, feed, and supply storage, leaving the third bay open for the farm tractor. She spent the days arranging and rearranging the spaces, and had enough time left over to transform the horse barn's small tack room into a first-aid station. On New Year's Eve day, seated at her bruised but sturdy antique pedestal desk, which she'd barely managed to wedge between empty water tubs, freshly laundered horse blankets, and gallons of fly spray, she placed her first official business order of horse feed and supplies.

The store's owner answered the phone pleasantly but mechanically after several rings. "Deal's Feed and Seed."

She guessed Dan Deal was sitting in his office chair at the back of the feed store, his feet—wrapped in seasoned, lace-up roping boots—propped up on the desk. He was holding an ancient black dial telephone to his ear—the same phone his father had answered for forty years—in one hand. With his other hand, he was either unwrapping, lighting, or already smoking one of the short Nicaraguan cigars he always carried in his shirt or jacket pocket. Wherever Dan went, he left a faint wake of cigar smoke. Rory guessed that he was in his early fifties, based on a comment he'd once made about retiring after nearly thirty years in law enforcement. The aging process was taking its time with him, so far delivering only fine crow's feet around his clear aqua eyes and more substantial smile lines at the corners of his mouth. His mouth. Usually set in a neutral expression, but with lips just short of full, which he flicked with his tongue sometimes. After that he'd usually break into a half-smile. It was that half-smile that had recently started screaming out at Rory to walk right into his arms and grab onto him. She battled against that image every time it bumped up against her. Some gray intermingled with Dan's close-cut dark blond hair, which was in short supply around his temples. His straight brows were more often than not raised at the inner edges, resulting in a contemplative look. It was as though he was always one thought ahead of everyone else. Rory attributed the current fitness of his six-foot-three-inch body to decades of the physical demands of police work followed by the daily labor required to run the feed store. He usually stood in a slight "huddle" position, leaning down and toward the person in front of him, like a football player on the field, strategizing the next play. He spoke with a barely perceptible Southern drawl delivered from between snow white teeth.

She cleared her throat. "Hi, Dan. It's Aurora—I mean, it's Rory, Rory Fielding."

"I'd recognize that voice anywhere, Aurora, *Rory*," Dan said, his voice gaining energy. "Now, tell me there's something I can do for you."

She lost her breath at the sound of his voice. "Yes—there is," she said, choking on the words. She forgot why she had called, despite a typed list laid out on the desk in front of her. "Okay, well"—she cleared her throat again— "I have some business for you."

"Lay it on me, dear." His accent made two syllables of the word *dear*.

His tone threw her off. From anyone else, the term *dear* would have sounded patronizing or inappropriate. From him, it sounded . . . stirring.

"Are you sitting down?" she said, laughing a little to mask her nervousness. "It's a very substantial order. My first for the new horse business—farm—or whatever it is I'm attempting to do over here."

"Congratulations!" he said cheerfully. "My pen is in hand, and I've got a nice cross draft in the office. Go ahead. Shoot."

She wondered how Dan maintained his perennial good mood. Surely he had a dark side, a secret life beyond what little she already knew about him, which was only that he had left Southern Point for college and a career in law enforcement thirty years ago, and now he was back to stay, apparently content to assume the life of a country merchant.

"Am I billing you, personally, or the new farm?" he asked. "Because it'll only take me a few minutes to set up a new account for your boarding operation, so you can keep your finances straight."

"I guess this should be run through the farm," she said, "but I don't have a name yet. How about NHF for now?"

"NHF? What does that stand for? Someone's initials? Or, two words followed by an expletive?"

"Very funny," she said, laughing. "No, it's the Nameless Horse Farm for now."

"You can do better than that! Come up with something fitting," he said. "Something that'll suit the place. You may have to live there a little while. You know, get the lay of the land. Let the earth and the fields speak to you—tell you their story."

"The earth and the fields?"

"Yes, ma'am. Everything begins and ends there."

"They haven't seen fit to share anything with me yet," she mumbled. "While I'm waiting for that, I'll give you my supply order."

Rory ticked off the items she needed from her list, and Dan scheduled a delivery day and time. After hanging up the phone, she pulled a copy of the farm's site plan out of a desk drawer. The plan consisted of a twenty-stall, center-aisle barn; a covered, lighted arena for year-round training, and a half dozen pastures. The barn was the project's largest monetary investment but could go up in less than three months, barring any unforeseen setbacks. Her biggest challenge wasn't going to be buildings or fences or riding rings, or anything drawn on the blueprint. It was going to be grass. Well-established, deeply rooted grass, from a specially formulated seed mix shipped in from Kentucky. Without it, she would have no pastures—no main food source. That meant no horses, and no horses meant no business.

A few days later, when Dan showed up with Rory's feed order, she asked him if she could pick his brain about her plans to clear, seed, and manage the pasture portion of her project. "I never thought I'd be this stressed out about damned grass," she said, throwing up her hands. "I think my timeline's off!"

"For optimum returns, fall's really when you should have done it, but you've already missed that deadline," Dan said, his tan boot propped up on the fender of his delivery truck. "I wish like hell you'd come to me sooner, but I guess you couldn't have, since you didn't live here then." He scratched his head and put his hands on his hips.

"I kept the property purchase quiet, Dan," she said. "And, I don't like asking people for things."

"You mean asking for help, don't you? We all need that sometimes, dear. You've got to give your turf six or eight months after you plant it. It's damned ambitious to think about bringing in horses before the next annual growth cycle. This land sitting fallow for as long as yours has—you've got to clear the debris, level it, trench out ditches, maybe—before you even think about amending and drilling seed."

"Drilling seed? What's that?"

"That's the way you seed pasture." They walked to the front of her shed-row barn, looking at the expanse of neglected farmland that lay directly behind it. Dan restarted his agricultural briefing, his voice animated, his hands drawing imaginary shapes in the air.

"You love talking about this," she said.

"Yes, yes, I love it." He pulled out a folded crossword puzzle, printed on plain paper, turned it over, and started drawing. "See, the seeds are drilled deep into the soil like plugs, so they establish stronger roots that hold up to the wear and tear of heavy livestock traffic." He indicated various points of his illustration. "Once you've done that, you'll have to give it the spring and all of summer before you put animals on it."

Rory's face fell. "How did I miss that? Nothing I researched indicated that I would need that much time."

"Hold on, Rory. Wipe that dread off your face. You can use that front pasture for a few more months, but even with a small herd, the long-term problem is still there: the previous owners planted plain old landscape grass seed. Safe enough for horses to eat, but not the right mix for real nutrition, and not able to hold up to their constant traffic." He pointed to the pasture's patchy ground cover. "See how sparse your turf is already? That's with just three horses and you supplementing with hay. You're going to have to rotate your horses off that area and fertilize and reseed it with some perennial orchard or timothy mix, designed just for horses. And if you get into breeding at some point, well, that requires another type of specialized grass."

"So basically, my entire future revolves around the next three months. I thought I'd done my homework on this. Now I'm starting to panic." She searched his expression for reassurance, even though he owed her none. "Hay is ten dollars a bale, Dan. Each horse can eat a half bale a day. That could be fifty dollars a day. "If that's all I have to feed them—they'll just—"

"Swallow up all of your profits?" He said. "Things change a hundred and eighty degrees when you go from horse owner to horse farm owner, don't they?"

"Oh, my god." She took a few breaths to center herself.

"Rory, you've got some major challenges here. No denying that. But *you* also have something else. Something that every farmer around here wants."

"Okay. What's that?" she asked, defeated.

"Something a little dirty, but priceless."

Dan grinned. Rory didn't.

"I'm not sure where you're going, Dan."

"L-o-a-m."

"Loam?"

"You have it here. A nice thick layer of it. And humus. From all the years the land has been fallow. Perfect for growing. You don't even need fertilizer. Everyone wants what you have.

That's your advantage. That's how you may be able to get away with this late start."

"Note you said I *may* be able...."

"My advice—don't start worrying yet. Figure out your barn and fencing. That'll distract you from the pastures for a while. But you've got to move on it now—get your contractors lined up."

They reviewed her timeline in detail. Loam or no loam, the back thirty acres had lain untended for decades, and required clearing, ditching and seeding, which would take about six weeks, followed by six months of turf establishment. During the growing season, she would build the barn, riding arena, and fences. In all, she was looking at three to four months of planting and construction, and another four months of crop growth and fine-tuning the buildings and arena. It would take every bit of time from mid-January to September to get the operation up and running in order to accept her new boarders. If she missed the deadline, she risked losing the farm, and no one would be coming to her rescue.

CHAPTER SIX

"Telephone poles?" Jane Simpson pulled her navy peacoat tight against her body and ducked into its collar, her light brown hair spilling out in thick waves. She extended her foot in front of her to stop the white wicker deck swing she and Rory were sharing. The swing, built under a wood pergola on Rory's back deck, served up a panorama of the farm's barn area and fields.

"Yes," Rory replied. "Telephone poles, and milled wood to use on the barn project. See, there's always something new to learn in the world of farming."

"Seems like it," Jane said. "How do they . . . harvest them? Is that the term?"

"Well, technically it's logging," Rory said. "I've had an official primer on selective land clearing. But, don't consider me an expert."

Jane looked unconvinced. "So, in the old days, all of this was farmland, and these trees just sprang up recently?"

"Most of them are Loblolly Pines. They grow fast, and I guess it's been twenty years or longer since these fields have been farmed. I'm having as few removed as possible. Just enough to get the barn and pastures on the best and highest site."

"Rory, you're really getting into this stuff. It's starting to scare me," she said, lighting one of her "diet" Marlboros. "Now you're a horticulturalist?"

It was too cold a morning to have coffee alfresco, but trying her best to accommodate one of Jane's few vices, Rory poured coffee into a couple of mugs, figuring they would serve double duty as handwarmers. The women's close friendship had begun ten years earlier at a fitness club in the city, when Rory rescued Jane from a runaway treadmill. The jogging belt had gone haywire, the power switch had frozen in the "on" position, and Jane panicked, afraid to jump onto the treadmill's deck. Two other women using the room ran off to find a manager as Jane struggled to keep up a single-digit mile pace. Rory walked over to the wall, made eye contact with Jane as she pointed to the power outlet, and then unplugged the treadmill, bringing it to an abrupt stop.

"Christ almighty!" Jane tripped and huffed as she hopped down. "Why didn't anyone else think of that? I owe you big time!"

Jane managed a special events company, a job requiring her to work most weekends, but affording her flexibility Monday through Friday. Jane and Rory usually met for coffee or lunch once or twice a week.

"Be honest, Rory. It's got to be weird living so close together when you're getting divorced. Your 'ex' is literally right down the road." Jane sipped her coffee and took a short, guilty drag on her cigarette. "I mean, won't you see more than you want to—comings and goings, other women, overnight dates—that stuff?"

"I have some doubts—I'm sure Tom does too, but we've agreed to try it for a year. If it gets too awkward"—Rory shrugged—"we'll have to try something else." She leaned back on the swing and crossed her arms. "You know what's been going on with Ian. I'm hoping that keeping our households close together and limiting changes to his routine will help him during the transition. Trust me, when parents divorce, they may lead separate lives, but their kids have to lead double lives. I want Ian to get through this with as little damage as possible. And there are two miles separating us, so we don't have to see each other if we don't want to."

"Christ, I'm glad I didn't have children with Lou," Jane said. "That would have been a nightmare." She rarely spoke of her ex-husband, an academia wannabe whose favorite pastime was tracing his lineage online through an ancestral website he had created, searching futilely for some royal connection. Theirs was a brief, shamelessly mismatched union. "And things are getting better with Ian?" Jane asked. "That runaway stunt he pulled last fall—Jesus!"

"I still haven't recovered from that," Rory said. "The hardest thing for me is leaving him alone in the house." She stood up and walked to the end of the deck. "I always wonder if he'll be here when I get back. Being home most of the day, I'm learning his afternoon routine. And I'm trying to talk to him more, even if it's just in the truck, running errands. I'm close now—minutes away from school—if anything happens. He doesn't have to go through the agency receptionist or voicemail and wait for a return call. My presence has definitely improved our communication. I think we're developing a better understanding of each other, common ground, a little more trust. Proximity breeds closeness; I'm banking on that."

"Except between you and Tom—" Jane blurted out. "Eeeff . . . did I just say that?"

"It's okay. You're speaking truth. In our case, constant togetherness veiled other problems. We evaluated our relationship from the outside in, instead of the inside out. I didn't know any other way. And Tom . . . I think he looks to *situations* rather than to relationships for his happiness. A depressing conclusion after twenty years, isn't it?"

"My friend, that's why you're here and Tom's not." Jane stopped the swing, carefully crushed her cigarette under her shoe heel, blew on it a few times to cool it down, slid the butt under the pack's cellophane wrapper, and pressed it flat. She looked up at Rory—caught running through her cigarette disposal ritual.

"God, wouldn't it be easier to just quit?" Rory asked. They laughed so hard that Rory had to sit down on the deck steps to catch her breath.

Jane walked to the edge of the deck and sat next to her to survey the property. "Wow, this place is really—big. And all of that space back there is going to be corrals or whatever you call them after the trees are gone?"

"Pastures."

"Right. Pastures."

"And that's after they've all been leveled and planted," Rory said. "That's another issue—that we can talk about next time."

"Okay, then," Jane said. "Change of subject. Ian's needs aside, are you going to be okay at home all day long? Cut off from the social part of being a fish in the giant sea of humanity twelve hours a day?" She rolled her eyes.

"It's kind of strange. I've worked full-time since I was twenty-two, minus a few weeks of maternity leave, and a vacation here and there. It's really an adjustment. But the upside is, I feel like I've joined this private society of people who aren't tied to everyone else's workday schedule. I can shop when I want to, plan my own day. I already see a difference in myself. My head is starting to clear—I actually have time to organize my thoughts, my house, even my purse, for God's sake! I can't wait to get the boarding business going, but I also don't want to waste any of the next six months before then. I'm using it as an opportunity to regroup, make a fresh start, cliché as that sounds."

The horses barreled up the front pasture, skidding around the bend behind the garage before landing in front of their barns.

Jane jumped up and moved toward the French doors. Rory stayed in place.

"Don't be scared. They do that almost every time a car comes up the driveway."

"Who's coming up the driveway that you don't have to open the gate for?"

Dan Deal's red truck slowly led a trailer packed tight with hay across the yard and back to the barns. Curiosity and greed prevailed among the horses, and they stood their ground by the gate, waiting for a handout.

"Oh, that's Dan Deal. He owns the local feed and farm supply store and he also has a lot of expertise in land management because his dad's a farmer here. He's helping me plot and plan out the land portion of the boarding operation. He was a police officer before, and I think he went to UVA. I told you about him."

"Does he just come and go as he pleases?"

"When I was at the agency, I was gone all day, and he would deliver and unload orders of hay and feed free of charge. He's still willing to do it, so I'm not going to turn him down. I ordered a load of hay from him last week, but it didn't come in until yesterday."

Dan jumped out of the truck and waved at Rory and Jane before evaluating how to back up to the paddock gate.

"Happy New Year, Dan!" Rory called out as she waved at him.

"Happy New Year is right! Holy crap, are you serious?" Jane's jaw dropped. "A guy like that just happens to be your little deliveryman? Wait—did I say little? There is nothing little about that man—I'm certain of that! No wonder you don't want to leave the place. I wouldn't either."

"Jane! He might hear you."

"I'm surprised you never said anything before," Jane whispered. "I mean—look at him! Yeah, I'd definitely let that guy come and go as he pleases 24/7."

"It's not like that," Rory insisted. "I'm just one of his customers. And . . . I'm—was—married before."

Jane shook her head as she tracked Dan with her eyes. "If you're telling me the truth, that's a damn shame, Rory. Now, let's talk about your birthday."

They walked into the house and sat down in the living room.

"So . . ." Jane said, gathering up her purse and gloves. "I'm thinking a few friends, a few drinks . . . we torture some men for a few hours."

Rory cringed. "Mmm, I don't think so. Not this year."

Jane was unrelenting. "Come on, you're turning forty-eight in three days! I'll call Liz and your other friend out here—what's her name again? Gatsby? We'll take you out and make some trouble and toss back a glass or two."

"Gabrielle Rawlins . . . her name's Gabrielle. She goes by Gabby."

"Okay . . . Gabby. I'll call Liz and Gabby and we'll go up to the oceanfront and eat some oysters and cause some trouble. Life is short, my friend."

Ian spent Friday night at a friend's house, leaving Rory no excuse to turn down Jane's birthday offer. Dinner and cocktails with her friends at a crowded raw bar along the beach resort strip was as loud and distracting as the drive home from her first post-separation solo outing was solitary. Once she left the oceanfront and suburbs behind and hit Southern Point, she chased a full moon. Clear orange yellow, it tracked her around every curve of rural two-lane roads, finding and then losing her again as it ducked behind dark gray clouds. Toward the end of her solitary drive, she turned onto Rock Creek Road, and wondered if Tom was still awake, lonely—it was too soon for another woman—bitter, hating her. Then she chastised herself for ruminating about the past, and vowed that starting that night, she would take a different route back and forth to her new farm. No more driving down Rock Creek Road.

CHAPTER SEVEN

Monday morning, a line of trucks, two surreal green-and-yellow combines and a tank-like vehicle Rory couldn't quite identify, began a delicate squeeze through her driveway gate. Jason Grimes, a friend of a friend of Scott Smith's, had agreed to selectively clear as much of Rory's back pastures as needed. Some of the oldest trees, not poisonous to horses, would remain in each segment of the pastures. Jason would use some of the cleared trees for power and light poles for the farm and pay her for the few remaining harvested trees. The brush and saplings would be mulched for use around the farm.

She held her breath while the alien-like fleet barely cleared the open front entrance, inches from shearing one of the black gates away from its attached pillar. That didn't happen, and watching the convoy make its way over the front lawn, she realized why Scott had warned her that he could not guarantee that all of her land could be cleared. The sodden, quaggy earth at the rear of the farm could swallow up the tires and blades of the mammoth vehicles.

Another five minutes had the caravan drifting past the edge of the mowed green turf and rolling into the brush. The crew disembarked to huddle for a moment at the back fender of one of the idling trucks before vanishing on foot into the maze of trees and thick bracken. They had refused Rory's offer of extra pay to check each tree for resident animals, assuring her that they would be humane and report back on any live sightings. She left the men to their work and headed out for the day's farm errands.

A week later, the farm looked as though it had doubled in size. Twenty acres behind the house now presented more than a mile of visibility, bounded only by the Stark Farms crop fields and woods in the distance. Rory's six-acre back woods remained unscathed, along with a two-acre tree line along the southern side of the property. A series of deep ditches running north-to-south created four, five-acre rectangular pastures. Ian was ecstatic to have room to ride his dirt bike, and the dogs rooted around and rolled in the half-frozen dirt fields as though they were filled with buried treasure.

No longer impeded by underbrush and crowded saplings, a steady breeze swept across the land day and night, something Rory knew all of the farm's residents would appreciate when the thermometer shot well above ninety degrees in the coming humid summer. For now, the ceaseless wind created new sounds in the house and in the barns as it lifted shutters and stall door latches and found its way into windowsills and under roof shingles. With a generous dose of oil, the barn's dormant weathervane came back to life, bobbing and spinning with the wind's changing velocity and direction.

For the first time since moving in, Rory could see farm lanes and neighboring properties, imagining what it must have looked like back when it was a working farm. She considered paying homage to the former owners by titling it Whistler Ridge Farm, then decided to take Dan's advice and hold off on choosing a name until she got a better feel for the place.

It was six thirty on Saturday morning—half an hour before dawn—Rory's new favorite time of the day. While the dogs snored and whimpered through one last dream, the heat pump's low hum canceled out the house's random creaks and thumps. Ian was sound asleep down the hall; Rory's own drowsiness insulated her from the impending day's anxiety and doubt about barns, deadlines, money, and parenting. She wondered if in time, the feeling would fade away, and she would become accustomed to being alone. In the meantime, her horses and dogs didn't differentiate between married or separated, or weekdays, weekends, or holidays, so she got out of bed to attack her morning routine. She brushed her teeth and put on lipstick, mascara, and perfume, a daily ritual instilled in her by her mother, Elise. "Aurora, you should look beautiful for yourself, and for other people," Elise recited to Rory daily while positioned at her dressing table, applying near-theatrical makeup to her lovely, taut face. "It's a responsibility. It makes them feel better—the other people—to look at someone who's beautiful. You'll be beautiful too—someday. Not as beautiful as me, but still . . . you have to do it." Rory, like so many others, including her father, Jack, adhered to Elise's mandate for emotional distance. In retrospect, she questioned whether anyone had known her mother intimately. Elise had made a career out of guarding the secrets to her soul. No one in the family had seen her cry—ever. Not when she was fighting with Jack over custody of their children, property, or retirement accounts. Not when Jack died a shockingly swift death at forty-eight during routine gallbladder surgery—a botched job by one of his colleagues. And not even when she was dying from breast cancer—semi-comatose, jaundiced, and in unbearable pain, unable to tend to her looks. Elise had refused life-saving chemotherapy because of what she termed "disfiguring" hair loss. The fact that the hair she lost would eventually grow back did nothing to sway her from her decision. She was fifty-two when she died.

Standing now in her walk-in closet, Rory surveyed barn uniform options—a polo shirt or blouse, jeans or breeches, and black paddock boots or lace up field boots—doubting Elise would approve of any of them. She chose the tall field boots because it was muddy outside, and jeans instead of breeches since she wouldn't have time to ride. At her heels, Al and Rocket scrambled through the house and sat, excited yet obedient, in front of the living room door, their haunches barely touching the rug. With a turn of the brass doorknob, Rory released them into the frostbitten morning. Confronted by a blast of frigid air, lacking the benefit of a built-in fur coat, she opted in favor of coffee and breakfast before joining them outside.

A toilet flushed, drawers slammed, and Ian shuffled past the kitchen in warm-up pants, a corduroy jacket, and bare feet, his hair like yellow steel wool.

"I'm going upstairs to play a video game," he mumbled.

Rory resisted the urge to criticize his bizarre clothing and uncombed hair. "Do you want some pancakes?" she asked, deciding on the menu only as she spoke the words, desperate for a positive dialogue. "I'm making breakfast after I clean the kitchen."

"Sure," he answered.

"I'll call you when our food is ready."

She sprayed down the counters with bleach and detergent solution and separated the dirty dishes into batches, positioned a dry dish towel on the counter, and filled the sink.

Calm overtook her, brought on by the simple kitchen routine. She had just started washing dishes when the reflection from her engagement ring flashed in her eye. Lately she wore the ring, that which she had once vowed never to take off her left finger as long as she lived, on the fourth finger of her right hand. She removed it now, placed it in the zippered compartment of her purse for safekeeping, and returned to the sink. Staring past the countertop and out the adjoining breakfast room's bay window, she saw the reflection flash again in the early morning light and realized that it couldn't have been her ring after all.

"Mom!" Ian yelled from the top of the stairs. "Is it time to eat yet?"

"I said I'd call you when it was ready!" Rory returned. She dried her hands and turned to the stove to start breakfast.

On weekends, Rory turned out the horses between seven and nine a.m., after the sun had burned off some of the morning's crystalline dew. She would feed and hay them in their stalls, wait an hour, send them off to pasture, and then muck out the barn and clean up the feed and storage rooms.

Wind burned her face and neck as she walked to the paddock, her gaze fixed on clouds high in the mid-January sky. *White alligator scales,* she thought. *Miles of them.* Cold as the morning was, in a few days it would be warm again. Winter weather, especially on the bay of Southern Point, was the definition of mercurial: thirty degrees and overcast one day, sunny and sixty the next. Rory's boots caught on frozen hoof-shaped divots stamped deep in the mud during the last day of rain. She nearly lost her balance but managed to catch herself just short of falling on her butt. The first stall she reached was Titian's, where he waited for her, impatient, gnashing his teeth, his copper-red head and neck extended as far out as the open top of the Dutch door would allow.

"Hold on, you monster," she scolded as a strand of slobber trickled from his lower lip into his empty feed dish. He pinned back his ears and exposed the whites of his eyes menacingly. "Knock it off!" she shouted. "Or I'll clock you!" He ducked into his stall.

Rory's lifelong affinity for horses revolved around her appreciation of their elegantly packaged yet awe-inspiring strength, their keen sensitivity to their environment, and their responsiveness to human influences. It did not involve idolatry.

She believed that a horse's greatest strengths lay in its uncomplicated brain: an excellent memory of both good and bad experiences, the ability to form simple associations—to trust—and to mistrust. These reactionary mountains of graceful power, fueled by a steady supply of adrenaline, prepared to outrun any stealthy predator, real or imagined, seemed the very opposite of her.

Titian, her thirteen-year-old gelding, exemplified the best and worst of the equine species. At well over sixteen hands high and fourteen hundred pounds, the Appendix Quarter Horse, named for his brilliant russet coat, balanced on well-formed but massive hooves, all the more noticeable because of their licorice-black color. They supported a dense, muscular body atop solid legs, the back right of which had a white sock. Titian's slightly feminine, pretty head was stamped with a dainty white star. A huge, square rump and ground-sweeping tail dominated his back end. He had competed successfully for years in regional field hunting trials, until his former owner suffered a stroke and listed him for sale in the *Virginia Horse Journal*. That was where Rory found him, a few months after her grandmother Priscilla died, leaving Rory and Mad thirty thousand dollars each, with the stipulation that the money be used for nothing practical, essential, or of primary benefit to anyone but themselves.

Unless prevented from doing so by humans, Titian bullied his two barn mates out of feed, hay, grazing space, and water. If he wanted something out of his reach, he quietly pushed through people, fences, and doors to get to it. One day he even broke down a pasture gate, miraculously negotiated his way up three deck steps, and guzzled a feeder full of birdseed. For all of his size, he had a morbid fear of needles, rearing and galloping away from the vet when confronted with his annual round of vaccinations. He nipped at anyone in the process of tacking him up for a ride. He refused to stand at a halt for a rider to mount. For passengers managing to make it on board, however, Titian carried them as precious cargo. He responded to voice commands to walk, trot, and canter, and would halt and stand as still as a stone for as long as requested. His past life of competing in dressage and field hunting had rendered him virtually bombproof. As gluttonous for attention as he was for food, he unfailingly answered Rory with a loud, heaving whinny every time she whistled for him or called out his name.

One of Titian's main pastimes was leading his herd of two, Olga and Mystic, on panicked gallops across the pasture at the first sound of geese honking overhead, motorcycles buzzing down the road, or any car breaking gravel in the driveway. Rory wondered how well he would adjust to a new life among a dozen or more horses, and to the possibility of losing his leadership status within the herd once she opened her barn doors to boarders.

Her arrival at the barn signaled the arrival of food, and all three horses began to weave and paw in their stalls in anticipation. As she doled out rations into each rubber feed tub, they nickered softly until their mouths were too full to form any sounds. Titian gobbled his food ahead of the others, and then began drooling into his feeder, creating a syrupy slush of saliva and any remaining bits of grain, which he sucked up noisily. While she admired his efficiency, watching him complete the feed-time ritual always made Rory gag.

Once she'd turned the horses into the pasture for the day, she pulled out a large four-wheeled blue muck cart and basket-shaped manure fork. It amazed her that thousands of years of animal husbandry had not yielded any major innovations in the most critical daily task of barn management—shoveling backbreaking loads of manure.

To prepare for the reality of the boarding business, she timed her morning barn routine. At approximately twenty minutes per stall to muck out, refresh bedding and change water, she estimated a minimum of six hours per day with a new barn full of boarders. She figured on an additional two hours when blankets or fly spray were necessary. With part-time help it should be workable. Her potential employee pool included Ian, who wanted to save up for a new guitar, and Diane, who was always looking for opportunities to spend more time with Mystic and could use the extra cash.

The Barnetts had done a decent amateur job equipping the existing barns. The three-stall shed-row barn featured a small storage room with plank floor, shelves, and a functional window. Next to it were two twelve-by-twelve-foot stalls suitable for large horses, and a pony-sized end stall. The smaller barn, housing Rory's horses, had three large stalls and a cantilevered four-foot overhang. Each stall included a hayrack, a sliding Plexiglas window facing the woods, a ceiling light, and a commercial-grade fan affixed to the wall.

Rory's original intent was to demolish the two small barns once the new one was built, but after settling in, she decided to leave her horses and Mystic where they were, close to the house, and accommodate her new boarders in the larger barn and back pastures. Creating a separate driveway leading to the boarder barn would allow her to maintain a little balance between business and her personal life.

She wheeled the muck cart, heaping full, through the paddock, parked it on the other side of the fence, and closed and locked the gate. Then she remembered that she hadn't put her rings back on after she'd finished the dishes. *Why do so many divorced women relegate their rings to their right hand?* she wondered. Wasn't that just a way of advertising a failed marriage? The idea of making the rings into some other piece of jewelry struck her as equally distasteful. The more she thought about it, the more inappropriate it seemed to wear them at all. Maybe the solution was to retire her rings to her jewelry box and offer them to Ian when he was older.

As she walked back to the house at seven thirty, a flash of something bright caught her eye again—the same light she had seen an hour earlier that morning, standing at the kitchen sink. This time, there was no mistaking it for the glitter of her diamond ring. "What the hell is that?" she muttered.

Back inside the house, she scouted out her birdwatching binoculars, focusing the lenses on the shiny object that looked like it lay just inside the wood line, behind the last field. The source was bright and flat, more a reflection than an illumination, on or near the ground. She scanned outside with her binoculars again at eight o'clock. The reflection was gone. With no sign of it later in the day, she concluded that whatever it was, its visibility depended on her vantage point and the position of the morning sun. Any further conclusions would have to wait a bit longer.

CHAPTER EIGHT

A balmy mid-January Wednesday arrived in Southern Point. Rory considered it a housewarming gift, officially marking six weeks at the new farm on Whistler Ridge Road. The melodic calls of robins, bluebirds, and one illusive meadowlark competed with squawks and gurgles exchanged by grackles and starlings—all mimicked by the farm's resident mockingbird, which surveyed Rory from rooftop to fencepost to treetop as she completed her afternoon tasks. Only the intermittent boom of shotgun fire interrupted the pleasant scene, as hunters picked away at wintering snow geese roosting in the bay marsh across the road.

Rory filled bird feeders in front of the house, watching for Ian's bus, glad to be home when he arrived, within minutes of his school during the day, present when needed. The yellow bus made its way down Whistler Ridge Road with one stop left before the farm, prompting a duet of barks and howls from the dogs as they watched from the dining room windowsill. A few minutes later, Ian made his way up the drive and into the house.

"Why don't you take Rocket for a walk to the back of the property and see if you can find out what that thing is in the woods?" Rory asked, as he began to unfold his lean body onto the living room sofa. "Al can stay here with me."

"But, *Mom*," he protested, "I just got home from school."

"You know she loves to go outside with you. Take her for her walk now—before you get too comfortable. I'm going to do a little cleaning—and I'll make something for you to eat when you two get back."

Ian's jaw stretched into a gaping yawn as he lumbered over to the kitchen pantry, grabbing Rocket's green harness and leash from its hook inside the door. When the puppy heard the leash hardware clinking, she began a slippery, noisy dance across the wood floor, simultaneously yapping, jumping, and wagging her otter-like tail. She wriggled through Ian's legs as he struggled to secure her leash, and then dragged him through the French doors leading out to the deck.

Boy and dog headed across the newly mowed fields, leaving Rory to survey the condition of the living room they'd left behind. Tufts of woolly brown and black dog hair coated the navy-blue oriental area rug. A green silk pillow rested on the floor next to a manure-caked riding boot of Rory's that Rocket had recently pilfered from the laundry room. Two of Ian's balled-up grass-stained crew socks served as a makeshift centerpiece for the marble-topped coffee table. The mummified remains of a hapless tree frog lay splayed under the leg of an antique rocking chair. Effective warfare against this reality of country living required the employment of state-of-the-art appliances combined with a vigorous application of elbow grease and an infusion of hope that this time, the house might stay clean for a day or two.

She gathered tools, rags, and a bucket in the home's central hall and concocted mixtures of lavender-scented household cleaner and lemon furniture oil. For half an hour she labored between the kitchen, dining room, and breakfast rooms, dusting, wiping down shelves and chair rails, and vacuuming. Finally, she made her way to the living room's large corner windowsill, which also served as Al and Rocket's favorite place to rest drooling jowls and muddy paws while they scanned their world for invading rabbits, deer, and twice-weekly visits from Diane's dog, Aggie. Rory had just knelt down to begin work on removing the thick film of dried saliva and hair from the windowsill, when, through her peripheral vision, she caught the blaze orange of Ian's hoodie streaking up the center of the muddy back pastures. He wore a look of stark terror on his face as he and Rocket cleared three drainage ditches in record time. Rory jumped up, dropped the rag she was holding, and ran for the door, tipping over the bucket of sudsy water on her way. "Shit!" She hopped in stocking feet across the living room rug as water flowed in all directions.

Dragging her leash, Rocket bounded through the distance, pink tongue flapping out of the sides of her mouth, tail spinning like an out-of-control hand crank that was propelling her home. Ian's speed knocked a few serious injuries off Rory's possibility list. She scanned his clothes for signs of dirt or blood, saw none, and wondered if he had run into some hunters, or stumbled upon an injured, or worse yet, rabid animal in the woods. "Oh, god, don't let it be a snake bite," she prayed. Ian and Rocket exploded through the door, tripping on each other, as Rory opened it.

"Mom! Rocket found a bone!" He spat the words out between heavy breaths. "I think something out there died—I'm serious!"

"What?" Rory thought she'd heard him wrong. "What did you say?" She tried to steer him clear of the wet spots on the floor.

He put both hands in the distended front pocket of his hoodie and struggled for a moment. "Here!" he exclaimed, retrieving a bone infused with dirt and roots from inside the pocket, and slapping it into her open palm.

"Ouch!" Rory cried. "Careful with that, honey." She cradled the bone in both hands. "Let's have a look at it."

Childhood impromptu anatomy lessons by Rory's pathologist father left her with more knowledge of the human body than she thought she would ever possibly need or use. Until now. While other kids played Operation, Rory identified the bones of the human body on a synthetic skeleton that hung in the corner of her father's study, in exchange for squares of Bazooka bubble gum. She had a working knowledge of most of them by the time she turned twelve—the same year her father had died.

Ian was right: it looked like a human radius bone, about six inches long, from an adult, she guessed.

"Okay, calm down. Go sit and catch your breath." Rory threw some dry dish towels on the floor. "This is probably from an animal," she lied. "A deer, maybe a cow. But I think to be on the safe side, we should call the police and have them check it out."

They went into the kitchen where Ian settled on a barstool at the counter. Rocket circled the stool, waiting for him to pass her back her treasure—the bone. But he was agitated and out of breath, oblivious to the dog's begging.

"Mom, maybe there's a—a—poacher or even a serial killer out there or something. . . ." he said, his voice trembling.

Rory tried to be reassuring. "Honey, look how dirty it is. I'd say that it's been there for a while. You know that when wild animals die, their remains, over time, return to the earth."

"And, people, too—when people die."

'Yes, right. Don't worry. I'll be right back." She found one of Titian's leg wraps in a basket of clean laundry and began loosely wrapping it around the bone.

"Aren't you going to wash it off?" Ian asked, calmer now.

"No, we need to leave it undisturbed if we can." She slid the swaddled bone into a brown paper bag.

"But don't you want to get a better look at it?" he asked. "See what kind it is?"

"Even if I did, the roots and dirt might actually help the police figure out how it got there. They're like clues. Handling it could destroy those clues. It's out of our hands now, literally." Rory searched her phone for the Southern Point Police Department's non-emergency phone number.

"Mom, you know that shiny thing you saw back there?" Ian asked, pulling off his hoodie. "It's a piece of metal from a car or something." He swallowed hard. "I think something real bad might'a happened back there."

A white police cruiser waited up at the front of Rory's security gate. She ran out of the house and down the driveway until she reached its midpoint, repeatedly pressing the pager-sized gate remote control. Her high-tech entrance had one hitch: the remote worked up to a distance of seven hundred feet, but her driveway was a thousand feet long. And she'd forgotten to give the entry code to the police dispatcher. The gates swept open and the car streamed over the gravel, slowing to an idle in the parking circle in front of the house.

Its lone occupant was a well-padded sixty-ish male officer wearing a slate-blue uniform, gold-rimmed aviator sunglasses, and a visored cap that covered most of his close-cropped silver hair. Rory recognized him as Sergeant John Adderson, the same officer who'd helped her when Ian had run away in October. The sight of him induced an immediate sense of relief. She waved at him as she walked to meet his car.

"Good afternoon, Mrs. Fielding. Nice to see you again," Sergeant Adderson said through the open driver's-side window. "So, your son's found a bone, has he?" The policeman was matter of fact, discreetly chewing on some gum while he waited for her answer.

"Actually, one of our dogs found it, Sergeant. Rocket, our black Lab puppy. Back in the woods."

"Lab puppies—those devils. They love to root around and dig, don't they?" He shook his head while mincing the wad of gum in his cheek. "And, those devils need jobs! Otherwise, they'll make short work of whatever's within reach. Shoes, boots, pillows—I've lost them all."

She nodded in agreement. "Thanks for getting here so fast. The bone is human from what I can tell. Do you want me to lead you back to the woods, or should I stay out of your way? I'm not sure what to do."

He got out of the police car and removed his cap. "Well, first I need to get some information from you. Then, based on our protocol, we can decide how to proceed from there. Is the bone here at the house?"

"Yes, in the house."

"Have you handled it?"

"Minimally. I have it wrapped up for you."

"Why don't you bring it out here to me and we'll get started?"

"Okay. I'll be right back." Rory went to the house and retrieved the paper bag. "I thought this would do the least damage." She passed him the bag. "No fragrance or chemicals."

"Thank you for doin' that." He took the bag and opened it, then drew his visor cap back on. "Can I ask you to show me where the dog found it, so I can get started on figuring out if a wrong's in need of righting?" he asked kindly. "Oh, and is it muddy back there? Should I change into my boots?"

Rory found the man's kind manner and tact comforting, this rural policeman whose sole precinct occupied three rooms of a small building it shared with a senior citizen day program. He had exercised the same balance of competence and empathy when Ian ran away.

"It's not bad back there, Sergeant. Stark Farms ditched behind the woods a few years ago, and we just repeated the process in front of the woods two weeks ago. It's starting to dry out pretty quickly. Let me get Ian and we can head back." She started walking to the house. "We can drive part of the way," she called out. "Otherwise, it's a ten-minute walk."

After running through the details of Rocket's discovery, Ian, Rory, and Sergeant Adderson drove as far as the side tree line and hiked the rest of the way to the back woods.

"Ian, can you show me exactly where you were when you—Rocket—found the bone?" Sergeant Adderson asked. He took photos with his phone while they walked.

Gingerly retracing their steps, Ian explained how he and Rocket found the piece of metal that Rory had seen from the house, just beyond the last cleared pasture. "Rocket kept pulling on her leash like she wanted to get at something, so I followed her," he said as the three of them entered the woods. "She came to that tree over there. . . ." He pointed to the base of a fifteen-foot gum tree, stripped bare of its leaves and gum balls by the winter wind and rain. "She was sniffing around and digging like she does in the yard. Then she pulled up that—that bone I brought back to the house." He pointed straight ahead at a small hole, a foot or so deep. "See? I think there might be other stuff down there."

Sergeant Adderson froze in his tracks and held up his hand like a traffic cop. "All right then, I think we oughta stop right here. I need to make some phone calls and take a few more pictures. Why don't you two wait for me by the car?"

"No problem." Rory thought about it for a moment. "Sergeant, we'll just walk back to the house."

"If you're sure. Otherwise, I'll only be a minute."

It was forty-five minutes later when Sergeant Adderson made his way back to the house. Ian coaxed the dogs upstairs and secured them in the room over the garage, yelling "all clear!" to his mother. Rory ushered the policeman into the dining room, where he pulled out a chair, leaned back, and removed his jacket and rested his battered silver field clipboard on his lap.

"Mrs. Fielding, the bone does appear to have been attached to a human, so we have to investigate this a little bit more."

"I understand," she said. "We'll just wait to hear what you find out after you examine the remains."

He shifted uncomfortably in his chair. "Uh, well, now, we're going to have to investigate right here—on your property. That means I'm gonna need you to bring some of your farming and construction activities to a temporary halt."

She felt her heart stop and skip at the suggestion of delays. Her schedule allowed few, if any. "Some? Can you be more specific? Which activities?"

"Well, pretty much all activities. No disturbance of the soil anywhere in the vicinity of the discovery. No blocking authorized access to the site. And we'll need exclusive access to the scene until we figure out what's going on here—what that dirt back there can offer up. Strange how much the ground can tell you—if you listen. Our first step is to send the bone to the medical examiner and possibly schedule a grid search of the area."

She sank in her chair. "What's a grid search?"

"It's where we bring in a team of officers—or county police academy recruits in this case—and the team performs two parallel line searches of an assigned area, first in one direction, and then in another, at a ninety-degree angle—like mapping squares on a sheet of graph paper. It allows us to utilize many sets of eyes at once, hopefully picking up on more evidence than we could with one or two people. It's not a sure thing yet, but until I know whether the grid search is a definite, I have to ask you to keep your dogs and horses out of the area, since right now it's midway between a curiosity and a crime scene."

"Anything else?" she asked, contemplating creating a list of do's and don'ts.

"I think we'll run some plastic fencing around the area of discovery just in case any deer, foxes, or other animals—especially nosy humans—take to wandering around back there. No one should be, since all the farm lanes are private. But you never know. All of our people will phone your house and give you a password before we enter the access code at your gate, so you'll be sure who we are. Think up a code word for me to disseminate. If anyone tries to talk their way in without the code, call 911."

"Okay." Up to this point, it hadn't occurred to Rory to be uneasy. He read her mind.

"Now remember, this is not a body. The bone looks like it's been here for some time, and it could have been carried here from somewhere else. Southern Point is full of old graves and cemeteries, some pretty informal, if you know what I mean. Years ago, an elderly migrant worker was found by a building contractor, buried in a simple grave."

"Someone mentioned that to me," she said.

"It was an unspoken practice in Southern Point, Ms. Fielding. The undocumented workers were transported into the area from across the US border in trucks, where they remained for the duration of whatever crop planting or harvest they were working, with no way home. If an older worker died of natural causes during the season, the other workers would bury him or her in a simple, unmarked grave, and continue their work until season's end. With tens of thousands of acres of land to choose from, chances were good that the graves would never be known to anyone outside the migrant workers' group. And it was rumored that their hidden cemetery network consisted of hundreds of secret migrant graves. It still might—if you ask me. With so much more land than people out here, anything can happen. If no one sees, if no one talks, we'll never know."

"I'm beginning to believe that," she said.

"Yep, the smaller the town, the bigger the secrets—if you ask me," Sergeant Adderson said. Then he motioned to the camera and alarm keypad by the front door. "Looks to me that with this alarm system and your dogs, your biggest threat is going to be the local media if they have a slow news day." He snapped his writing case shut. "I'll be in touch. Good day to you."

Ian helped serve dinner that night without any complaints. Rory sat down with him at her left, leaving four empty places at the white-clothed table Sandy had spent an hour arranging and fussing over. Silverware and china clicked and chimed as the two pushed chicken, and fresh vegetables from the self-serve farmers' market down the road, around their plates. Half an hour passed before Ian started asking questions.

"Mom, what do you think happened back there?"

"Honey, I have no idea, but it had to be a long time ago. I'm going to ask Sandy and Mr. Deal if they've ever heard of anything going on in the woods. They grew up here—they might know something."

Ian sneered. "Do you have to ask *him*?"

"Ian, what is your problem with Mr. Deal?"

"He bugs me. He always stares at you when you're not looking."

"I think you're exaggerating," she said.

"Yeah, right," he mumbled back. "Well, I guess I can't ride my dirt bike anywhere around here now. It's too weird."

She rolled her eyes. "I'll get some more information from Sergeant Adderson about that. I don't think they'll prevent us from using all of our property. I imagine they just need clear access to travel back and forth with their vehicles. And maybe to fence off the area around the . . . evidence . . . for a few days while they're working in the woods."

Ian slept on the living room sofa with Rocket that night, disregarding Rory's assurance that the alarm system was armed, and that Al could easily fend off any unwelcome visitors. A protection-trained dog, Al was usually quiet and aloof, but responded to several secret word commands in emergencies. Rory purchased her, as she had the dog's late aunt, from a local breeder specializing in canine protection training. Any intruder trying to break into the house would have to go through a hundred pounds of overly protective German Shepherd first.

Despite his anxiety, Ian was out cold minutes after he settled into his makeshift sofa bed, but Rory chased sleep unsuccessfully that night, unsettled as the bone whose rest in the back woods had now abruptly ended.

CHAPTER NINE

"Miss Rory, folks 'round here are sayin' that it's the McCullough girl—that it's Kerry." It was Tuesday morning, and Sandy had let herself into the house to a chorus of barking dogs. She found Rory standing at the living room window, sipping a half cup of espresso—her heart condition dictated limited consumption of caffeine—as she stared out at the cordoned-off woods. Sandy leaned against the kitchen counter and cleared her throat conspicuously. "Miss Rory," she repeated louder than before, "they're saying that maybe Herb might'a took care of things like he always said he would."

"Who—who are you talking about, Sandy?" Rory asked in a sharp tone without turning around. It was the jumpstart of a new day, peppered thick with speculation about the "big find" in her back woods. She had spent the much of the last week maneuvering around inappropriate questions from neighbors and store clerks. She'd fielded a string of bad jokes from friends suggesting that she had knocked off Tom and that the bone was his.

Ian declared he was "totally creeped out" by the thought of a body, or part of one, buried on the farm. While Rory didn't admit it to Ian, or anyone else, she was creeped out too. Then there was the delay the police investigation was causing in opening her business. The very activities Sergeant Adderson had ordered to a halt were those most critical to her construction timeline.

"Sorry, Sandy," Rory said, her bitchy tone in check. In the six years Sandy had worked for her, the woman was, even at her most invasive, well-intentioned. Perhaps in this case, those good intentions might yield some helpful history or insight. Rory turned away from the window. "What do you mean—took care of Kerry? Took care of her when? Who is she?"

"Well, somebody's dead down there in that dirt, and they've been there awhile," Sandy answered. "You know that place over on Goose Pond Road?"

"You mean that farm with the cluster of houses where the tractor-trailer's always parked?"

"Yeah, that's owned by the McCulloughs. Course, it's only Joe and his mother, Sally, livin' up there now."

"Why do you think they're connected to the body—bone?"

Sandy slid onto a kitchen barstool and wrapped her hands around the water bottle filled with sweetened club soda that she always brought with her to Rory's house.

"Down here, people don't mix like they do in the city and up north—where you're from. And back then, in the seventies, early eighties, things were even more split up. It was okay as long as they didn't cross that line."

"The line. Were 'they' Black people?"

"Well . . . yes, ma'am," she said, averting her eyes.

"Go on, Sandy."

Apprehensive about continuing, Sandy stayed silent.

"What were you going to say, Sandy?"

Sandy took a swig from her bottle. "Well, uh, I remember way back my younger sister, Susan, met a boy—in high school—the only boy in the whole school who wasn't White. He took a likin' to 'er. When he saw our mother at the school's fall pageant, he asked her for permission to call on Susan. Momma had to tell him to keep to his own people. It was for his own sake. There would'a been trouble."

After Sandy cited examples of trouble in the form of racial intolerance in Southern Point, she announced, "It's even more separate down on Fisher Island, you know."

"Worse than this? Christ."

Fisher Island was a small landmass connected to the southernmost point of Southern Point by a marshy two-mile causeway. A major waterfowl migration hub, its economy revolved around fruit orchards, fishing, crabbing, and duck and swan hunting. The island had one dilapidated grocery store, which also sold gas, fishing permits, and bait. A rotting plywood breezeway connected the store to Ida's Bar, an equally unappealing establishment featuring twelve stools and one table for four. Rory and Tom made the mistake of going into Ida's once, thinking they might get pizza or a sandwich. They ended up walking backward all the way to their car, vowing that in the future they would only head to the island with full stomachs and a full tank of gas.

Sandy was on a roll, and not about to stop. "About twenty years ago, my Ray had to follow two Black sailors off the island when they tried to get a drink in Ida's."

Rory sat down at the breakfast room table, anticipating another tale with an unsavory outcome. "What happened?"

"Ray was there for his daily afternoon beers. He knew better than to drink at a bar up here 'cause I'd a heard about it. Two Black sailors walked into Ida's, uniforms and all. The bartender told the sailors he could sell 'em a beer at the bar, but they'd have to *drink* it outside. The sailors said they paid for it like everyone else and they should be able to drink it inside. Ray saw trouble comin' and told the two of them to leave the bar, for their own safety. Somehow, he got them to go outside and then followed them all the way back through Southern Point to make sure no one did anything crazy. I mean, anything could'a happened to them between that marsh and the mainland."

"That was in the nineties? God, Sandy, I feel like you're off by three decades."

"I'm not sayin' that's how *I* think. It's not. There's good folks and bad folks—black and white. I'm just sayin' that's how it was here back then. Still is—to some. Still to this day." Sandy fidgeted a little in her seat. "The Black folks—they never had a place with the whites down here in those days."

"What are people around here saying about the bone?"

"Well, Herb Whistler—his family owned the largest farm around here way back when—most of the land between here and Goose Pond Road. The road was named for his daddy back in the 1930s. Herb was mean enough sober, and even meaner drunk. Most people tried to stay clear of him. His wife, Julia, had that disease—the one they got that big telethon for."

"You mean . . . muscular dystrophy?" Rory guessed.

"Uh-huh. She was from St. Louis, didn't have any family here. No one to help her. She was a real pretty woman and sweet, too. They had one child, Jimmy. I think havin' the baby took a toll—made her worse."

"Was she hospitalized for her disease?"

"Sometimes, here and there. Hers was the grown-up kind—I guess that ain't as bad as if they find it when you're young. Julia couldn't do no heavy work, but she did her best on the farm. And, she had to use a wheelchair on some days. It seemed like Herb blamed Jimmy comin' into the world for Julia's sickness. He was so hard on that boy." Sandy shook her head. "Anyway, the lane that the Whistlers used to get to their house ran right by Joe McCullough's place. Kerry McCullough was a couple'a years younger than Jimmy but in his class 'cause she was so smart—smart enough for college. Those two walked the same road home every day for more than ten years."

Rory thought for a moment. "The entrance to the McCullough place isn't really near where the Whistler's old house is. . . ."

"Not now. In those days it was. The Whistler farm took up just about every bit of free space out here, near a thousand acres. Their farm lanes—there were lots of 'em, includin' the dirt roads off the back of your place—ran behind everybody else's houses." Sandy finished her drink and tried unsuccessfully to suppress a burp. "'Scuse me! People always thought that Jimmy liked Kerry. Some even said they were up to no good."

"Do you think they were in a relationship?" Rory asked.

"Oh, they had a relationship all right. Everyone knew that. They'd been close since they were kids. Were they messin' around? No one knew for sure, but most folks thought so. The last summer Jimmy and Kerry were here was, maybe, the late 80s, and there were lotsa rumors that they ran off together and their families were too ashamed to admit it, but I know that didn't happen."

"You mean because of the racial issue?"

"Oh no, it wasn't just that. Joe McCullough wouldn't have stood for Kerry taking up with Jimmy any more than Herb wanted Jimmy to be with Kerry. Jimmy drank just like his dad, and he was always in trouble. But he wasn't mean—at least not that I ever saw. Jimmy was more . . . sad. Sad and quiet—like his mother. The alcohol is what did it to him, if you ask me."

"What do you think happened?"

"Joe McCullough always told folks that Kerry went to Baltimore to finish school, 'cause it was easier up there for, you know, jobs and all. Herb told Ray that Jimmy went off to see the world, went out West or something. Both of 'em? The same time? It was all real strange." Sandy stood up and turned to Rory. "I wouldn't put anything past Herb."

"You talk about him like he's still alive."

"No, ma'am! This sounds bad, but thank the Lord he's dead and gone. If he didn't like you, he'd ruin you for sure. I remember hearin' something about a family down the ridge who refused to sell him their hundred-acre place. For a time, hog farmin' was good business here—before the big companies took it over. Back when I was younger, there were maybe twenty family farms around Southern Point. The rumor was, Herb had his eye on one of the local farms, but the owner wouldn't budge. Wouldn't sell out to him. Next thing you know, all their hogs turned up dead. Every single one. Someone put antifreeze in the water troughs. It was never traced direct, but everyone knew Herb did it, or paid to have it done. They say the family went broke and was forced to sell their farm to Herb after all. Don't know exactly who it was—a buncha hog farms shut down around that time. And that's only one example."

"You're telling me that people around here believe Herb hurt or killed Kerry McCullough?"

"Oh, Herb wouldn't dirty his own hands. He'd get someone else to do it. What I'm tryin' to tell you is that Herb Whistler would never have let those two be . . . together, you know. And one day, Kerry went away"—she snapped her fingers—"just like that. I guess we'll see what the police dig up back in those woods."

"I guess so," Rory agreed.

Sandy got to work on the house, leaving Rory to review budget numbers. She sat down at her desk in the den and printed out the barn contract draft, emailed to her earlier in the day, but couldn't concentrate. Sandy, by way of telling tales about Herb Whistler and Kerry McCullough, had explained why the McCulloughs seemed hesitant to respond to her friendly waves when she passed by their houses. For the past five years, Rory had assumed their frosty reaction to her waved greetings was because they considered her an interloper in their small community. It hadn't occurred to her that they viewed themselves as outsiders. She forced herself to look over the contract again, scrutinizing numbers and notating revisions so she could overnight the package by noon.

Rounding the final turn of Goose Pond Road on her way to the post office, Rory cruised slowly by the McCulloughs' place, a three-acre compound cut out of the dense, surrounding woods, consisting of one decaying white clapboard cottage with red trim, one immaculate asbestos-sided house painted mint green, an old red barn, some chicken coops, and a steel building seemingly the size of an airplane hangar. Behind a row of neatly trimmed azaleas, she saw a tall, muscular older man in overalls and an elderly woman wearing a pink housecoat puttering together in a small vegetable garden. Based on her conversation with Sandy, she concluded they were Joe McCullough and his mother, Sally. Rory waved as always, but Sally returned only an upraised palm without making eye contact, the same as every other time Rory had waved, and probably the same as she'd done thirty years ago.

CHAPTER TEN

As was the case on most days, things at the post office were quiet. Toby Pierce, the postmaster, stood behind the counter just past a wall of brass-fronted postal boxes and next to a live and very agitated rooster, preoccupied with pecking its way out of its cardboard delivery crate.

"I think Foghorn Leghorn had a rough trip," Toby said, scratching his head. "I sure wish his new owner would get on in here and retrieve him. He's startin' to stink up the place somethin' fierce." Toby showed Rory his new model train set and passed her a bowl of leftover Christmas candy while he processed her overnight package, politely refraining from any comments about her recent move and change in marital status. She had one hand on the glass entry door when he silently passed her a change-of-address form with her receipt. "No rush. We know where to find ya," he said. She walked to her truck, holding her receipt and address form tight in her hand. Once inside, the finality of her decision to leave Tom hit her. The truck windows were closed tight. No one else was in the parking lot. She put her face in her hands, unable to stop the flow of tears.

The midafternoon temperature in Southern Point shot up to a comfortable seventy-five degrees, thanks to a cloudless, sunny sky, which also burned away the shadow of Rory's earlier funk. Once the dogs returned from their pee-and-romp session in the yard, she started up the tractor and set out to mow the front pasture. The loud drone of the Kubota's diesel engine drowned out all ambient noise, so she didn't notice a *Shoreline News* van pulling into the driveway. It was only during one of her mowing passes in the direction of the road that she saw a lanky young man with a fake tan and noticeably plucked eyebrows frantically waving at her from outside the gate. A reporter, she guessed. In the past week Rory had counted a dozen or so cars, most of them media, idling at the edge of the driveway, held at bay only by the front security gate, whose iron and stonework formed a formidable barrier between her family and intruders of all kinds. She continued her work, ignoring the reporter's animated pleas for access or information, until he finally gave up and left, just as Ian got off the bus.

"God, let me have five peaceful minutes with Ian, and I promise not to swear this week," she prayed aloud to the cycling tractor engine. She pulled out of the pasture and rode back to the house alongside Ian as he trudged up the driveway, looking glum. He'd turned down her offer to let him hitch a ride on the running board.

Their daily arguments were becoming exhausting and discouraging. Tom insisted that the two of them clashed because they were so much alike. Rory believed the real reason was Ian's assumption that she had single-handedly destroyed their family. The fracture in the mother-son relationship had deepened following the move to Whistler Ridge Road. Technically, Ian was right: Rory had initiated the legal separation. What he didn't know was how long she had lived unhappily in her marriage, for him—in lieu of personal fulfillment. Right or wrong, she would never tell him that her sadness had become hazardous to her own well-being, that she'd mused about bloodless suicide scenarios. That sometimes she'd stood in Titian's stall when he was eating his feed, wishing that he would make the decision for her by delivering one well-placed kick to her head. Or that, in the end, it was fear of finding the courage to realize her ideations—not selfishness—that forced her to end her marriage.

"I want to live at Dad's house. This place freaks me out," Ian announced as he walked up the front steps. Rory jumped down from the tractor and followed him into the house.

"Ian, your dad is traveling too much right now for you to live there."

"Why can't I stay over there while he's gone? I have my own room—I know where everything is."

"Not alone, Ian. You're only fourteen."

"I hate this. Why do you have to get a divorce now? Everyone's asking me questions about why we moved, and about the whole corpse thing."

"First of all, it's not a corpse. It could just be an old grave for all we know. Secondly, your dad and I have discussed you going back and forth between houses, and we can talk about it some more—when he gets back from DC. In the meantime, you live here. Get on your homework and I'll take you out for dinner later." As soon as she said it, she asked herself why she'd thrown a reward into the expectation of civility and appropriate behavior. Invoking the rule of getting back on a horse after being thrown, so its last memory of the ride is the rider being the one in control, she coughed up a weak mitigation of her blunder. "We're going somewhere healthy. No junk food. No burgers."

CHAPTER ELEVEN

Rory closed the truck windows as she coursed the dirt lane leading to Deal's Feed and Seed, a green Quonset building fronted by stacked water troughs, hayracks, and neon-colored plastic buckets. Tawny dust, stirred to life by her truck's tires, filmed over its hood and doors, nullifying the previous day's ultimate car wash from the Southern Point Gas-N-Go. She opened the glass entry door to the sound of a cowbell and was in the process of scanning the disordered interior for signs of life when she heard shuffling noises coming from somewhere behind the pet food section.

"Dan?"

A voice pierced the neck-high wall of dog chow bags. "Hello! What's going on at Churchill Downs?"

"Very funny," she said, continuing her search for the body that went with the voice. "Things are at a standstill at the farm. I'm here to go over my numbers and my schedule one last time if you have a few minutes."

"You come on back here," he answered, appearing in front of the store's curtained-off office area in his standard issue—jeans and a gray snap-front shirt with its sleeves rolled up to the elbows. She made her way toward him, stepping around bags and crates of store inventory, her pulse hammering against her veins. Was it an electrical cardiac misfire, or raw sexual longing? Unsure which of the two, she breathed in through her nose, counted to fourteen as her doctor had instructed, and held in the breath for a few seconds.

"You okay, dear?" Dan asked. He stood in front of his desk and lit a cigar while he politely waited for her to sit down.

She nodded, repeating her technique.

"Well, then, have a seat."

Notepad in hand, Rory settled on one of two tired white plastic lawn chairs. Next to her, a small black-and-white television served as the centerpiece of the old desk, piled high with file folders and papers. Dan caught a momentary wave of revulsion passing over her face.

"Look, I have a legitimate office at home," he blurted out. "I just keep the one here for show." He bit his lip as he stared down at the desk with a new perspective. "I can't have customers thinking I'm too successful, can I?"

"I think you're safe from that happening," Rory said, balancing on the edge of the chair to minimize the transfer of dirt and dust to her new breeches. With the police-ordered work stoppage at her place in full force, the price of everything was now an object, and her new hundred-dollar breeches had to last her for a while.

Dan sank into a maroon steno chair, its shiny, cracked upholstery revealing lumps of gray stuffing. "I just need another minute," he said, picking up a pen and hunching over a *Washington Post* crossword puzzle. "What's an eight-letter word for 'romantic complication'?"

"Oh geez, where to begin?" she pondered out loud.

"Starts with a *T*," he said, his eyes volleying over the squares of the puzzle.

"Can I think about it and get back to you?" she asked.

"Don't take too long, Rory. I have to finish this one before I start a new one—I'm addicted."

"Let's see the puzzle," she said, standing up and walking to the other side of the desk, where she leaned over his shoulder. She caught the smell of shampoo and sun, mixed with a trace of tobacco and some unknown aftershave, wafting upward from his head and neck. It made her feel physically hungry.

"Well?" he said, turning his head and looking up at her.

She jumped back as their eyes met. "Uh, I can't think of anything right now."

"Eight letters . . ."

Rory returned to her chair. "Dan, what is it with you and crossword puzzles, anyway?"

"They keep the wheels turning. I approach my work in the same way. You don't get all of the information at once. You have to keep filling in the blanks, working it from the outside. Every little scrap of information . . . leads to something else. Sometimes, you get more to work with, other times, the clues—the leads, take you down the wrong path entirely. . . ."

She leaned forward across the desk and rifled through a stack of completed puzzles, all of them neatly folded, out of place on the messy work surface. "You've given this a lot of thought."

"That's precisely what they make you do, Rory. Think." He turned toward the window and away from the front of her scoop-neck T-shirt, which presented an unobstructed view of her breasts, barely contained by an embroidered lavender bra. "No distractions."

Rory tapped her lower lip. "*Triangle.*"

"Huh?" Dan muttered, fixing his eyes on her face.

"Is it *triangle*—the romantic complication?" she asked, leaning farther over the desktop.

"Maybe—okay, let's think—talk—about something else," he said loudly, standing up. "Let's confer like the farmers that we are."

"Right," she agreed. "Or, in my case, aspire to be."

They reviewed all things agricultural: soil amendment, fertilizing, and pasture rotation. Dan sketched out a working timeline of seven months. With her land cleared and checked off the list, she still had to plant grass before the first of April to establish pastures in time for September boarders. Delivery and completion of the fencing and barn construction could wait until early summer if absolutely necessary. When they finished talking about horse business issues, Dan proffered the police investigation.

"How're those Southern Point coppers—the police—treating you?" He lit a half cigar.

"The assigned officers have been respectful and try to stay out of our way, but I need access to all of my property now. You and I revised the timeline a minute ago. It's almost February and the clock is ticking."

"You can spare another few weeks before planting without any major problems, but that's about it." He delivered the statement with a note of caution. "If you're going to make this work, they need to button things up—sooner not later."

"I think they're trying to get through it. They show up early and work late. Don't say much to us—mostly polite reminders to stay out of the cordoned-off area. The police have got the bone Rocket dug up, and I don't know about the metal thing I saw. They say it's from a vehicle of some sort. Let's see what else. Oh yes, my son has now informed me that he hates living in a graveyard, and I'm not crazy about the rumors floating around Southern Point."

"Rumors about what? How the bone got there?"

"Yeah. Sandy Cross told me about a girl who disappeared decades ago—a girl named Kerry—she thinks suspiciously. She also filled me in a little bit on the Whistler family and Southern Point's history of racial relations."

Dan didn't react with the surprise she'd expected. "Chances are whatever Sandy told you is true. The smaller and more isolated a place is, the longer it takes to accept new ideas, even today. That's why I didn't follow my father into farming." He took a long draw on his cigar. "I had to get out—adopt a more global view of the world. Trust me, I could write a book about some of the things that have happened out here."

"It's all true then? Do you have your own ugly tales to tell? Your own theory about who was—is—in the back woods of my farm?"

"Let's just say that a lot's been buried around here over the years. Hell, Rory, I remember back to the '70s, my mother decided to go out into the world on her own. Translation—she got a job at a drugstore in town."

Their shared laugh was brief. Then Dan's smile faded.

"She met another new employee who worked her shift at the same store sometimes. Turned out—he lived here in Southern Point. He didn't have a car—his was in the shop because of an accident or something, so Mom offered him a ride with her on the days they worked the same hours. When she picked him up the first time, he got into the back seat of her car. She told him to ride up front with her. Well, he told her he didn't want any trouble for her from the people in town. She insisted that he get in the front seat, and eventually he did. It caused a small scandal, Rory. All because she was white, and he wasn't. If our family hadn't been considered "respected" and off limits for harassment by a certain group of 'ole boys around here, who knows how bad it could have gotten?"

"But it died down after a while?"

"Yeah. Coincidentally, my mom got pregnant with my younger sister and had terrible morning sickness. She quit her job. It was probably for the best."

"That reminds me of what Sandy said. 'It was for his own sake. It was for the best.'" She couldn't hide her disgust, as much for what she perceived as his open acceptance of unfair treatment as much as for the act itself. Maybe she'd thought too highly of him.

"Rory, it doesn't mean I condone it; I condemn it. That's history—the truth. That's the way it was. And some folks around here still have that attitude. Look at the proudly displayed Confederate flags you pass when you drive up and down Southern Point Road. Here's another story for you. When I was seven or eight, my brother, Rick, and I decided to go into the big woods behind our farm that led to the waterway. Everyone assumed that it was swampy and full of snakes. No one ever went back there. Or that's what we thought. Our mother gave us permission, but told us we had to mark our way, we had to take a watch with us, and we had to be home before dark. Now, these were our own woods, bought by my dad a few years earlier, sight unseen. Rick and I were, oh, maybe a half mile or so in, and what happened? We stumbled right onto two small cabin houses and an outhouse, furnished and outfitted like the people had left with no warning whatsoever. There were clothes in trunks, dishes, everything. We ran home like our pants were on fire and told our mother what we found. She said the houses must have belonged to a Black family that was run out of the area years before."

Rory disregarded her dust-laden seat, leaned back, and braced her arms on the sides of the chair. "Dan, I'm not naïve. I've lived in the South for twenty-some years, and in Southern Point for almost six. But I didn't pick up on the pockets of casual segregation and racism that still exist here until now. When I worked at our agency, five days of the week I was gone more than I was here. Now that I'm immersed in the community—I've had the time to discover it."

"Did Sandy tell you about Fisher Island? To this day, you won't find a single Black family down there. And what about the case of that Black girl who was stabbed to death decades ago by two white men, all because she tried to sell encyclopedias in a white neighborhood? That case went unsolved for thirty years because no one would come forward. Neo-Nazis? Klan rallies? Charlottesville? Racism is revived alive and well—exalted. Not just here. It's risen to the top—to Washington, for God's sake! Who knows what could happen next?"

"A family not taking action if something so horrific—shocking—happened to their daughter? Think about that." She crossed her arms in front of her. "I've tried to put myself in their position—"

"Useless!" He cut her off. "Rory, you can't. Neither one of us can do that. We've never lived in fear of our neighbors, or with the fear of not being protected by the law. I've seen plenty of people in that situation—here and when I was on the force—afraid to come forward, afraid to tell the truth."

"You're right," she conceded. "But still—his *daughter*."

"Anyway, the McCulloughs don't talk much with their neighbors, and the Whistlers aren't around here anymore. The son took off, like so many of the young people around here did as soon as they were able. Herb died—I don't think anyone cried over that—and the wife may still be with us, I'm not sure. She went into a nursing home years ago. If I can find out where, maybe we can see if she remembers anything about the property."

"Shouldn't I just leave it to your brethren, the police?"

"Absolutely, if your business plan can withstand interminable holdups. I don't think at this point the authorities consider this the highest priority, because the remains appear to have been there for a while and no one was ever reported missing. The bad news is, with the county involved now, they're going to wade through protocol because they have to, which means indefinite status quo for your farm. Your call, Aurora."

CHAPTER TWELVE

Three days later Rory sat in what she privately called the Mamba's lounge at Moby's Music Store with two other women her age, taking note of their nearly identical wardrobes featuring suede track shoes, jeans from a big box store's juniors department, and faux shearling jackets. They had parked themselves at opposite ends of an old plaid couch that was positioned squarely in the center of the lounge, making them and their rant about the logistics of juggling playdates with one child versus two or more, and attempting to personalize their cell phone rings with Top 40 songs, inescapable. Rory considered it a safe bet that they were the proud owners of the vehicles bearing the SPOILDHER and KIDSMOM license plates she had passed in the parking lot on her way into the store. For the first time since Ian had started his guitar lessons six months earlier, she prayed that today's lesson would end early.

At this point, music represented a small patch of common ground between Rory and Ian, and his weekly guitar lesson provided them with a two-hour reprieve from conflict. Ian's fourteenth birthday, five months earlier, was the last Rory and Tom had celebrated as a couple, and they went a little overboard, buying him a guitar signed by Pete Townshend that Rory had found on an online auction, along with a year of guitar lessons. They were both shocked and happy that Ian had practiced daily since then, demonstrating a level of commitment they hadn't known he possessed.

Rory had held back one present from his birthday. When she ordered the guitar, she'd also bought a dozen collectible picks, planning to pass one along to Ian every month he progressed on the guitar. So far, he had five, his favorite being a black logo pick apparently thrown offstage by Jimmy Page at one of Led Zeppelin's last concerts.

Her prayer to escape Mamba's lounge conversation was answered when her phone beeped; she welcomed any excuse to grab her purse and leave the building.

It was Dan. "I discovered the whereabouts of Mrs. Julia Whistler."

"I've thought about it." Rory leaned against the storefront window and played with the buttons on her ivory trench coat. "Dan, the last thing I need right now is to get charged or whatever you call it for interfering with the police investigation or they're doing in the woods. I can't afford any more setbacks."

"Okay, Rory, but there's no law against you visiting an old lady in a nursing home. You bought a piece of land she once owned. Besides, you can ask her about that second water well on your property that no one has been able to find for years. Locating it will save you the expense of drilling a new one for the boarding barn."

"I didn't know anything about that."

"See, it pays to commune with the locals. There's supposed to be a second utility well on your property. Do you want to head down to North Carolina tomorrow and find out from Mrs. Whistler where it is?"

"How about Thursday?" *Did I just say that?* she asked herself. "Um, would we be back by four?" she asked Dan. "I want to be home when Ian gets off the bus."

"That shouldn't be a problem. It's only a couple of hours each way. I was told that, in her condition, Mrs. Whistler may not be able to tell you much, but we can try. Since I'm retired police, I think I can bluff our way in there if necessary."

"Let me think about it and I'll get back to you tonight."

At ten o'clock on Thursday, Dan Deal arrived at Rory's farm in his red Super Duty pick up. He leaned on the passenger door, ready to open it for her when she met him at the foot of her front steps. Standing in front of her now in brown lace-up work boots, well worn, but immaculate jeans and a pale blue chambray shirt, Rory couldn't deny his attractiveness or her attraction to him. She still hadn't cracked the Dan code, and figured he must harbor some serious personal issues or be a closet serial killer or all of that and more to have remained single twenty years after his wife had left him.

"Good morning, Aurora. Are you ready?" he asked.

Aurora. No one had called her that since she was a girl. Each time he said the name, it disarmed her. Not because she found it patronizing or presumptuous. Because she found it intimate. "Are you sure I'm not going to get into trouble—be arrested for this?" she asked.

Dan laughed. "I promise, if you go down for this one, I'll go down with you. If you only knew what happens in the police department every day, you might feel scared—instead of protected. Trust me, this is nothing." He saw her camera bag. "What's the point-and-shoot for?"

"I always carry it in case I see a bird or deer or . . ." She reached for the back door, but he beat her to it.

"Or what?"

"I've been photographing some of the old houses and barns around here. Even in their decrepit state, I think they're beautiful. And we both know they won't survive the developers' bulldozers much longer. I also document their location and any other details I think are noteworthy. I was thinking of putting together a book someday, although I'm not sure it would have much of an audience. Not terribly relevant, I guess."

"I think it's relevant. I like that you see beauty in overlooked places."

"Is that old place I see off in the distance behind my farm the abandoned Whistler house?"

He closed the back door and took his keys out of his pocket. "What's left of it."

"I thought the Whistlers were the local land barons around here back in the day. I'm surprised, Dan."

"You mean because it's so small and humble?"

The remains of the Whistler's narrow, asbestos-shingled beige house, flanked by opposing chimneys, sagged into the surrounding landscape like an overburdened hammock. A large rusted propane tank teetered on three legs against what looked like a utility room, waiting for one more Southern Point rainy season to attack and fell it, returning its mineral alloys to the ground. In front of the house stood a lone camellia tree, its huge pink blossoms softening the wretched scene behind it. Rory had noticed the house the first time she rode Titian out through the back of her property after it had been cleared; she'd taken a photo of it that day.

"Herb made a shit—er—an s-load of money, but he wasn't a generous person—not even with family. His father built that house, and it's doubtful Herb improved it much beyond plumbing and appliance updates. The barn and outbuildings are long gone. It was all about the land."

They got into the truck and set out for North Carolina and the Brook Manor Rehabilitation Center. Rory slipped on her sunglasses and prepared for a potentially awkward road trip.

Dan broke the silence as they ascended the Intracoastal Waterway bridge, connecting the lower end of Southern Point to the neighboring mainland. "You talked about getting into trouble earlier."

Rory nodded.

"Well, I could get in some trouble for what I'm about to tell you, but here goes. The complete analysis on the arm bone isn't back yet, but Dr. Kelsey, the anthropologist that forensics always works with on these cases, said that at first glance, the remains look like they're from an adult. He said he's not sure exactly how old, and based on the length of the bone, he thinks the person was above average height."

"So, Sandy's Kerry McCullough theory may rest on how tall she was. I have no idea what she looks like—looked like."

"There could be more bones, identification, another body, who knows what else."

"Let's hope that they find out before I go broke from construction delays. Or my son disowns me, which is looking more probable every day." She hated hearing herself whine and lowered her voice. "You know, I've started to feel uncomfortable being at home alone at night, knowing that something violent probably happened back there. I can't really blame Ian for not feeling comfortable at home either."

"That's natural, Rory. Your entire life has been disturbed, with the whole bone issue. I've been thinking: there are hundreds of graves out here—most of the old family farms had their own cemeteries."

"But there's nothing on my survey indicating a gravesite, and who would put one in that swampy place? You said yourself that my woods were a throwaway then, not even used by hunters."

"It could be a homeless person from years ago, or a migrant worker. You city types are paranoid. Let's wait for that analysis and any other evidence they've got. And you shouldn't worry about your safety on the farm. Southern Point is still the safest place to live in the entire state, and everyone knows the police are all over your property. I can't imagine anyone bothering you with that monster dog of yours and a top-shelf security system. Now, if you want guaranteed security, get yourself a special friend."

Rory wasn't sure what he meant. "A special friend?"

"Yup, a special friend. That's what we call our personal protection devices."

"Personal protection devices? You mean a *gun*?"

"Are you against firearms?"

"Not as long as they're owned and operated by sane people."

"Then you should think about it. Out here we even name them. I can teach you to shoot yours if you like—if you're open to giving it a try."

"Believe it or not, I can shoot a rifle, shotgun, and assorted handguns. My sister and I grew up in a rural area, outside of Philadelphia. We . . . did a lot of outdoor stuff . . . at my parents' house."

Dan smirked. "You're trying to tell me you're a simple country gal?"

"Yes, in a way. Our . . . uh . . . house was next to a dairy farm." She didn't mention that the house had been six-thousand square feet. Or that it had included a tennis court, a swimming pool, a housekeeper, and a collection of horses. Or her parents' multiple affairs, separation, and attorney-brokered reconciliation, finalized one year before her father's death.

"Okay, then, Annie Oakley," Dan said as he pulled out a cigar from his jacket pocket. "You mind if I smoke?"

"I like the smell of tobacco, even though it's politically incorrect these days. Besides, it's your truck," Rory said. "I used to love an occasional cigar, so did Tom—my husband—Ian's dad."

"Why'd you quit?"

"For years Tom and I threw a big annual tree-trimming party for our friends and clients. A lot of guests would bring cigars, and near the end of the night, a group of us would end up on the deck, smoking and drinking coffee or tea before everyone headed home. At the party a few years ago, a friend asked Tom and me how we expected our son not to smoke if he saw his parents smoking. Neither one of us had a good comeback for her, so we caved in and gave up smoking."

"Interesting," he said, lighting up.

Rory thought she detected disapproval in his voice. "Why is that interesting?"

"Well, it's just that, as an adult, you are entitled to do things, legal things, that your child isn't."

"So, you're saying you think our decision was wrong?" She wasn't sure he had earned the right to judge her.

"No, it's not my place to make that call, which is my point. I'm saying that your guest was completely out of bounds to question your parenting skills, especially in front of other people, while she was eating your food and drinking your liquor."

"I never thought about it from that angle."

Dan reached into the center console and turned to her with a cigar encased in a clear glass tube and sealed with a horse-and-rider finialed cork. As she took it, he passed her his well-worn silver butane lighter. "Here, horseperson, I'll never tell." He smiled as he returned his eyes to the road, then noticed her trepidation as she stared at the bourbon-infused corona. "Look, Rory, it's a cigar, not a crack pipe."

She knew he had gone well beyond Southern Point to find the Blanton's infused cigar. "Thanks. I've never seen one of these."

"But?"

"It's the smoking issue," she said, tapping the cigar tube on her knee. "Ian has such a problem with lying and hiding things right now; I don't want him to see me as hypocritical, and I told him I don't smoke. I guess I need to know that he can trust me, that I'm setting a true example, being consistent in my own life. I don't want to add any fuel to his angst fire. God, shut me up."

"You worry too much about your son. I think he's edgy because he's worried he won't be able to handle being the man of the house. He's probably worried about you. Boys his age only want one thing—okay, two. But seriously, they want to be in control, to not look dumb to anyone. Come to think of it, that doesn't really change with age. If we're smart, when we're adults, we become more adept at hiding that fear."

"I'd love to think he's concerned about someone or something besides himself."

"Believe it. You'll see. You've taught him all the important stuff already. He'll come through this fine. Look how I turned out." He took a long draw on his cigar. "Hang on to that cigar I just gave you. With everything that's going on in your life right now, you may change your mind."

CHAPTER THIRTEEN

A few miles into North Carolina, the highway opened up into level, fallow farmland, making it appear as though Dan's truck would eventually slip off the edge of the horizon. The newly laid glassphalt sparkled like diamonds under the clear sky, offering a break from the bland winter landscape that stretched out in all directions. Dan combated the glare with a pair of aviator sunglasses, then turned on a satellite bluegrass station to a nearly inaudible volume and cracked his window, contentedly smoking and navigating the quiet road.

The highway abruptly closed in around the truck, presenting a strait of forty-foot pines lining both sides of the road. Rory felt the small space that separated them, a foot or so of gray stitched leather and some slightly smoky air, contract and compress with each breath she exhaled. The urge to reach over and grab his strong arm, to make physical contact with him and hold on to him, overwhelmed her. She laced her hands together and clamped them tight between her knees to stop herself. She clenched down on her jaw and stared out the window at the blur of passing trees, desperate to get out of the truck, to be anywhere but where she was.

"You okay over there?" Dan asked.

"Fine," she lied.

The open space of the rehabilitation center's half-empty parking lot granted Rory some needed distance from Dan and her impulses, and she focused again on the purpose of the trip. After she left the truck and stretched her legs, she slipped off her trench coat and laid it on the back seat. She adjusted the open collar of her white blouse and searched her black pinstripe trousers for omnipresent dog hairs and wiped her shoes with her hand. Using the truck's side mirror, she smoothed her hair and pushed it back from her face.

"You look exquisite to me," Dan said after watching her entire grooming session. "You dress a lot better than the rest of us out our way."

"That's only because I have to watch my budget now, and I've still got a closet full of business clothes. I have to wear these out before I can buy anything new. Who knows? I may walk into the feed store in a ball gown one of these days."

"I think I'd like to see that. I'd escort you to a ball anytime. And then escort you home."

At that comment, she felt as if her clothes had just fallen away and she was naked in front of him.

"Okay, you're who you are and I'm someone else—your cousin," he said as they walked through the nursing home's glass entry door together. "We'll see if they'll let us visit her."

Rory braced herself for the universal nursing home smell: floor wax, urine, and steamed meat. She was hit instead with a light breeze of—nothing. Just fresh air. She looked around and then at Dan. "Either no one lives here, or they're doing something very right."

"Hold on to that in case things go downhill from here," he said, easing her into the lobby with a hand at her waist.

They approached the receptionist, who didn't ask for their names or any identification, and pointed to the nurses' station directly behind her.

"Things seem pretty informal here," Dan whispered. "I think we're in."

They passed a woman in a white uniform, and Dan hailed her with a wave. "Excuse me," he said softly, "we're here to see Mrs. Julia Whistler."

The nurse looked surprised. "Mrs. Whistler? Really? She hasn't had a visitor except for her social worker since I started here, and that was eight years ago." She started walking them down the hall. "Come on with me. She's in her room. Are you long-lost relatives? Is this a special occasion?"

"No. We're . . . neighbors. We live in her old town."

"That's nice. Well, Mrs. Whistler doesn't really talk much, and she's not very oriented, if you know what I mean. We haven't gotten much sense out of her for years. Try to keep it simple. Oh, and she doesn't like to be touched. We have a heck of a time getting her into the shower." The nurse led them into a small, tidy room flooded with sunlight, its walls painted the color of the innermost stalks of a head of celery. "Mrs. Whistler? Mrs. Whistler? There're some people here to see you," she said before closing the door partway behind her.

In the corner of the room, next to a white-paned window, slouched a tiny figure wrapped in a colorful crocheted afghan, bobbing her head. Looking closer, Rory saw an old woman, her thin, matted gray hair in desperate need of a shampoo. The woman didn't look up but managed to aim a feeble wave from her bruised, purple-splotched hand in Rory's direction.

"Mrs. Whistler, I wonder if I might speak with you briefly?"

"Do I know you?" The words came out in a high rasp. "Are you here to take me home?"

Rory knelt down in front of Julia Whistler's chair. "No, ma'am. I live on your old farm on Whistler Ridge Road in Southern Point. I was trying to get in touch with someone in your family to ask a few questions about the property."

"Have you seen Jimmy?" she asked, and then demanded, "Who's that man with you?"

"I'm Rory Fielding, Mrs. Whistler, and this is my . . . cousin . . . Dan. No, I haven't seen Jimmy. Is Jimmy your son, Mrs. Whistler?"

"He'll never come back home. After all that trouble."

Flabbergasted at Julia Whistler's immediate reference to her son, Rory looked over at Dan and reached for chair that was pushed against the wall. He grabbed the chair for her, shrugging.

"Mrs. Whistler, I bought the piece of your old farm that covers the top ridge, over near the McCullough place, and I wondered if you knew of any old gravesites in the back woods there."

"I knew Jimmy took too long getting home after school, and when McCullough came to our house, it all broke loose. They should've known better. Nothing good could come out of it." She sank back in her chair and closed her eyes.

"Mrs. Whistler, maybe this isn't a good time—" Rory managed to say before Julia Whistler jerked forward in her chair and cut her off.

"You don't know! You don't know what our life was like!" She started coughing violently. Dan stuck his head out the door and called down the hall for help.

"It was—he—hell—" Julia choked out. "It was hell in our house. I did what I could!" she screamed.

A nursing assistant arrived with an oxygen tank and mask. Rory and Dan waited in the doorway, exchanging guilty glances, while the nurse worked to return Mrs. Whistler's breathing to normal.

"Don't feel bad—this happens all the time. It's part of her condition. It's worse when she hasn't slept much, and she's been having problems sleeping lately, haven't you, Miss Julia?"

Julia Whistler struggled to straighten up. "I don't want to talk to him—just her. The woman can come back tomorrow," she snapped.

Rory wasn't sure what to say. "I can't come back tomorrow, but I'll come back as soon as I can."

The nursing assistant walked with Rory and Dan toward the front desk, pushing the green oxygen tank. "That's more talking than she's done in years. Who are you people?"

Rory got into Dan's truck and put on her seat belt, then took it off. "Did that just happen? What was she talking about?"

"I guess she saw something in you and needed to talk. You know, sometimes older people feel the need to clear their conscience, before . . ."

"Before?" She knew that was what he was thinking. "Before they *die*?"

"Well, she is very ill and old."

"What is going on? You're the police officer here. What's your take on her story?"

"I think she was remembering something about her son, or her husband. We'll figure it out. I recorded it."

"What?"

"I turned on my phone recorder when we entered her room. It's a carryover from my police days. Don't you hate it when you try to remember a conversation and can't?"

"I don't have much experience in that area—recording conversations, I mean. Dan, she's probably delusional, right? Even if we listen to the conversation again, it's incoherent, disjointed."

"True. Which means you could do nothing and see what the police come up with. Or you could talk to her again or talk to Joe McCullough and see if there's something to this idea of his daughter disappearing. Maybe prepare him for the result of the analysis of the remains, if he really doesn't know where she is. I've got to say, something is definitely off about all this. Why don't we stop for some lunch before we head back home, and we can mull it over some more?"

They ate at a small coffee shop near the waterfront and were just past the city limits when Rory spotted a commotion in an abandoned cotton field along the highway.

"Look at that!" she said, lunging over her seat to get her camera from the back of the truck.

"Just some vultures . . ."

"Wanna bet? Stop the truck."

Dan obliged, watching from the truck as Rory picked her way in high heels through the rotting cotton plants, trying to avoid cutting her ankles on their sharp spikes, while inching as close to the birds as possible without scaring them off. Two juvenile bald eagles, dirty brown in color, were playing with a leathery rabbit carcass. She took several pictures before navigating back through the field to the truck.

"Good eyes. I would have driven by," Dan said, looking at the pictures on the camera's display screen.

She put the camera back in its case. "You never know what you'll discover on a road trip."

"Dead on," he said, watching her as she reviewed the pictures again. "You're right about that."

Dan was true to his word, delivering Rory back home to her front door twenty minutes before Ian's school bus was due.

"Let me grab my camera from the back." She opened the rear passenger door, leaned in, and pulled it by its strap from the floor. Without turning around, she sensed he was there. Her heart was in her throat as she pursed her lips and tried to take a deep breath before facing him. His left arm spanned the door opening, blocking any chance of an uneventful exit. She stared down at her red shoes for an instant, and then he was there, facing her, against her. It was a fast first kiss. Firm, lips closed, more of a forceful embrace. He supported her back with one hand and grazed the contours of her body with the other. She instinctively grabbed at the fabric of his shirt and kissed him again, loving the faint taste of tobacco in his mouth.

"I need to stop things here," she blurted out, trying to push back from him and free herself.

He looked confused.

"I'm not saying this was a mistake. . . ." She reflexively smoothed her hair, certain it was as out of control as the rest of her at the moment. "I just don't want to go into this backward."

"I'd say we're both moving straight ahead right now, dear." Dan carefully adjusted the collar of her blouse, testing her composure. "You know I want you, and you know I can wait."

She was staggered by his frankness. "I—I have to get my . . . house in order. And I think I could get lost in this—with you—right now."

"Let's put it away . . . for now." He put on his sunglasses and ran his hands through his hair, unfazed. He stayed where he was and smiled again. "Rory, I can't leave your driveway with you standing inside the truck door."

She stepped back and closed the door, an infatuated teenager in a woman's body.

CHAPTER FOURTEEN

Rory sat at a small table at the Blue Heron Grill, one of Southern Point's two small restaurants, slugging clumsily from a glass of scotch. "Jane," she moaned, "what am I doing? I must be crazy."

Jane slid into the chair across from Rory's. "I don't know. What exactly are you doing, and what in the world are you drinking?"

"Mad called the other day, and we were talking about how our dad used to drink a scotch and water every night. Under the current circumstances, I thought I'd better bring out the big guns, alcoholically speaking."

Jane snorted in response. "I've got to take this in. I've never seen you drink any more than a single glass of wine in one sitting. That heart thing—how many drinks have you had?"

"This is my first one," she replied. "My only one." She tapped her chest above her heart.

"Amateur! Don't make me call 9-1-1."

Rob White, owner of the Blue Heron, walked over to the table, took Jane's drink order, and returned promptly with a light beer. As soon as he left, Jane leaned across the table.

"Did you do the deed with that feed store–police guy or whatever he is? Is that what this is all about?"

"Not quite, but I—I—wanted to. It was mutual."

"What did he do, offer to show you his pitchfork or something?"

"Very funny. Nothing like that. You know he's helped me a lot with the whole boarding business thing. I honestly don't think I could have done it without him. And I told you that he suggested we go talk to the woman who used to own my place." She took another swig of scotch and then sat back in her chair, gripping its arms tightly. "Jane, when we were driving down to North Carolina the other day, I felt like I was possessed. I wanted to crawl across the truck seat and jump into his lap. I think I'm losing my grip."

"I love this place." Jane lit a cigarette and took several deep drags. "You're not losing your grip. You're a horny bitch, and you like him. I've seen him, remember? You'd be crazy not to want him. We should drink a toast to your rediscovered libido. Exactly when and how did you attack him?"

Rory corrected her posture, back rigid, a rider's Hunt Seat. "When we got back to the farm, there was a moment—I could have stopped it—I didn't. We kissed."

Jane almost spit out her beer. "One measly kiss? What are we, twelve? That's all? *That* was your attack?"

"That's all? Now we've crossed that line," Rory insisted. "God, do you really want to hear this?"

"I'm glad you told me. Keep going."

"It could confuse things, hurt people."

"Like who?" Jane's eyes met Rory's. "You're not talking about Tom, are you? Is it because you have lingering feelings for him—that you're not sure about your decision?"

"That's just it. I don't feel much of anything about Tom. It's almost too easy. And I am still legally married."

"Well, you two had serious problems years before you formally split. And you kept it clean until the separation. Credit where credit's due—I respect ol' Tom for that. You know how most men his age can be. Trade down to another model, even while they're still married. Not that Tom will ever find anyone to rival you. However, Rory, you do realize that he's going to find *somebody* sooner or later. You have to let yourself move on. There's that non-interference thing in your separation agreement. You're both allowed to date."

Rory forced down another gulp of her drink. "Even so, with all of the other changes in my life, it's just . . . not the right time."

"Geez, girl, I feel like I'm peeling back the layers of an onion here."

"What do you mean?"

"I mean you. I'm seeing a side of you I haven't before. You're so logical about other things—business, for example. I never thought I'd be giving you advice."

"In business you have a plan. I didn't plan on anything like this."

"Now you sound like Tom. I don't think that you can predict or plan these things, can you? In my opinion, that whole 'timing' thing is a bunch of crap. Do you have any idea what it's like out there—in the dating world? Bars? Forget it. Singles events? They're still the meat markets they always were. I even tried what I thought was a low-risk way of meeting some men I'd have something in common with. You know, swipe right, match your chemistry, get to know each other through messages, then meet and maybe walk off into one little sunset. Rory, I got some promising matchups—until we made contact. They wanted pictures of me in underwear, naked, with toys. They wanted me to define my 'sexual appetite' to assure them that they'd get plenty of action if we went out on a date. They got miffed if I wasn't jumping all over the prospect of giving them my home address. I wanted to puke! Finally, in the midst of the motley crew of lecherous grandpas, scammers, and wannabe sugar daddies, one guy messages me: handsome, polite, from a small town a couple of hours north of here. I thought maybe this one could be viable. Maybe we'd see each other once a week or so, have some fun. He seemed sweet, safe—he was a teacher for God's sake! He'd lost a few family members at a young age, appeared all the more sensitive and considerate for it. Yeah, right. For a solid month texted me for several days straight to get to know me—the perfect gentleman—and then promised me he'd call to set up a date the next day. He never did! Five more frickin' times he pulled the same stunt. He'd apologize and suggest texting. Then finally, he wanted sexting. I guess he just liked the game of it. Screw it. I decided, that if that's who's out there, I'd rather be alone. Do you know how lucky you are that Dan walked into your life? What if he's the right person? He's here now. He's real. Take him!"

"Jane, when I met Tom, I thought he was the right person and it failed."

"Both of you were young. Too young, if you're honest about it."

"You know how Tom proposed? He said, 'Marry me. I'll never leave you.' I don't recall him saying he loved me when he asked me. I'd felt alone for so long—my parents dying young like they did—so much of it was about feeling safe—being safe. And I didn't want to hurt him. I never wanted to hurt him. And now I have."

"Whoa, Rory. Being safe is not the same as being in love. I understand you not wanting to hurt Tom, but I also know you thought the divorce decision through. You agonized over it."

"A hundred times I rehearsed telling Tom that we needed to separate. I imagined every response, every possible comeback. Then, when I actually said it, all of that preparation fell away. I couldn't think past the words I heard myself saying. It was awful. I think I've ruined two peoples' lives. No—three." The scotch pulled at her inhibitions and sense of order. "If I lose everything, if this fails, I don't know how I'll start again. I've got Ian to think about too. What if I lose him in the process? I'm terrified. Maybe Tom was right, and I'll wake up and realize this was crazy—me thinking I could do this horse farm thing. He's the mastermind businessman. I should have listened to him. Been more sensible. Just sat on the money. Invested it."

"Rory, if the world was full of Toms, it would be a bleak landscape. You can have a dream, take a chance, add the color to this whole life thing. It's entirely legal. It's called the pursuit of happiness."

"I'm still not sure I can, or should, pursue anything with Dan."

"You're just scared."

"Jane, you know what I hate most about being around Dan?"

"Wait, now we're in the realm of hate?"

Rory lowered her voice to a whisper. "When he laughs, it hits me in my gut. Knocks me off center. When he looks at me—really looks at me—I feel the intention. He could ask me to do anything and I would do it. No shame, no hesitation, no doubt. I met him years ago, see him every week, but hardly know him. It makes me question everything I thought I knew about relationships. I never felt that kind of passion or excitement with Tom. Have I ever been actually loved by a man, or was I just *maintained*? Needs met, comfortable, no deep dives into my soul?"

"Wow, that's a lot, girl. I agree there are absolute reasons you should divorce Tom now. But, what about when you first met? I mean, we've talked openly about men—sex. It always sounded to me like things between you two were, you know, really good. Like there was some passion there once upon a time."

"It depends on your definition of *good*. We had a good sex life, in the technical sense—mechanical sense. Got each other to the orgasm goal—got off. In fact, our sex was all about the goal. Another checklist. We were good partners, but probably not really lovers at all. Ironic, isn't it? Me, the one you used to come to for relationship advice."

"And the advice you've given me has actually been good," Jane said firmly. "Maybe you gave me the advice you wanted to take for yourself." She hailed Rob for another beer. "How deep does this Dan thing go with you, anyway?"

"I'm not sure, Jane. All I know is, when I'm with him, I don't want anything else. And when I'm not with him, or I don't hear from him for a few days, I feel empty—stranded. And I think I'm starting to . . . *need* him around me."

"Sounds like a serious case."

"Serious case?"

"Of extreme like that's moving toward love, dummy."

"Don't use that word. When I'm with Dan, it's like I'm starved for him. And he's so wide-open about everything—his life, his feelings. No guile at all. I want to be with him. I just want him. It seems dangerous."

"And you know everything now? Okay, we'll nix that word *love*. Obviously, you like each other, and there's major sexual chemistry, and probably something more. But you'll never know unless you see it through."

"I don't know what I'd do, if it failed like my marriage."

Jane tapped the table with her menu. "You had twenty years with Tom, some of them good, and you have Ian, so it wasn't really a failure. Now's your chance to live the next stage of your life a little differently. You may have two hours, two nights—who knows how much time with Dan? There are no guarantees in relationships, and not every relationship has to be long term."

"But the timing—God—why now? I never looked at him that way before."

"It's happening now because you never had a moment to notice him before with the agency and driving thirty miles each way to Ian's school games and being wrapped up in the stuff with Tom. Come on, Rory. Were you planning to live the next forty years as a celibate farmer?"

"I didn't consider my personal life in my decision to leave. I never looked that far off into the future."

Jane drained her beer glass. "When I was a basket case during my divorce, what did you tell me? To stop doubting myself, to trust in my decisions. It became my mantra. Well, now it's your turn." She played with an unlit cigarette. "Look, Rory, I don't think the guy has any agenda. He's full-on, he tells you how he feels, and you're responding. It's completely normal, natural. You should just enjoy it. Go with it. And stop analyzing it to death. Now, enough about Danny boy. What did you find out from that woman you went to see? Or did that turn out to be a dead end?"

CHAPTER FIFTEEN

Rory pulled into Joe McCullough's driveway and parked next to an old red Mustang held in place by concrete wheel chocks. A plump orange cat, sprawled on its back across the car's hood, looked up from licking its paws and watched her crunch her way across the gravel to an open outbuilding that sheltered a bright purple tractor-trailer. As she neared the building, she saw a man she assumed was Joe, stooped half in and half out of the driver's side of the semi-truck's cab, stuffing a khaki duffle bag behind the seat. His navy work pants and a red-checked flannel shirt met at the base of his barrel chest, held in place by a pair of red elastic suspenders. A black mesh trucker's hat covered most of his cropped gray hair. He was a goliath of a man; she had no doubt that his size and strength had shielded him from countless altercations over the years. Even as a senior citizen, he was a daunting figure.

"Mr. McCullough, Mr. Joe McCullough," Rory called out, making her way toward the semi. "I'm Rory Fielding." She was apprehensive about invading a stranger's privacy because of a confusing conversation with a senile old lady, but after several days of internal debate, her gut instinct prevailed, and she pressed on. Joe said nothing, his blocky six-foot-six-inch frame now directly opposing her. She tried again, hoping the Whistler name might evoke a reaction from the man. "I live over on the ridge, on one of the old Whistler parcels, and wondered if I could . . . talk with you briefly."

"What would you want to talk to me about?" he boomed in a deep voice. "Ma'am, you can see I'm working—getting ready for a two-day run up north." He tipped his hat back with square, thickly calloused hands. "Good day to ya." With that, he turned away from her and stuck his head in the open truck cab.

She cleared her throat. "Mr. McCullough, you may have heard on the news—or around Southern Point—that some remains were found on my land."

"Whad'ya mean by remains?" he asked, fiddling with the driver's-side doormat. "I don't hear much'a what goes on 'round here. Keep to myself."

"A bone fragment. A bone fragment that the police think is human," she said. "They're working to see if any other related items may be in the area. Mr. McCullough, I had a conversation with the property's former owner, Julia Whistler, and she mentioned you by name."

He wheeled around and put his hands on his hips. "I don't know nothin' 'bout that," he said, frowning. "And I got somewhere to be."

"Mr. McCullough, Mrs. Whistler also talked about her son and your daughter—Kerry."

His face hardened. He reached in a pants pocket and pulled out a clean rag and ran it over his face, wiping away growing beads of sweat.

Rory wasn't sure where to go with her line of questioning. "Would it . . . be possible for me to speak with your daughter—with Kerry?"

"She don't live here. Long gone. Long gone." He was visibly agitated. "I think you better take your questions and go home. I got to get on the road."

"Sorry to have bothered you," Rory said, holding out her hand to Joe. He put his hands in his pockets, refusing a handshake.

Backtracking to her truck, Rory felt eyes on her. She turned around, sure it was Joe, but he was nowhere in sight. A hand pulled back a curtain from the front window of a white bungalow—one of three houses on the property. It was Sally McCullough, spying out through a pair of black horn-rimmed glasses that rested midway down her nose. The instant her eyes met Rory's, she released the curtain and vanished from sight. Trying to talk to her would be futile, Rory decided. Whatever secret the McCullough family held, Sally McCullough was no more ready or willing to reveal it than Joe was. She would have to try another approach. She waved a couple of times in the direction of the window and then headed home.

"Rory, this is getting interesting," Dan said over the phone. "The greatest challenge I've had since I retired. Well—almost."

Rory had promised him she would call after her visit to the McCulloughs' place. "I'm not seeing it, Dan," she argued. "Joe didn't tell me a thing. The whole idea—a family allowing their daughter's murder to go unreported. Come on, it's like a bad movie."

"Wait a minute now," he said. "Sometimes what a person says is less important than what you see or feel when you're with them . . . when you're questioning them. In police work, people follow gut feelings or hunches every day. For some cases, it's all you've got to go on."

She took a pause, mentally rewinding her trip to Joe's place. "Well, I'm not a detective, but I will say, Joe McCullough was extremely defensive—nervous. And he was sweating—in forty-degree weather. That struck me. If he isn't hiding something, he should be."

"See, that's what I mean. The idea of something happening to his daughter is plausible after all."

"I think I should wait for news from the police," Rory said, still on the fence about digging around where she didn't belong. "Hopefully they're moving along with that bone analysis, and this will all be over soon."

She heard static over the phone. It lasted a little too long. "Dan, is there something else going on?"

"Yeah, I'm afraid so. Now is probably not a good time to be the bearer of bad news, but my inside sources tell me that the grid search Sergeant Adderson talked to you about is a definite, so be prepared for a full-scale invasion of sorts. I'm sure you'll be hearing more about it from him."

"God, any idea when?"

"Before long."

"And you think he's the best person to handle this?"

"Yes, not a doubt. Trust me, having him in charge is a good thing. He understands how things work out here in the county. He'll make sure no one jerks you around."

She was about to say goodbye but changed her mind. "Hey, Dan. I keep forgetting to ask you exactly what you did with the police force before you retired."

"Detective. Homicide. In Richmond," he said in a clipped voice. "Murder capital of Virginia when I was there."

"I should have known," she said. "Did you like your job?"

"Some days, yes. Most of the time, it was like no matter how many battles we won, we always lost the war."

CHAPTER SIXTEEN

"Before long" turned out to be two days later. Rory waited on the sidewalk as Sergeant Adderson's pale blue cruiser crawled up the driveway before crunching to a stop in the gravel parking circle. He hung one arm out of the car's window when he saw her approaching, as though he knew he would be sitting there for a while and wanted to get comfortable.

"Hi, Sergeant," she said, working hard to sound unconcerned. "Do you have any updates for me?"

"Well, yes," he answered. "The preliminary analysis of the bone necessitates a grid search. We talked about that before."

"I remember," she said, leaning one hip against the car. "There's no question—the bone is human?"

"Yes, but that's about all we know at this point."

"Who will conduct the search?"

"Police academy recruits, with supervision by my precinct. We'd like to start on January twenty-fourth—that's next Monday—if possible."

"The sooner you start, the sooner you'll finish, right?"

"Right. I'll let you know as soon as we set it up." He started to close his car window and then stopped. "Oh, I almost forgot. The medical examiner's office is sending out a specialist."

"What kind of specialist?" Rory asked.

"They're sending a forensic excavator," he answered.

Rory hoped she misunderstood him; the word *excavator* connoted bulldozers, razed trees, and scarred landscape. "Did you mean to say forensic *investigator*?"

"No, she's a forensic excavator. There are only a handful of them anywhere, and we happen to have one here. She used to work on the historic Jamestown site. A few years ago, she decided she wanted more of a challenge. Seems the Jamestown site gave up its best artifacts a while back. She uses archeological methods to collect and document evidence at crime scenes or, in this case, death scenes."

"Is that what she's going to do on my land?"

"Yes, and she'll also help us to determine whether we need to remove any significant vegetation to help the case along."

"Wait, Sergeant." Frustration struck again. "What do you mean, 'remove significant vegetation?' She can do that on *my* property?"

"She uses very conservative methods, Mrs. Fielding, and maintains the integrity of the site as much as possible. We may have to take out some brush or trees if it looks like they're impeding our investigation by preventing us from reaching evidence. I don't know for sure, but I think she's on another job until the first of February. Let's wait and see what the grid search turns up."

As soon as Sergeant Adderson left, Rory made a note to call Scott Smith and push back the start date of the barn site survey and pasture work—again.

Two emblemed vans full of blue-suited police academy recruits arrived at the farm early on Monday morning. Rory watched from a window as the young men and women filed out of the vehicles and huddled in the drizzle in a tight cluster, waiting for instructions before entering the woods. A stocky, middle-aged female officer stood in front of the group, gesticulating wildly as she paced back and forth. Judging from the recruits' nods and raised hands, Rory surmised that she was giving them a primer on the grid search process.

Ian walked in the rain to meet the bus, protesting Rory's offer to drive him in the truck. With him gone, she straightened up the house, recovering a basket full of hairbrushes and shoes that Rocket had "retrieved" and stashed under various pieces of furniture, and then started a load of laundry. Eight o'clock came around fast. It was time to go outside.

It happened quickly, as she was wheeling a garden cart filled with feed and hay from the garage to the barn. The familiar catch in her chest, and then straight into breathlessness. She leaned forward, squeezed her eyes shut, and made herself cough. Then she reflexively took a step backward. By the time she comprehended she'd lost her footing, she was down on the ground on her right side. She managed to keep running through her maneuvers for three or four minutes, gasping with relief when she felt her heart bounce back to its normal pulse and rhythm.

At first, her right shoulder didn't hurt at all. It was more like muscle stiffness. She got up and rubbed it, struggling through her chores using her left arm. Over the next hour, she lost more and more mobility in her shoulder and the pain became excruciating. By the time Gabby Rawlins came by to drive Rory to the doctor's office, the rain showers had moved out of Southern Point. Rory couldn't move her shoulder at all; it had completely frozen.

"What happened?" Gabby asked, helping Rory into the car.

Rory recounted her fall as briefly as she could. As Gabby stood next to the car, listening, she spotted the white police vans and blue-uniformed officers at the edge of the woods. "Well, let's hope it's something minor—not a rotator cuff or something. Hey, what's going on out in the back today?"

"Oh, they've started the forensics work where the bone was found," Rory explained. "They'll be searching for a while, looking for more remains."

"I heard a brief story on the news this morning. They said an unidentified Southern Point farmer had found a skeleton. Nothing about foul play, though. I guess it's official—you're a farmer."

"An out-of-commission farmer," Rory added. "And I love how it's miraculously grown from one bone into a skeleton. All I need now is media attention to slow things down even more."

"How's your planning coming along? Mike and I were thinking maybe we'd get a pony for the twins and board it with you."

"I have to ask you to hold that thought. I've only got six weeks left to plant and fence twenty-five acres and get going on the barn construction. I've got no food or shelter for your pony."

Gabby helped Rory with her seat belt. "Well, right now let's go get you patched up."

Half an hour later, Gabby parked her minivan in the Eastern Orthopedics' parking lot and began a search of its back seat for an umbrella she and Rory could share. The rain showers that passed through Southern Point earlier in the day had found their way twenty miles north, with no sign of abating.

"Oh well, it's better than nothing," Gabby said as she opened her daughter's minuscule pink-handled umbrella, featuring a silk-screened image of Cinderella. The two women huddled together and scurried into the building.

Rory's friend Paul Edwards, managing physician of Eastern Orthopedics, got straight to the point. "Technically, Rory, it's an Acromioclavicular Joint Sprain, Grade I. You've got trauma involving one of the ligaments, but it's not completely torn, more like frayed. We'll treat it with rest, ice, and an NSAID for pain and swelling. We're going to put your arm in a sling for a few weeks."

"Paul, you're kidding, I hope."

"No, I'm not kidding. Total recovery can take four to six weeks. And if you don't rest and recover fully, you may be looking at surgery and months of rehabilitation, my friend." He tried to sound stern. "Now, I'm going to give you something for pain that will also help you sleep during the next few days. You can alternate it with your over-the-counter pain reliever. Rest is key here, so get some help around the farm. I can give you a pain pill now. I'm assuming that you didn't drive yourself here."

Rory and Gabby stopped at the pharmacy and filled her prescriptions before heading home. She called Diane from her cell phone to arrange for her to manage the barn for a few days but got voicemail and didn't leave a message. When Dan called a few minutes later to see how the investigation was going, Rory babbled freely about her injury, helped along by the codeine-laced painkillers. He proposed taking on the barn chores, and she accepted his help.

"Are you sure you'll be okay?" Gabby asked as she helped Rory up the front steps and into her house. "I can stay for a while, make you some tea or soup."

"Thanks Gabby," Rory answered sleepily. "I'll be fine. Ian will be home in a few hours, and right now"—she let out a yawn—"I just want to crash." She made her way into her bedroom, Gabby following closely behind.

"Rory, call me if you need anything. I'm only a few minutes away." She stood in Rory's room, picking at some fuzz on her sweater, stalling. "Before I go, I want to say something."

Rory pushed herself onto the bed and leaned her back against the headboard. "Sure, Gabby. Just don't expect . . . too coherent an answer. I'm . . . a little spaced out."

Gabby sat on the edge of the bed. "Rory, I know when people divorce, there's always the question of who gets custody of the friends—"

"Custody of the friends?" Rory couldn't help giggling. In her altered state, it sounded funny. "Sorry. Go on."

"You've been a good friend to me, and of course Mike and I love Tom as a next-door neighbor, but I guess what I'm getting at is, you've got custody of us. We've talked about it—Mike and me. We're closest to you. If it's easier for me to come over to your place so you don't have to run into Tom, I will."

"Thanks, Gabby. Your friendship means a lot to me."

"I just wanted to tell you, because we haven't seen much of you since you moved out."

"Oh, Gabby, that's not it," she said. "Things have been out of control over here with police all over the place." For a moment she wanted to tell Gabby everything—make her confession about Mrs. Whistler, Dan, Joe McCullough—but forty years of clutching her fears and emotions tightly against herself prevented it. Instead she said, "Thank you for hanging in there during all this. I'll call you tomorrow."

"Promise?"

"I promise."

It was two in the afternoon when Rory woke up. Sitting on the edge of her bed, she had an unobstructed, if somewhat groggy, view of both barns and the garage. The storm had finally passed, leaving a clear sky in its wake. In the searing daylight, no one could see in through the white bedroom sheers. The dogs were alert but silent as they tracked Dan's truck, which moved slowly past the side of the house to its final destination at the garage entrance. She felt like a voyeur, taking furtive pleasure in watching him as he extinguished his cigar in the truck ashtray and then went to the fence rail to check the water level in the pasture trough. After hoisting the overhead garage door wide open, he moved back and forth, gathering feed buckets, loading hay, and mixing supplements. He pored over feeding instructions on the dry-erase board and talked to the horses over his shoulder as they watched him from the pasture, their ears pivoting like antennae in response to the rise and fall of his voice.

Attempting to stand up brought on a spell of light-headedness, so Rory sank back down on the pillows, studying her surroundings. The bedroom was obviously built for two, with matching floor-to-ceiling windows spaced just far enough apart to accommodate a king-sized bed. A pair of walk-in closets led to a large bathroom with a Jacuzzi tub, double-headed shower, and a linen closet. There was room for duplicates of everything—bureaus, nightstands, dressing tables—with wall space left over for a full-size sofa. She imagined what it would have been like to move into the house with Tom, wondered if new surroundings could have made any difference in their failing marriage, then remembered that they'd already tried that by moving to Southern Point in the first place. In the last year, especially, he had been disengaged, complacent—accepting whatever fragments of her came his way. No objections, no demands, no passion. Their mundane sex life had surrendered to an effortless death a year before that, buried beneath the benign routines of daily life.

She closed her eyes for a moment, too tired to ruminate any longer. When she woke up an hour later, Dan's truck was gone.

CHAPTER SEVENTEEN

After more than a week of prescription painkillers, heating pads, and home improvement shows, Rory was desperate to rejoin the living. Convinced that she had learned every one of Dan's facial expressions and idiosyncrasies from covert observation through the vantage point of her bedroom-window, she now concentrated on identifying the visiting law enforcement vehicle license plates on sight. They routinely rendezvoused on the parking pad by the garage before heading back to the woods.

Today's winter weather crapshoot dealt Southern Point a dreary gray dawn. As Rory pulled open one of her bedroom windows a few inches to let in some fresh air, two police vehicles came to a stop in the usual spot, next to the garage.

"This is a fuckin' cakewalk," a male voice said loudly from inside one of the idling SUVs. "I get a paycheck just for sittin' here, dickin' around with myself all day."

"What the fuck? It's probably some drunk dumbfuck redneck who got lost back there takin' a piss and couldn't find his way out," said another voice, laughing.

"Well, FYI, watch yourself around that old fart from the local police department. He won't even let you *spit* in those fuckin' woods. Says it's disrespectful to the homeowners."

You go, Sergeant Adderson, Rory thought. He rose up another notch on her scale of good guys. She made a point of slamming the window shut so the uniforms would know she had heard them.

Sandy had stopped by each day that week, preparing simple meals and babysitting the dogs so Rory could rest her shoulder. It worked; she now felt like a paroled prisoner waiting for the cell door to open.

"Mom, are you better now?" Ian was standing in the laundry room, half-asleep, wading through a sea of clothes he had dumped onto the floor.

"I'm getting there. Have you been checking the farm's emails?"

"Yeah, and some guy named Jason Grimes sent you about ten of 'em." He yawned and stepped out of the swirl of colored fabric. "Who's he? Another guy who wants to date you?"

"No, Ian. He works with Scott Smith. He's the man who's going to seed the pastures."

"When's that gonna start?"

"Not until the investigation is over."

She searched through stacked-up emails, clicking on the last one sent by Jason Grimes. He was looking for a timeline to start the pasture work, holding off other jobs in an effort to accommodate her schedule. She responded to his email by explaining that she would check back with him in a few days, although she knew it would take a miracle for the police to have their work finished by then.

Ian announced his intention to take a shower as though it was a monumental event, ambling through the house in his underwear before finally arriving at the bathroom door, which he slammed behind him, more for dramatic effect than malicious expression. Rory took advantage of the twenty-minute reprieve from his semiconscious presence and let the dogs out. Minutes later they both sounded off, sending her to the front door to track down the source of their agitation. This time it was a white SUV at the front gate. A quick inspection through her binoculars confirmed it was from the state medical examiner's office. She brought both dogs back into the house and checked the driveway again. "Hmm, it gets better and better, doesn't it, girl?" she asked Al, who sat up and barked. Rocket wagged her tail and peed on the floor. Rory checked her watch. It was barely seven o'clock.

Five minutes later, the house phone rang. The caller was Shelly King, driver of the SUV, the much-anticipated forensic excavator, a title Sergeant Adderson had had trouble defining and which Rory still couldn't quite comprehend. As promised, Shelly was prepared to recite the gate access code.

"Zero-three-one-one, Mr.—uh, Mrs.—Fielding," she spouted into the phone without first saying hello. "Zero-three-one-one."

"Excuse me?" Rory answered, put off by her terseness.

"Shelly King. Need access to the dig site, please. Zero-three-one-one."

"Okay," Rory replied. "Follow the driveway to the garage and then drive over the grass along the tree line to the back. Please drive in low gear. The ground is soft right now."

"I'll try, but my priority has to be gaining access to the site." She paused. "Oh, did I see dogs? You'll need to keep them away. I don't like animals."

And I don't think I like you, Rory thought. "I'll do what I can, but they live here. They will be outside from time to time," she said, watching Shelly's SUV drift by the house, unable to make out what Shelly herself looked like. The scene repeated itself at precisely seven o'clock each day that week, despite weather conditions.

On Thursday, Rory felt ready to test her healing shoulder with a ride. Titian was fairly cooperative when she tacked him up, making her suspect that he was using all the cells in his lemon-sized brain to plot against her. She clipped her camera to her saddle's D-ring and mounted up. They walked to the first stand of trees on their way to the back of the farm, the leather from Titian's saddle and Rory's field boots squeaking rhythmically with each rocking step. She loved the sound, one that a rider takes comfort in and longs for when they've gone too long without it. Horse and rider negotiated their way along the pasture ditches and past Shelly King's parked vehicle to the wood's edge. From there, Rory thought she could better scrutinize the grid area for property damage.

"Ms. Fielding!" Shelly King called out, "I cannot allow photographs of this area." She was a few yards inside the woodline, next to a small plastic tent-like structure, kneeling atop a small blue tarp, and wearing a matching blue muumuu. Only her head and hands, flushed pink from the exertion of sliding around on the tarp, were exposed within the sea of blue. Wiry white hair, a few inches long, stuck straight out in all directions. On her feet were old green gumboots. Shelly's pastel-blue eyes stared out at Rory, unblinking, from behind round wire-framed glasses. She was either in her mid-fifties or mid-sixties, Rory estimated. Her full face and neck, virtually wrinkle-free, made it impossible to narrow her age down any further. Lined up by her side on the plastic tarp sat a box of sandwich bags, a children's sand bucket, and a slotted metal kitchen spoon. In front of her, a large bottle of Mountain Dew with a straw duct-taped to its top nestled inside a U-shaped terrycloth pillow—the kind used for airline travel. She pursed her lips in frustration. "Did you hear me, Mrs. Fielding?" she scolded. "It's a restricted area. Stay out!"

"Ms. King, I'm aware of the limited access. My camera is for photos of birds, although I doubt I'll see many with all of the racket from the work back here. While we're on the subject, I need to adjust the time you arrive in the morning. From now on you can access the site after nine a.m. Before then, consider it a restricted area, or take your chances with my dogs. Thanks." She clucked for Titian to walk on, proud of herself for finally exerting some control over the small army that had commandeered her farm. She sensed Shelly King's contemptuous gaze following her, and then heard her voice.

"Humph," Shelly grumbled. "This is a first. No cooperation on a dig."

Rory wheeled Titian around and faced Shelly dead on. The horse snorted and pawed the muddy ground. Shelly's eyes widened as she crawled backward on the tarp, her face now bright red. Rory almost burst into laughter. Titian's show of force was purely serendipitous—probably a cranky response to being kept out of the pasture half an hour past his afternoon hay ration—but nonetheless effective. "Ms. King," she said, measuring her words out carefully, "this isn't one of your deserted settlements or abandoned burial sites. This 'dig' is also a family's home—my family's home. I'm raising my son here, and we've tolerated weeks of a total loss of privacy, interruptions, noise, and property damage. Now it's your turn to be flexible. Have a good morning."

Shelly's mouth hung open as she sat, frozen in place, on the tarp. Without waiting for her to respond, Rory turned Titian in the direction of the house. "Good boy," she said as she patted his neck. "Good job."

Friday morning was quiet, with no phone calls or visits from forensics personnel. The February rain had fallen all night long, and even though the farm was on high ground, large shallow pools of rainwater dotted the yard and pastures. But the sky was high and blue and cloudless, and the air was pristine, a crisp backdrop for the blossoming trees and shrubs. Something set off the dogs at just before eight o'clock, but they stopped barking almost as soon as they'd started. Rory was both pleased and perplexed by the short-lived ruckus—until Ian left through the front door on his way to the bus.

"Mom, you'd better come out here." He was standing on the front porch next to an open box. Inside was their weekly milk delivery, daily newspaper, and a five-pound bag of carrots with an index card attached.

Taking today off—sorry about yesterday.
Too much time on archeological and forensic digs—I forget to consider the living!
We all need our privacy.
—Shelly King
PS Please don't send your attack horse after me—bribe enclosed.

It was Shelly who had alarmed the dogs earlier.
"Is it from *Dan*?" Ian asked sarcastically.
"No," Rory told him, "it's from Shelly King—the woman who's exhuming whatever is buried in the back woods. And I think she may have restored some of my faith in humanity. Now go to school."

After he left, Rory pulled together the unlikely combination of cobalt-blue riding tights, tall black rubber boots, and an oversized red-and-black soccer jacket of Tom's that had somehow evaded the personal belongings editing process she'd completed before moving out of the Rock Creek house. She slogged around the flooded yard and paddock, resembling a psychedelic jockey of sorts, and was slowly working through her tasks when Dan's red truck appeared in the driveway. She wasn't prepared for callers, especially him, and hurried to the garage to grab some folded sheepskin saddle pads from a shelf. She clutched them to her chest, hoping the cream-colored fleece would diminish the impact of her clothes. She was too late.

"Good morning!" he said cheerfully, walking over to her. "You could direct traffic in that ensemble."

She wanted to crawl under the palette of hay bales and stay there. "I . . . wasn't expecting anyone."

"Oh. I didn't hear from you about not coming over to help," he continued. "I figured I'd keep coming back until you told me to stop. How are you feeling today?"

"Trust me, better than I look." She put the pads back on the shelf, feeling her face flush from embarrassment. "It hurts when I overdo it, but otherwise I'm okay."

"Good." He pointed to Titian's saddle and bridle, both on the floor, leaning against the wall. "Looks like you've been cheating a little, Aurora."

"I got a bit ambitious yesterday, checked out the goings-on in the back. My arm gave out before I could get them back up on the saddle rack."

"I'll take care of it. No investigators out here today?"

"Everyone took the day off. I think they were afraid I was finally going to crack and become violent." She laughed and stretched out both of her arms, rubbing her shoulder and flexing her neck.

"I'll finish up for you, Rory. What's left to do?"

"Only the best part . . ." She held up a basket fork, a variation of a pitchfork, designed specifically to muck stalls. It was universally recognizable to any horse owner.

He took it and stepped into the garage. "You're sweet. Thanks for that."

She stepped backward toward her desk to make some space between them, reaching for the coffee cup she had left there earlier. One of them needed to say something to break the tension; neither did. Breathless, she stood with him in the crowded garage bay, which seemed to get smaller and smaller as the seconds ticked by. The air felt thick and heavy, as it had on their drive to North Carolina. Out of excuses, she made one last attempt at decorum before the inevitable occurred. "Thanks for everything you've done around here lately. Maybe we should talk about the other week, the trip to North Carolina."

"Only if you feel you need to," he said softly, taking a step toward her, erasing the thin line of personal space she had maintained until now.

She turned away and arranged some files on her desk to avoid facing him. "I've told you how I feel about doing anything right now that would cause more confusion or conflict with my son."

"You can't give me more than you have to give, Rory. My goal is to make your life a little better—not to interfere with your other relationships. I've gotta say, I think you're working this thing too hard."

"You mean my divorce?" she asked, facing him now, half-sitting on the edge of the desk. "I just think I need to finish one thing before I start another."

"You're already legally separated, aren't you? I understand wanting to protect your son, but you can still have something for yourself—of your own."

"Maybe we got ahead of ourselves the other day."

"Why? Because of a kiss?"

She knew he was going to smile before he did, and as he stared at her, she felt stripped to the skin, as though she were standing in the bright, hot sun with no escape to shade or shelter.

"Rory, you can analyze the hell out of this," he said, reaching behind him and lowering the garage door, leaving them in the few strands of muted daylight that filtered through the small window. "But sometimes you just can't stop the train."

He took her hands in his, pulling her close. She swallowed hard as adrenaline began flooding her veins. A hint of cigar and some unfamiliar aftershave mingled with the smell of his hair as he leaned down and unzipped the top of her jacket, kissing one side of her neck. He drew back, took her face in his hands, and then kissed her on the lips, exploring her mouth with his tongue. She reached under his shirt and felt the muscular lines of his back and shoulders. Pushing books and files onto the floor, his warm hand moved between her legs as he stretched her back over the desk. Her riding tights slid off easily, leaving her half-naked on the cold, hard surface. Dan grabbed a folded turnout blanket from the pile next to the desk and slipped it underneath her, then resumed stroking and caressing her with his hand until she could hear her own panting against his freshly shaven cheek. Her excitement mixed with fear. Not of the consequence, but of giving herself over to him. A vision of sex with Tom flashed through her mind—their tempered, bed-borne ritual, usually scheduled into a weekend evening here and there along the monthly calendar. This was different—unscripted, overpowering, consuming.

"Sweetheart," Dan asked, his voice husky from arousal, "do you want me to stop? Am I hurting you?"

"No," she gasped before he covered her mouth with his. Rory fought her excitement until she couldn't hold back any longer. Her pulse pounded in her ears and she moaned uncontrollably, beads of sweat on her bare skin mixing with the cold air. She felt exhilarated, spent—like he'd broken her.

"Are you cold? Your shoulder . . ." he whispered.

"I'm okay—it's okay." She didn't say any more.

She threw both arms around him and held him tightly, feeling his hardness. He pushed up her bra so her skin met his, and eased himself out of his jeans, moving inside her with his eyes fixed on hers, forcing her to watch him. It felt like a death when he finished—the end of something she was afraid she could never repeat, except in her memory.

They lay together for a few minutes, until Rory began to shiver in the drafty garage. Dan helped her into her jacket, and then sat up on the side of the desk and buttoned his jeans. "Is this where we smoke a cigarette and think about what to say next?" he asked.

Right then she had no regrets about what they had done—didn't care that she was lying nearly naked on a hairy horse blanket.

He persisted. "I've left you speechless?"

"Not completely." Her voice was hoarse.

He studied her body from head to toe. "You sure are beautiful, inside and out."

She finished pulling on her clothes and stood up, their interlude suddenly striking her as impulsive and risky. "Dan, maybe this was a mistake. . . ."

He ran a hand through his hair. "How? What do you mean?"

"Now that we've done this, I can't say I know where it's going—where it *can* go."

"I haven't planned it out, either. Some things are destined. Not meant to be reasoned out. This will go wherever we want it to."

"I just don't want awkwardness between us." She knew it was probably already too late for that.

He kissed her softly. "Horseshit."

"What?" she asked distractedly, wrestling with a tough knot of anxiety that was forming in her stomach.

"Horseshit." He pulled a cigar from his shirt pocket and lit it. "With your permission, I'm going to take a few pulls on this stogey, and then go shovel some." He ducked out of the garage and stood in the driveway.

"Don't start any fires," she called after him.

"My dear, a bit late for that now, isn't it?" he called back.

CHAPTER EIGHTEEN

A pileated woodpecker, dead set on drilling a hole through one of Rory's pine trees, cocked its crested red head to the side each time she shoved the push broom out of the garage, assessing whether she might scale the thirty-foot tree at any moment and steal its cache of insects.

Looking up from her work, Rory caught sight of Dan's truck in the driveway. He parked the truck and trotted toward her, waving a thick manila file folder back and forth like a flag. Adhering to the ground rules of their week-old relationship, he made no attempt greet her with a touch or a kiss. But, once inside the garage, he stopped at the desk and slowly ran his fingers along its surface, as if in reverence to their recent encounter. Raw excitement ran through Rory as she watched him, remembering the feel of his hands on her body and the texture of his skin brushing against hers. A single word or subtle gesture of invitation on her part would set in motion another frenzied lovemaking session. She couldn't take that step. Rory envied his ability to accept the things given to him, without harboring expectations or regrets, without doubting himself. To her, he always moved in one direction—forward. No fear.

"You mind?" Dan asked, pulling out a chair from her desk. "Rory, dear, you know that I left for college in 1983, so I had to do a little asking around to get background on the Whistler family." He straddled the chair backward, wrapping his legs around its legs, hugging the chair back with tan rock-hard arms, sending her back to war with her sensibility.

"No, of course not," she answered, finding the corner of a hay bale to sit on. "Did you find out anything about them—any real connection to the investigation?"

"I turned up an altercation between Joe and Herb at the Southern Point Auto Repair Shop in 1979. The police were called because of alleged threats of bodily harm. Charges were eventually dropped, but the incident's still on the local books."

"Dropped by Joe?"

"Oh no—by Herb. Evidently, he approached Joe and provoked him, and Joe responded by what Herb reported as a threat. Another customer in the shop was afraid the two of them were going to come to blows, so he called the police. You know who might know more? Your babysitter, Sandy. If I remember correctly, her husband owned that shop at some point. Yeah. It was Cross Auto Repair back then."

"I'll ask her when she's at the house."

"And there seem to be quite a few people around here who believe that the two kids—Herb's and Joe's—were involved in some kind of intimate relationship as teenagers. You know, I'm a few years older than they are, so I was long gone before they were in high school, and my family being the way they are, my mother wouldn't have allowed gossip like that in our house anyway. I never heard about it."

"God bless your mother. I think I'd like her. She was ahead of her time."

Rory pointed to the packet of papers in Dan's hand. "What do you have there? More about Herb Whistler?"

"You know some of the stories about him: poisoning livestock herds, strong-arming people into selling him their land. The worst of it was the common knowledge that he beat his wife and kid, probably his dog, and God knows who or what else. The problem was, Julia never reported it, and the son always denied it. Not the kind of family secret you should keep, if you ask me."

"What else do you know about Herb?"

"He died in 1986, of heart failure—sort of."

"Sort of? What does that mean?"

"Well, he died at home, in the bathtub of all places. I guess he finally drowned his sorrows—in alcohol and bathwater. The thing is, his autopsy showed that he was headed to greener pastures anyway."

"He was sick?"

"You might say that. He had advanced cirrhosis of the liver—common with alcoholism. Untreated, from what the autopsy showed. They also found gallstones, jaundice, and an enlarged spleen. The man must have been racked with chronic pain at that stage. Maybe even neurological problems—erratic behavior. Systemic toxicity."

"So what *was* his cause of death?" she said, hearing her physician father's voice in her head.

He recited from the report: "Heart failure secondary to hypothermia."

"Hypothermia? I'm confused. You said he died in the bathtub."

"Yeah, he did. At least that's where they found him. The police concluded that he was so drunk, he ran a bath and lost consciousness, and that eventually the water went cold, and he slipped into hypothermia, which leads to heart failure. It's all right here." He slapped the papers against the chair back. "My question is, if he was conscious long enough to turn off the water, wouldn't he sense that it was getting uncomfortably cold? Who climbs into a tub of ice water willingly?" Dan's train of thought kept rolling. "I know what you're thinking. Hear me out. If he passed out before the tub was full, if he was relaxed in warm water and somewhere along the line passed out, why wasn't the bathroom flooded? It didn't make sense then, and it still doesn't, but the finding of accidental death wasn't contested. Whistler's wife was disabled, and his blood alcohol was through the roof."

"Are you saying someone . . . did him in?"

"Don't quote me on that, but I think half of Southern Point's population would have lined up to do the honors if fate, or whatever—whomever—hadn't intervened first."

"The son, maybe."

"Jimmy Whistler? Don't think so. By all recollections, he was long gone by then—out West somewhere. I don't think anyone around here's heard from him in decades. Can't say I blame him for trying to get lost, with kin like that."

He stood up and handed her the file. "This is a copy of the autopsy report, for your . . . personal use, if you follow me."

"Thanks." She took the report. "I'll keep it away from prying eyes—i.e., Sandy."

He laughed. "You read my mind. Where's that son of yours today?"

"He's in Washington for a long weekend with my hus—I mean—with his dad. They're going to catch a D.C. United game while they're there and check out the spy museum."

"Sounds like they'll have a good time. Today's Thursday. What are you doing for fun this weekend?"

"Louisville."

"Louisville, Kentucky? As in bourbon central?"

"Yeah. There's a model barn out there nearly identical to the one I plan to build, and I'm going to tour it to get a better idea of what mine may be like. Since I can't start construction on schedule, at least I can fantasize about what should be going up on my property right now. It will also give me a chance to see if I need to customize my plans more, rearrange anything."

"Fantasizing. Splendid idea!" he said. "I travel well . . . and I'm good in strange surroundings."

She saw hope in his eyes. "It's three days, Dan. I'll be there three days, and I leave tomorrow morning. How can you leave the store on such short notice?"

He wasn't budging. "That's not your problem to worry about. What airline?"

"Delta, but, well, there's one thing about that."

"Okay . . ."

"I'm flying first class." She felt self-conscious saying it. "I'm so tall, the seats are more comfortable. And I believe that half of any trip is how you get there. Thank God for reward miles."

"You don't have to rationalize how you travel. I'm intimately familiar with first class, have plenty of banked airline miles, and I do earn a living. Tell me the flight number and I'll book a seat, hopefully next to you. Where are we staying?"

"The Brown." She knew she'd missed her chance to say no, but she wanted him to go with her. "More points—American Express has its rewards."

"The Brown? Now you're talkin' first class." He started toward his truck. "Oh—and, Rory?" he called out.

"Yes?"

"Happy Valentine's Day, sweetheart, a week late."

Norfolk International Airport was noisy and crowded when Rory arrived for the Louisville trip. She checked the airline's flight status monitor, found the last empty seat near her boarding gate, and put down her carry-on bag. After debating for a moment, she called Sandy to remind her about keeping tabs on Shelly King. There was no answer. She ducked her head down and cupped her hand over her phone to block out the overhead announcements and crying babies to leave a message. "Sandy, it's Rory. Feel free to call me if you notice anything strange going on out in the woods—you know that whole forensics dig thing—" She cut herself off as her eyes met with the tips of two tan Frye boots directly in front of her own shoes, so close to her that she couldn't stand up.

The boots led to dark jeans and a fitted chocolate sweater over a white crew-neck T-shirt, animated by Dan chewing the life out of a piece of gum. Dan. Unbridled. No guard rails. And, no evasive maneuvers within her reach.

"Excuse me, is this the morning commuter to Louisville?" he asked, tapping a rolled-up newspaper, certain to contain a crossword puzzle, against his thigh. His blue eyes locked down on hers.

She presented a thin smile, one formed from wanting to be with him, combined with guilt over engaging in anything remotely close to dating a few months into her separation. It made her want to run for home before it was too late. Dan read her mind.

"Second thoughts? Doubts?" he quizzed her as she remained motionless in her chair. Then: "Let's get some coffee or something, so I can continue staring at you from across the table for an extended period of time."

She shook her head. "Dan, where do you come up with these things?"

"All from you, sweetheart. You inspire it. Come on." He held out his hand and pulled her from her seat.

For all of her misgivings at the airport, there were too many moments during the Louisville weekend when Rory wanted to cancel her return flight. All of the Brown's single rooms were booked, blocking any pretense of a friendly business trip. She and Dan checked into a two-bedroom suite and changed for dinner in separate bedrooms. He'd brought along a perfectly tailored dark gray suit and a sky-blue poplin shirt with French cuffs, which he secured with a pair of cufflinks bearing the UVA Cavaliers' crossed-saber logo. His pre-departure appearance at Rory's bedroom door caused her to consider whether they should just order room service and stay in.

They did go out, exchanging the historic hotel's opulent chandeliers for a dusky six-table Asian restaurant near the waterfront. On the way back from dinner, they ducked into a bar on Fourth Street to sample some Kentucky bourbon and local jazz. They finally left the place at one thirty in the morning, when Dan had exhausted every bourbon flight worth its paddle.

It wasn't until they'd returned to their suite and undressed by the light of a lone table lamp that they saw each other completely naked for the first time.

Rory knew nothing of Dan's history with women, other than the fact that he was once married and that he definitely knew his way around the female body. She'd had twenty years with the same man, a man who hadn't felt the desire or necessity to acknowledge or praise any aspect of her physical appearance, who didn't ask if what excited her five years ago, excited her now. She held a limited perspective of herself. As Dan stood in front of her, his eyes grazing point to point on her body, she wondered if the unfiltered reality of being with her was a disappointment, or if she met his expectations. Were her breasts too small, too large, high enough? Was her stomach flat? She cursed herself for eating an enormous plate of pad Thai at dinner, loaded with shrimp, noodles, and peanut oil. With no clothes or covers to hide behind, she shied from direct eye contact, focusing instead on a battered Celtic cross, suspended by a length of rawhide, that he wore around his neck.

"Confirmation gift," he said softly. "From 1979. I take it off only to change the rawhide."

With a few steps, he closed most of the distance between them, stopping inches short of touching her. "I knew exactly what you'd be like here. I could feel it," he said, and then pulled her to the bed, exploring her body with his hands and mouth before moving on top of her. "I know I already said this, but you're so damned beautiful." He tucked her hair behind her head, kissing her face and neck before moving back to her breasts. "You're like some rarified, perfumed air that's permeated my being, my life, and I can't shake you off." His lips moved downward again, grazing the contours of her stomach.

"But I haven't done anything—" she answered, breathless.

He positioned himself directly over her, propping himself up on his elbows, and kissed her lightly on the lips. "It's not about what you've done. It's about who you are—what you're made of. For me to see that, all *you* have to do is breathe."

"I wonder if you see more in me . . . than I am."

"Impossible," he said, gently lowering himself onto her body until she could feel his heart thrashing against his chest—and hers. "And now I think . . . I'm going to make you very happy."

"Please, just do it," she begged as she watched him move over her, reveling in his smell and the crush of his weight. She held off as long as she could, trying to stay with him. He grabbed onto her tighter, more forcefully, moving faster inside her, the silver cross rhythmically undulating upon her chest.

"I'm not stopping until you give in to it," he whispered hoarsely. The words were like a trigger. She lost herself in a violent rush of pleasure. Within seconds he followed her, calling out her name to the shadows lining the walls of the dimly lit room.

As they lay together on the bed, Dan kicked the damp top sheet to the floor and put his hands behind his head, staring at the ceiling. Rory moved in closer to him and rested her head on his chest.

"How's that shoulder? I didn't hurt it, did I?"

She shook her head.

He followed the lines of her upper arm and shoulder with his fingers." So why don't you tell me about this heart condition of yours?" he asked. "In great and vigorous detail."

She sighed. "Let's see . . . I was born with it. SVT. Supraventricular Tachycardia. Atrial. Left side origin."

"What happens when you have an SVT attack? In the event I have to intervene?"

"Paroxysmal. As in episodic. They're called episodes. When I have one, my heart goes into an insane, fast rhythm, I'm short of breath, there's heavy pressure in my chest—it feels like what I imagine a heart attack must feel like. When I was younger, I thought I *was* having a heart attack."

"And what sets off an episode?"

"Specific things—nothing at all. Running as fast as I can, pulling up a saddle girth too fast and hard, jumping out of bed without sitting up for a couple of minutes first, overhead lifting, things that cause a dramatic increase in pulse or a blood pressure shift. And then, other times—do you really want to hear this?" she asked.

"Absolutely," he said, smiling. "If we're going to spend time together, I need to know how to take care of you in a crisis."

"Okay," she said with a sigh. "Well, sometimes, it happens for no apparent reason. Those are the worst, because I can't predict them or try to prevent them, and I have the hardest time stopping those. Anyway, my condition—it's some electrical anomaly in my left atrium, the doctors tell me. And the maneuvers I use to stop them do something to the vagus nerve that reprograms the system. All very technical and fascinating, isn't it?"

"Yes, it *is*. Is it—could it be—serious?"

"You mean fatal? My doctors say not. According to them, I could lose consciousness, although I never have. If I did, the rhythm would restore itself, and I'd wake up and the episode would be over. Until the next one. That's what the beta-blocker is for. It lessens the intensity and length of the episodes. But I live my life always waiting, wondering when and where it will happen again. It's as though I'm always walking on a some very brittle, very sharp ostrich eggshells."

"It didn't seem to bother you just now, when we were making love."

"That's because I took some extra medication—after dinner. My doctor told me I could do that once in a while—under special circumstances." She looked up at him. "I think I knew you'd probably be a special circumstance."

"A special circumstance. I kind of like that idea." He smiled again. "How long will the effects of the extra medicine last?"

"You mean the extra dose I took? Full effect for another couple of hours, I guess."

"Good. Very good," he said, rolling back on top of her. "Let's not waste it."

In the early morning, just before full sunrise, she watched his bronzed body shift in the stark white sheets while he slept, wondering if they would have one more day together like the last. Even when she and Tom were young, in the earliest stages of their relationship, they would make love one time on a weekend morning and then quickly get on with the day and move around with the rest of the world. Here, in this room, she was with a man whose sole focus was her. For now, she alone seemed to be enough for him. She wanted to stay in that place—in that space of just the two of them. No one else.

The plane sat on the Louisville runway, waiting for take-off clearance from the control tower. With three hours of air travel ahead of them on the trip home, Rory took a chance and questioned Dan about his past. "Can I ask what happened with your marriage?"

"She left me, sweetheart." Dan leaned deep into his seat and closed his eyes.

"Why—what happened?" she blurted out. "Sorry." She immediately regretted her inquisition.

"It's okay." His voice softened. "It was because she couldn't have children."

"And you couldn't adopt, or—"

"It didn't matter to me if we had children," he interrupted. "I loved her, just as she was. I was blissfully, unconditionally happy with what we had. But she said she couldn't stand to live with me, grow old with me, wanting my child, a part of me, and not being able to give that to me. I told her that to grow old in love was all I wanted. She said that what I thought I wanted might not be what I needed, and that she'd end up hating herself for it—for staying and keeping me from being a father."

"I'm so sorry, Dan. Do you stay in contact with her?"

"We'd been married three years. One day, while I was at work, she vanished from our house—took next to nothing with her. Nothing. No clothes, no money, not even her purse. Only some pictures of the two of us. I never saw or heard from her again. You see, she knew I'd never leave her. I tried everything. All of the resources of the department, every lead. Nothing came back. Not to this day. Eventually I had to have her declared legally dead. I had to accept that she didn't want to be found. So, when you ask me about Kerry McCullough or Jimmy Whistler? I know that people can absolutely disappear—no trace—no shadow—when they want to." He turned away from her.

"I'm sorry, Dan," she said. Before now she'd felt like he had no scars, and so couldn't understand the depth of hers. His history proved her wrong. As the plane left the runway and began its ascent, she leaned her head into the curve of his shoulder. He kissed her forehead and cradled her with one arm, using the other to retrieve a crossword puzzle he had stashed in the seat-back compartment. Silence. She understood that segue. No more questions for now. She closed her eyes, grateful to be sheltered by him, encircled by him, for a few hours more.

CHAPTER NINETEEN

"How was your trip?" Sandy asked, mixing one of her club soda concoctions on Rory's kitchen counter. She held the bottle up to the light to check its content level. "I guess it's full of antioxidants, 'cause it's purple!"

Before Rory could answer, Sandy had moved to the living room's French doors, eyeing the activity outside. For weeks, her speculation about the remains found in the back woods had ebbed and flowed, urged along for a time by Cindy Staab, a young newspaper reporter set on exploiting the situation to make a name for herself. Fresh out of college and hungry for her first big break, Staab had decoded Sandy's routine and begun a regular vigil at the driveway's end, offering her a few minutes of fame in exchange for leaking some tidbits about the investigation. In the end, Sandy resisted Staab's scheme and stayed loyal to Rory, telling the reporter to stop harassing her. With Sandy no longer on the line, Staab moved on to staking out the police department—specifically Sergeant Adderson—who likewise ignored her micro minis, thigh-high boots, and pestering, diligently marching on with his investigation.

"Lord, it'll be a shame if they make a mess of things back there," Sandy lamented. "Have they told ya how long they're keepin' the woods roped off?"

Rory sighed. "Well, Sergeant Adderson says they should finish processing the bone that Rocket found within a week or two, but that the forensic excavator, Shelly King, is going to be here for a while. And *she* may decide that some of my trees have to be removed."

"I know ya won't be happy about that!" Sandy made a half-hearted attempt at dusting the window frame as she talked.

Rory twirled the rod for the window blind in her hand. "Whatever happens, Sandy, whatever they're looking for, I'm not letting them raze the woods to get to it."

Sandy put her hands on her hips. "And I'm telling ya, they don't need to do any fancy test on that bone! Who else could it be but the McCullough girl?"

"Sandy, your husband owned the auto repair shop years ago, didn't he? Cross Auto Repair?"

"Sure did."

"You don't by chance remember hearing about a fight between Joe McCullough and Herb Whistler, do you?"

"Oh, that was the fight over the land. Everyone heard about that. Had to be ripe in the grave not to hear that one."

"What land were they fighting about?"

"Didn't I tell ya this story before? Herb wanted that piece'a land that Joe owned—still owns—and Joe wouldn't sell it. Somethin' about frontage—sub dividing—some such thing. Well, Herb said he was gonna find a way to get it from him anyway. Joe wouldn't back down. He told Herb he'd shoot him dead as a Christmas turkey if he ever set foot on the McCollough property."

Rory backed up and raised herself onto the kitchen counter, then winced with regret as her shoulder spasmed in pain.

"Is that arm still bothering ya?" Sandy asked. "Want some of my drink?"

"No, thanks. I'm good. I overdid it on my trip, I think," Rory said, remembering her two nights with Dan. "Back to Herb and Joe—people say those things without literally meaning them."

"Let me help you with these chores!" Sandy left the room briefly, returning with the vacuum. "Yeah, but Herb was in cahoots with the sheriff then. In those days, Southern Point only had a county sheriff, not a real police department. I think those two had the same, how do ya say it, racial opinions? The sheriff arrested Joe for the threats Herb said he made against him and his family."

"How did it end?"

"The sheriff held Joe overnight, but then had to release him. It was common knowledge that Herb and the sheriff also led a group of . . . white knights."

"White knights? You mean the KKK—the *Klan*?"

Sandy nodded. "For the longest time after Joe's arrest, the sheriff or some of his friends would park across from the McCullough place and just sit there, ya know, to try to make him nervous."

"What was Herb's story? I mean, how did he turn into the cruel bastard that he was?"

"Well, I know some but not all. . . ."

"Like what?"

"Like, Herb's father, Herb Senior, was a farmer before him—built the house they all lived in."

"All of them in that little place?"

"For a while. And it didn't have no indoor plumbing in those days. Herb Junior met Julia at a conference in St. Louis. She was there with a group from a young women's home; they cooked and served the meals for the conference guests. With no folks of her own, she must'a thought Herb was a way out, a way to be part of a real family." Sandy tsked and shook her head. "She sure picked the wrong family. Herb Junior hated bein' a farmer's son, but that was his lot in life; his father surely wouldn't let 'im be anything else. And he was the weaker of the two of 'em. He took to drinking young and never stopped. Then he brought Julia back here, and they all lived in that little house his dad built. The Lord alone knows what went on there—behind those walls."

"What happened to Herb's parents?"

"Herb's mother died of lung cancer at forty and Herb Senior drank himself to death, in a way. He didn't believe in doctors, wouldn't get treated for . . . I think it was liver cancer. He was dead at forty-five. Then it was just Herb Junior and Julia, until Jimmy came along."

Sandy plugged in the vacuum and peered out the dining room window as Dan's truck bypassed the turnoff to the barn area and came to a stop in the front parking circle. "I think your gentleman's here," she said, watching Dan get out of the truck. "Lordy, there sure was a line of ladies around here who tried to get with him when he came back here to live—if ya know what I mean. But he's different, getting that big-time education and all—going to work up north in Richmond, an' all the other things. Not that he ever acted like he was better'n anyone else around here. I think he needs someone special in the romance department. I can see why he chose you."

"Sandy, he's probably got some news from the police front—or he forgot to drop something off with my last order."

"No, there ain't nothin' in the bed of his truck," Sandy insisted. "I looked."

"Well, I'll go outside to talk to him anyway, so the dogs don't go crazy." Rory squeezed through a narrow opening in the front door and across the porch with deliberate slowness, aware that Sandy was observing all of the action about to play out—analyzing the scene to broaden her collection of material for use in future speculation and theory-building about the "romance department" or the "bone situation," as she called them.

Dan approached the front steps, his open face and rolling gait a study in boyish self-effacement. She wondered if he was about to mention their weekend in Louisville within earshot of Sandy, who was most likely standing just to the side of the open dining room window.

"So, Rory," he started as he led her away from the house and onto the front lawn, "you live your life surrounded by water, but do you enjoy actually being on it?"

"You mean . . . as in a . . . boat? It's been a while," she answered.

"Well, we can change that," he said. "Go out with me on Redhead Bay tomorrow. We'll cruise around for a few hours and pretend to fish." He read her uncertain expression. "Don't worry. You'll be back before Ian gets home. I'll pick you up at the Southern Point dock."

"If I can make it, what should I bring?"

"You're more than enough for me, all by yourself."

His grin weakened her resistance. "Okay, what time should I be ready?"

The next morning was cloudy and cool. Rory needed both of the old sweaters she had grabbed before leaving the house and struggled to layer them over her short-sleeved T-shirt as she drove to the town's public boat ramp, which was really just a crumbling wooden dock at the water's edge of an abandoned fishing cottage a half mile across the road. Dan's thirty-foot

Boston Whaler idled restlessly against a soggy piling, held in place by one rope and his strong right hand. In his left hand, he held a yellow windbreaker.

"Wasn't sure if you brought one of these!" he called out, grinning. He passed her the jacket and helped her onto the boat. She thanked him as he began to untie the mooring line.

"Are you ready?" He gestured to the passenger seat.

"If you are," she said, sitting down. "Darn, I'll be right back." She climbed off the boat and ran to her car, returning with her camera bag.

Dan chuckled. "You really do take that thing with you everywhere, don't you?" He sat down and took the wheel.

They cleared the dock and cruised out onto the bay in uncharacteristic silence, Dan's eyes never straying from the water in front of him.

"Is something wrong?" Rory asked.

"You mean because I haven't told you three bad jokes already?" he asked, swiveling his chair to face her.

She nodded. "I'm usually the quiet one."

"Nothing's wrong, sweetheart. I'm like this when I'm on the water. It's my church—my temple. Nothing but good can happen when I'm out here." He turned back to the water.

Fifteen minutes later Dan slowed the boat to a drift. "I have a job for you. Take the wheel for five minutes," he said, leaving the captain's chair and making his way to the boat's stern. "Just aim toward the sun."

Rory slid into Dan's chair tentatively, suddenly conscious of how long it had been since she'd been on a boat, out of reach of the pull and stress of her everyday life. The steering was tight; she was afraid to take her hands from the wheel. Behind her, she heard him light a cigar and then open a tackle box, then the hiss of fiberglass reels as he rigged and set four lines in succession. The soles of his battered running shoes squeaked back and forth across the textured floor as she righted the boat in choppy waves. She stayed the course for half an hour. They didn't speak once in that time, instead sharing the space in silence. If the bay had risen up, capsized the boat, and taken her just then, she would have given in to it, her soul satiated.

With no bites in more than an hour, Dan pulled in the fishing lines, still fully baited. "I think someone tipped off the fish," he said. "They knew we were coming after them. We'll concede for today, then. Let them think they've won." He took the wheel again and steered the boat toward home.

"Do you have a few more minutes before you have to get back?" Dan asked as the dock came in to view.

Rory looked at her watch and nodded.

"It's your turn."

He guided the boat in the direction of the landing, veering off at the last minute into a quiet inlet, and cut the engine. "Let's hope I don't run us aground," he whispered as they drifted several yards into a thick stand of tall sea reeds, bleached pale russet from four seasons of life.

"What are we doing here?" she whispered back. "Why are we whispering?"

"You'll see." Dan pulled out an air horn from a storage bench. "You'd better get out that camera of yours . . . right about . . . now."

She readied her camera, searching the faded reeds for any sign of life.

"God will forgive me for this one," he said. He aimed the air horn at the reeds and pressed the trigger. The deafening blast flushed several dozen Tundra Swans from their hidden roosts among the reeds. The huge birds were a stark, blinding white, with black beaks. Heavy and slow to take flight, they flailed their massive wings against gravity, producing a low, billowing whistle as they rose up, long necks craned, from the water.

"Oh my God, Dan," she gasped, snapping a few shots before dropping the camera into her lap and bringing both of her hands up to her face to cover her mouth.

"Are you okay?" Dan asked. "Is it your heart?"

She shook her head twice, and then returned to watching the ethereal spectacle of the birds ascending into the sky, straining to track the last of them as they were swallowed up by clouds and blue.

"Makes you feel . . . terminally ordinary, doesn't it?" he asked. "Grounded by that blasted earth we're all bound to."

Overwhelmed, she leaned over and kissed him on the lips. He accepted the kiss and caressed her cheek with his hand.

"Guess I know what buttons to push with you," he said.

Back at the dock, Dan's hands betrayed the slightest tremor as he tied up to a piling. With the boat secure, he walked Rory to her truck.

"So, Aurora, I have an extra ticket to the Southern Point Animal Shelter's annual fund-raising dinner. Their board of directors hosts it every year up at the old general store. I'm always an easy mark for the kids selling them." He looked at the ground for a moment, kicking some gravel with his boot. "They come into the store and surround me like they're a hunting pack and I'm wounded prey. Do you want to go—as my guest?"

"Umm . . ." She adjusted the strap on her camera. "When is it?"

"Friday. I know it's short notice, but I also know you have a closet full of clothes, so don't use that as an excuse not to come along." He pulled a white envelope out of his pocket, hands trembling again.

"Can I check on a couple of things and get back to you?" she asked.

"Here, take this." He reached into the envelope and passed her a brightly colored ticket covered in animal clip art. "If you can't make it, give me the ticket back by Thursday, and I'll pass it on to someone else. Otherwise, I can pick you up on my way there." He shifted his shoulders and tilted his neck to one side, waiting for her to respond.

"I'll meet you there, okay? If I can work it out." She took the ticket and kissed him again. "Let me get back to work with Sandy—I have to pay her for the month today. Thanks for asking me, Dan." She smiled and climbed into her truck.

CHAPTER TWENTY

Wednesday came, and with it, Ian's weekly guitar lesson. On the way home, he and Rory stopped at the Blue Heron Grill for a quick dinner.

"It's my turn to deliver an evening meal to a homebound parishioner tonight," Rory said as they finished their food. "Will you be all right at home for a couple of hours, or should I see if Sandy can come over?" She prayed he would decide on her second option.

"Oh, my gawd," he said, sighing and rolling his eyes. "I'll be fine, Mom. My friends stay home alone all the time. Nothing's gonna happen. I'm not gonna run away again, if that's what you're worried about. . . ."

"You told me not long ago that you felt weird about the bone thing, so I thought you might not want to stay home by yourself."

"I'm so over that, Mom. It's no prob."

"Really?" Rory asked, surprised.

"Really, Mom," he replied.

Wanting to trust him, she accepted his response. She signed the restaurant check and backtracked a few miles to the grocery store, where she scouted out a small potted plant. She liked to leave something colorful behind when she visited sick church members. Those on her list had no family close by, and she empathized with their anxiety and uncertainty. She was happy with tonight's find: a bright orange gerbera daisy.

All of the food, and the cheerful daisy, fit nicely inside a large cardboard box. Rory pulled her raincoat from the front closet and walked to Ian's room, where he sat inside a cloud of sandalwood incense practicing the "Stairway to Heaven" solo he'd learned at the day's guitar lesson.

"I'll be back at eight. Set the alarm and stay inside. You can rent a movie if you want to. Nothing R-rated. Don't let the dogs out after dark. Don't open the front gate. And keep your phone with you and turned on, okay?" Finished with her litany, Rory paused at the front door. "I love you, honey. Call me if anything comes up."

From the front porch security camera, Ian watched her truck pass through the front gate and fade into the darkening horizon, and then put his guitar away. He dug around in his backpack, pulling out his phone. Bypassing his orange hoodie for a black one, he disarmed the house security system and checked to make sure no police vehicles were on the property.

Al and Rocket waited by the living room door, following every movement of his hand on the doorknob, optimistic about a romp outside. "Stay," he told them, holding out his flattened palm in front of their muzzles. The sun had set by the time he'd made his way to the back woods.

CHAPTER TWENTY-ONE

Home from Washington for a long weekend, Tom picked up Ian at five o'clock on Friday, weaving his tank of an SUV around several local media vehicles idling along the edges of Whistler Ridge Road, inches from a straight drop into its six-foot ditches.

"What's with the circus?" he asked, looking well rested and uncharacteristically tan. Separation seemed to agree with him.

"Good word for it, Tom," Rory said, committed to holding up her end of an amicable exchange. "They wait for the police and medical examiner's office personnel to get to the end of the drive—thank God for that gate—and then they try to get information from them before they can turn onto the road." Rory leaned against the side of Tom's Suburban. "The police have been very good, though. A patrol car waits at the end of the drive with Ian every morning so the reporters can't bother him on his way to the bus."

"Seriously? The kid has to dodge the press?" Tom asked. He helped Ian load his guitar, amp, and backpack into the car. "Well, son, let's see if we can escape your mother's grand experiment to a paparazzi-free zone."

Ian smirked. Rory was glad to see him smile—at anything—and push back her anger at Tom's dig. "Ian, call me if you need me to bring over stuff for your room at Dad's house," she said. "You two have a great weekend."

"See you, Rory," Tom said, upbeat. "I'll have him back to you on Sunday."

When she had visited Rory at Christmas, Mad insisted upon setting up a small bar stocked with premium liquor in a locked cabinet in the dining room. "Trust me, Rory, with all you've got going on, there'll come a day—more than one—sooner not later, when you'll appreciate a good, strong drink," Mad had promised. "You'll only need one." That day was here. After taking care of all the animals, checking messages and emails, and straightening every room in the house, Rory mixed a dry vodka martini anchored by three massive stuffed olives. She stripped down, twisted up her hair, and slipped out the French doors and into the hot tub, grateful to the Barnetts for installing a lattice screen around the portion of the deck it occupied. Though they couldn't have known it when they built the house, the decorative screen was now serving double duty as a privacy shield against the police department minions engulfing her property.

Buoyed by the hot saltwater, she closed her eyes and mentally perused her closet, visualizing its organized formal-wear section for a dress to wear to Dan's charity dinner. She downed the martini in a few gulps.

Over the years, she and Tom had shored each other up at countless charity receptions and galas sponsored through their agency. After browsing predictable silent auctions, they sat through lukewarm dinners, smiling and chatting with their tablemates as though there was no place else they'd rather be. Tom always looked great in his tux, his collar-length hair a perfect contrast to the conservative suit.

Rory's weakness was ball gowns, most often silk or organza.

She'd always loved to dress up, and especially enjoyed the ritual surrounding a formal affair: a professional manicure early in the day, and a hot bath and hair and makeup two hours before leaving for the event. Once her jewelry was in place, she would put on a pair of beautiful evening shoes and remove the plastic from a new dress that was freshly pressed, and usually altered to fit by Veenie, the petite Taiwanese woman who owned Veenie's Tailor Shop. Veenie was a trained tailor, not a seamstress—a rarity in her culture at the time she was studying.

Rory never got the chance to wear the last gown she'd bought, intended for a pre-Thanksgiving ball benefiting a local home for disabled children.

"You look pretty—look good," Veenie assured her, and deftly maneuvered her bare razor blade, slicing through the hem of Rory's red hammered silk dress, somehow finding an extra inch of length. "You are getting skinny. Is everything okay?"

"I'm okay. Thanks for asking." She wasn't ready to make her marital problems more real by talking about them and changed the subject. Even she didn't know that within weeks she and Tom would have their tempered blowout on the sunporch. "Just busy . . . and my teenage son's driving me crazy."

"You will be okay—the best-looking girl there. Just don't get more skinny."

In the end, Tom attended that dinner alone, honoring their commitment, and dodging friends' questions about Rory's absence.

Rory's second martini hit hard. She knew when she mixed it that it was too much. Too strong. As she stood up to get out of the hot tub, the familiar lurching of her chest set in. Her heart rate hit its familiar racing pace—she couldn't find her breath. She shouldn't have had one drink with no food, let alone two, while in the scalding water. That was a sure SVT trigger. She made her way, soaking wet, hunched over at the waist, into the house and onto her bed. She grabbed at the ceiling fan cord and turned it on full force, lying on her side on the bed naked, shivering from self-induced hypothermia, restricting her breathing to a count of six seconds in and eight seconds out—her best vagal maneuvers—willing the episode to pass. She dumped her purse onto the floor, snatching her bottle of beta-blockers. She split one pill in two, held it under her tongue until it dissolved, and swallowed its bitter slurry without water. Then she started to cry, maybe the result of too much adrenaline flooding her system, or from witnessing Ian's apparent relief when he'd gotten into Tom's car to leave for the weekend, or, maybe, from her guilt about how easy it was to want Dan, to think about him, to be with him, and the wretchedness of what she could not stop herself from doing now. She lay on the bed, freezing, counting, waiting for normality. A few minutes later, she sensed her pulse slowing, sat up, and put on a robe. Her pulse was normal.

Standing in her closet, Rory couldn't bring herself to take her dress off its hanger. She delayed getting ready, unnecessarily sorting out dresser drawers until the clock swept past the window of time she needed for her hair and makeup. By that time, Dan would be en route to the dinner. She tried his cell phone. No answer. Now, too buzzed from alcohol and too spent from cardiac turmoil to drive, she had no way of contacting the old Southern Point General Store that the shelter was renting for the dinner.

As the hours crept by, she felt awful, beyond guilty—childish, irresponsible. She'd made a commitment. Then she shirked it. She imagined Dan at the fund-raiser, his blue eyes riveted on the double entrance doors, waiting for her. This would hurt him deeply. She wanted to go—she was afraid to go. She turned off all the lights and muted her phone, hoping for the chance to hide from her conscience in any kind of sleep.

By early morning, Rory counted six missed calls from Dan, the last at four a.m. She guessed he had lost most of a night's sleep worrying about her. She didn't listen to the voicemails he left, and dreaded calling him back, knowing she would have nothing to say to him if she did. No excuse she tendered could justify her actions. He solved her dilemma by showing up on her doorstep at nine a.m.

"What happened to you, Rory?" Dan blinked, frozen in place at her front door. "Is it Ian? I drove by last night—no lights on, gate closed. Checked police and hospital call-ins. Didn't want to trespass, but I have to tell you that I was worried."

Rory held the front door open and both dogs ran out past his legs, demonstrating full acceptance of him as a member of their pack by ignoring him. "It's not Ian," she said, pulling at the tied sash on her white silk robe, wanting to be anywhere but where she was. "He's fine—Ian's fine."

"Then what?" He tried to meet her eyes. "You didn't call me back—leave me any messages. What happened? Your horses—did one of them colic?"

She brushed her hair back from her face and nervously twisted it into a knot. "Dan, I planned to go—I was getting ready—really. Then I . . . had a heart thing."

His face went white. "Rory, was it bad? You should have called me!"

"Not my worst. But, well, then, after that, I . . . well . . . I . . . just panicked about going."

"About going?"

"About us being seen by everyone at the dinner—as being together—in a relationship."

"Hold on. It was your heart that kept you away—yet you were fine. You simply stood me up—for fear we'd be seen together—as a couple." He rubbed his forehead and put a closed fist over his mouth, holding in his next thought.

"Dan, things are moving fast . . . and with me still legally married to Tom . . ." She knew she'd pushed things too far.

"Oh, now you're married again. This is bullshit, Rory," he said, stepping inside the house and closing the door behind him. "I'm finished with breaking myself into little pieces and letting you pick and choose the ones you want—the ones you can handle. I'm not the problem; we're not the problem—you are. You think that if you arrange everything around you enough different ways, you'll make your life, your family, right again."

"Just because we've slept together, you don't have the right to assume you know what I think, what my husband thinks!"

"*Slept* together? We didn't get much sleep, did we?" He was shouting now. "Let's take it down one more level and just say we fucked! How's that? I'm sure that helps you to shove it away in some neurotic compartment of yours. And now you conveniently have a husband again? Wait, now. You left him because your marriage was dead. You moved out, bought a new house, started a new life. Has your husband once called or shown up on your doorstep begging for reconciliation? No! Because he's done with you. You're history."

He leaned against the closed front door and crossed his arms over his chest. "A gift drops right into the palm of your hand. Do you enfold and embrace it? No, you just watch it slip—

no, you squeeze the life out of it. Then you let it slip through your fingers."

Her eyes brimmed with tears. She clenched the ends of her robe sash hard in her fists to keep from crying.

"You know Rory, I'm torn—between anger and frustration over your refusal to accept and hold on to what we have and—" He sighed and shook his head. "Forget it. I'm wasting my time here...."

"And what?" she choked out. "And what?"

"I was going to say, torn between that and being humbled and grateful for you sidestepping into my life. For having a small part of you, for a little while, to myself. It's ridiculous. I'd choose talking to you on the phone over a night with any other woman I've known." He pulled one of her hands from her robe sash and gripped it tightly in his. "Listen to me. It seems that somewhere amid our fact-finding trips to North Carolina, helping you with your farm, that day on my boat, and the few times we've been alone together . . . that I fell in love with you."

"Love?" She pulled back her hand.

"Right now, I think *love-hate* more closely defines it. Rory, are you saying you don't feel the same way? That you don't love me?"

"Dan, I . . . didn't mean to . . . mislead you in any way. I told you—you knew my situation—early on. I'm not in a position to be talking about love, or that kind of relationship right now. I'm—I'm sorry."

"Sorry? Oh, please. Rory, your sympathy is not what I'm after here. I'm not going to chase you, and I won't fuel your penitence complex—don't need that kind of masochistic excitement in my life. Can you believe that there were times in the last month that I asked myself if you were too good for me? I questioned whether or not I deserved you? Christ, at least I don't deny my feelings. You can't admit the truth to yourself, so why in the hell would I expect you to admit it to me?"

Rory tried to respond, but her throat closed. She stood locked in place, glued to the floor.

"You know, 'we forge the chains we wear in life,'" Dan said flatly.

She found a small voice. "Did you come up with that one just for me, Dan?"

"No, not me. It's Dickens, Rory. *Charles Dickens*. People like me have been dealing with people like you for a long time." He shook his head. "It's funny. I'd forgotten how much pain relationships can cause—when you're honest and the other person isn't. When you assume the honesty you give will be returned. I thank you for reminding me of just how that incorrect that assumption is."

She touched his arm with her hand. He threw it off. "Uh-uh, sweetheart. It doesn't work that way. Don't worry. I'll leave you alone if that's what you want. If you can accept what I have to give you, you come to *me*—you ask me for it. My father always told me, 'Stand closest to the people who understand you best.' I'm too old for the drama of unrequited love. Guess I always have been. You find yourself in trouble—you call me. I know how to be there for someone when they need me. Other than that, I have nothing more to say to you."

He stepped through the door and smacked it shut. Outside, the dogs charged him, tails wagging, as he pounded the way to his truck. Rory watched him from the silent house, trembling, until she lost the battle she'd been waging with herself. "I ruined us," she whispered.

CHAPTER TWENTY-TWO

No more daily phone calls to slip her inside information on the police investigation. No email primers on agricultural tax programs or farm equipment financing plans, which ended in flirtation or downright propositions. No truck-side briefings on land management. Or, anticipating the next time she would see him, or kiss his cheek, or drown in the excitement of clinging to his warm, powerful body as he buried his face in the curve of her neck and moaned her name. That was the hollow that Dan's exodus—channeled by Rory's own hand—left in her life.

Spells of regret and self-doubt replaced the small slice of serenity she had found in the first part of each day after moving into the Whistler Ridge farm. She imagined Dan asleep in his bed, moving through his day at work, around his house. And then it struck her. His house—she had never asked him about it. Never thought to ask. She had no idea where he lived.

Ian returned from Tom's house, still convinced his life would be more "normal" if he lived with his dad. "Things over there are more like they used to be, Mom." He stood in front of the open pantry, perusing its shelves for junk food. "Oh, except that Dad's dating now."

"Really?" Rory asked from her perch at the kitchen bar, sorting through the stack of photos taken the day she and Dan had gone fishing out on Redhead Bay. They were some of her best. In one, she had caught a swan mid-wingbeat, its head raised arrow-straight upward, its feet just breaking the water's surface. Defying gravity. Limitless. She wanted that.

Ian shook half of a bag of chips into a bowl. "Some woman named Katie, or Kathie—from DC. I guess she's helping him get through what you did to him."

His comment dragged Rory down from her lofty interlude. "Hold it, Ian. Your father and I decided together to end our marriage. It was a painful, difficult decision—for both of us."

He took the bowl and sank into a chair at the breakfast room table. "Whatever, Mom. At least he seems happy."

She put the photos into an envelope and joined Ian at the table. "Look," she said, trying to detour away from more unpleasant dialogue. "I know you haven't seen much of your dad since we moved. Why don't I talk to him about you spending spring break at his house?"

Ian stopped crunching a mouthful of chips. "Will you be mad if I do?"

"Of course not. I'll miss you, but I won't be mad. You can see him anytime the two of you can work out your schedules. I already told you that, honey. I understand what you're going through. I've been there myself."

Ian didn't ask her what she meant, and she didn't offer up any more on the subject.

Another week began as the last one had ended: the early morning arrival of various configurations of police personnel; school, soccer, and guitar lessons for Ian; Rory half-heartedly tackling her daily routine of house painting, clumsy self-tutoring on tractor implements, massaging her business plan for any possible budget cuts, and watching and waiting for some—any—progress report from Sergeant Adderson. The police investigation had taken on its own plodding rhythm, and it was difficult for her to remember what life had been like before Rocket had found the bone, when all she had in front of her was old emotional baggage and newer calculated risk. She knew that without Dan around to analyze, theorize, and co-conspire, the chances were slim that she could discover more information about the bone any faster than the ensconced army of police could. As vans crammed with police personnel filed past the house each morning, she wondered if this day might be the day the bone gave up its story.

Thinking about it later, Rory guessed she should have known that one day it would happen, with so much traffic up and down the driveway early in the morning and into the night. Olga was a six-year-old off-track thoroughbred—hyper, paranoid, loaded with shotgun reflexes—and no match for Jake Karloff, a recent police academy graduate, newly assigned to the task of shuttling the forensics investigative team off the property at the end of each workday. One evening, Jake arrived outside the front gate in a department-issued white van and entered the four-digit security code. But instead of waiting for the gates to open, he hit the gas pedal and lurched forward. Realizing his error, he slammed on the brakes, skidding shrilly on the concrete pad and coming to a stop within inches of the iron gates. To Olga, it was the starting bell at a racetrack. She charged across the pasture at a full gallop, soaring over its single, grass-lined drainage ditch, her body a perfect arc. In her panic, she overshot the landing distance from the pasture's lone utility pole. As her front hooves hit the ground, she couldn't shift her weight fast enough to clear the pole. Her left flank slammed against it, sending her into a full roll—belly up, legs flailing. Seconds later she righted herself and shook it off.

Jake was shaken and apologetic, and the horse seemed more intent on getting back to grazing with her companions than standing around for inspection. Rory watched her for half an hour and then let her go. The horse seemed to be fine. Things were different an hour later.

"Mom, something's wrong with Olga!" Ian shouted as he ran into the house from soccer practice, his cleats digging into the wood floor. "She's holding her foot up."

"What do you mean? How?" Rory forgot about the cleats and the floor and jumped up from her desk.

"She won't put her one back foot on the ground. I can't remember if it's right or left," he explained. "She tries, and then yanks it up. Oh, and her backend is shaking like crazy."

They ran outside to the pasture. His description was dead on: Olga was in trouble.

It took Craig Leighow, Rory's veterinarian, an hour to reach the farm, by which time she had lured Olga into her stall with some feed and blanketed her trembling body.

"X-rays rule out a clean stifle break, but not a hairline fracture," he reported to Rory. "Definite deep bruising and a torn muscle. But her entire hip and flank is buried beneath massive swelling right now, making it impossible for me to determine the full extent of the injury."

He placed Olga on stall rest for several weeks. "Let's be honest. It's a wait-and-see situation. Right now, I plan to x-ray her again in a week, when the swelling's gone down. At any time, the scenario can change, meaning you'll have a difficult decision to make."

The mare's dapple-gray coat was dark and slick from systemic shock. Her brown eyes widened to the point of exposing their whites with each panicked blink. Rory stayed in Olga's stall until the medication calmed her, and for hours after that she watched her weave and paw futilely within her four walls, dependent and powerless. The display mirrored Rory's sense of time in her own life—slipping away, lost to no particular direction, with no next step, at least not any that she could see. And there was no getting that time back. That agreement she had struck with herself weeks earlier—to leave the police investigation up to the police, to wait things out—was wasteful. It was an agreement she had to break.

Three days later Jane called Rory to check in for their weekly coffee date. "How's it going out there?"

"Less than good," Rory groaned. "Olga had an accident."

"No!" Jane gasped. "Is it serious?"

"Yeah, it is. She was spooked by a van coming up the drive and injured her stifle."

"Her what?"

"Stifle. Think of it like a knee. I've been spending most of my time out in the barn. The police are paying her vet bills, and the recruit who was responsible for the accident has been pulled off the investigation. It's either going to get better or it's going to get a whole lot worse."

"Like, you won't be able to ride her?"

"Like having to put her down. There's no such thing as a three-legged horse, Jane. Rigid spine. It's physically impossible."

"God, I'm sorry. I understand if you can't get away—"

"No, I'm sorry—sorry for being a bitch. And, I absolutely need a break from everything going on here."

"That bad, huh?"

"I was supposed to save the horse that I adopted—not *kill* her. And this police thing just keeps dragging on. It's already mid-March, and I'm worried sick about the business—the barn construction and the land."

"What about Dan? What does he think?"

"I haven't seen him much lately." It wasn't quite a lie. And, it did head off Jane's inevitable questions.

"Well, listen. I'm here for another week, and then I've got to run that Navy reunion thing out in San Diego. I'll be gone on that gig for almost a month."

Rory had forgotten about that trip. "I'll call you tomorrow. I just want to check on something. I definitely want to see you before you go."

CHAPTER TWENTY-THREE

Awake at five a.m., Rory waited as long as she could before calling Jane. A gravelly voice, the result of a late night, too many cigarettes, and no morning coffee, answered her eight-thirty call.

"It's morning, isn't it, Rory?" Jane made a yawning sound. "And I overslept again. Or else, you under-slept." Another yawning groan. "So, what'll it be today, your one cup of coffee or your single glass of scotch?"

"Neither," Rory answered quickly. "Sorry I woke you."

"No biggie. I had an event last night that simply wouldn't end. I had to kick the rowdy bastards out at three a.m."

Rory sighed into the phone. "Jane, I need a favor."

"Umm, let me guess. You're eloping with Dan and you need me as a witness."

"Hardly. I did some things, said some things—it's over with him."

"Wha—hold on!" Jane blared. Rory heard the flick of a lighter and then a hissing exhale into the receiver. "It's only been a few weeks since he . . . you know . . . rocked your world."

"Can we not talk about this—him—right now?" Rory asked.

"Yeah, sure. I'm sorry."

"I'm calling about us getting together before you go out of town."

"Let's do it."

"How about making our weekly coffee 'to go?'"

"'To go' where, friend?"

Rory bit at one of her cuticles. "Jane, you know I went down to North Carolina to talk to Julia Whistler."

"North Carolina!" she shrieked. "Back there to talk? You told me the old lady was out of it—couldn't make sense."

"She was—that day. That's what I took away from it. But what if there's more to Julia's story—some sense—some logic—lodged in the middle of all of it? I want to try again. I've got to do something besides sit and wait while my bank account drains to nothing." She heard Jane exhale another lungful of carbon monoxide air into the phone. "What do you say, Jane?"

The line was silent for a moment. "Rory, I say supply me with good java, and I'm there."

Rory bet on traveling to North Carolina as a reprieve from the subject of Dan Deal, but his name surfaced almost as soon as she started up the truck.

"Rory, what's the current status of you and Dan?" Jane's tone held no trace of her usual sarcasm.

"I know I told you already. Whatever it was I was doing with Dan is over," Rory insisted, her hands tight on the steering wheel.

"You had a wretched falling-out. This will pass."

"It was more than that, Jane. A lot more. I wish I'd never met him. He's shown me parts of myself, places in myself, just by being around me. And not all of them are good. There are so many things I regret, and things I want to do now—things I have to say—to make up for a lifetime of keeping the peace—avoiding conflict. Maybe it's too late for all of that—too late for me. It's like I don't know anyone or anything anymore. Except for Ian. I know I love Ian. That's all I'm sure of." She forced back tears. "Being with Dan—it couldn't work. I was getting lost in it."

"Come on," Jane said encouragingly. "That's the beauty of a new relationship. Getting lost in the passion, the discovery."

"I can't reconcile the contradiction—the conflict."

"Conflict?"

"Yes. As undemanding as Dan was, I felt . . . pressured."

"Pressured? By that guy? About what, specifically?"

"Pressured to go in deeper than I wanted to, at the expense of other parts of my life. I'm not ready."

"Well, no one else can make you ready. Your emotions dictate what happens."

"Jane, relationships can turn on, and then destroy people."

"Relationships don't turn on people. People turn on people."

"Fine. I don't want to feel too much."

"'Don't want to feel too much'? Did you really just say that? Where is all of this coming from?"

"Jane, have you ever recalled a bad memory, one you'd forgotten, because something happening now triggered the memory?"

"Uh, yeah, I guess so. What's going on?"

"This is hard to talk about, but I've told you my childhood was . . . extreme. A handful of wonderful memories, but most of them, I've tried to forget. Anyway, one morning when I was in the fifth grade, I rode to school on the bus as usual. But that afternoon my mother arrived at school with a flourish in her red and black Mercury Cougar—she *loved* her sports cars. I remember her standing in the principal's office, waiting for me, wearing a pale green suit, her ivory headscarf wafting along on a breeze created by the secretary's desk fan. She didn't say where we were going—I assumed it was home. It wasn't. Instead we ended up at a small ranch house in a cramped development about ten miles away. No yard, no ponies, no space, just a bleak gray box my mother had secretly rented and moved into that day. For the next miserable year, my sister and I were weekend visitors to our family home, which was now occupied by our father. I remember him picking us up on Friday afternoons in his new car. He purposely bought a Cadillac because he knew my mother hated Cadillacs. My mother seethed with rage every time she saw that car—called him a monster. We started pretending we didn't like the car—in case she was watching us—to keep the peace. We did that with everything. Lied, pretended we were miserable when we were with our dad—that we didn't want to spend time with him. We had to pretend we didn't love him. No. Worse. We had to convince our mother that we hated him. It was our little secret—Mad's and mine."

"Rory, that's terrible."

"It was. My mother punished my father by dating men she knew he despised, and he retaliated by bringing other women into the house—never while we were there. His time with us was exclusive. But he let them play house, redecorate our bedrooms, and he let their children sleep in the bedrooms. They would leave toys and other things behind, maybe thinking they were going to live there someday. It was horrible—finding the stuff. Do you know, Jane, that I know exactly how much my weekly riding lesson cost? During the year my parents were separated, we were destitute. The only constant in my life was my weekly riding lesson. Each lesson cost thirteen dollars, something I'd never had to think about before. There were many weeks that loose change and birthday or Christmas money from my grandparents contributed to the fee."

"God, Rory, I could cry. But your dad was a successful doctor. How could your mother not have enough money to live on?"

"Because my mother tried to prevent my dad from seeing us at all, and I guess he thought that he could force her hand by restricting her support payments. We were like little pawns in their screwed-up divorce war."

"I've never heard you say that your parents were divorced."

"They weren't actually divorced. They technically resolved their problems, or as my mother described it: 'Your father and I have agreed to reconcile. He'll make the money, and I'll spend it.'"

Jane moaned. "Oh, that kind of true love."

"I actually believe that it was—love, I mean—on my father's part," Rory said. "He would have done anything for my mother. But nothing—everything—wouldn't have been enough. My mother couldn't love—I'm certain of that. Can you can see why I want to keep my own separation as clean as possible? Why I had to be so careful with Dan? I cannot allow him to influence any other part of my life—or Ian's life. I can't allow my emotions to alter any of my actions. I have to protect my son from what I went through as a child. I won't do that to him. If there was any possible way to make it work with Tom—to survive living like that—avoid the divorce—I would have. I would have—if only for Ian's sake."

"You should tell Dan what you told me. He'd understand you better—why you're so fucking terrified. I do. Listen, you're not your mother, Rory. I'm telling you—you should pursue this thing with Dan. He's been good for you. I've seen the change."

Rory shook her head stubbornly. "It's too late for that, Jane. I stepped too far over the line. The last time we saw each other, he made it clear—how much I hurt him. Me, the one who tries not to hurt anyone—look what I did. I don't deserve him, and I accept that I don't."

They drove on toward Edenton Bay, silent for a while. Then a sprawling horse farm came into view on Jane's side of the road. "Christ, look at that place," she said out of one side of her mouth as she lit a fresh cigarette with the embers of its dying predecessor. An older man in breeches and field boots pivoted in the center of an outdoor schooling ring, encircled by a half dozen adults on horseback. They were alternating between a sitting trot and a posting trot. "Excuse me, but what the fuck are they doing?" Jane asked, starting to laugh.

"Oh my god," Rory said, looking past Jane to the scene in the riding ring. "He looks just like my first riding instructor. . . ." She slowed down to get a better look. "It's an adult class."

The riders mesmerized Jane. "Can you do that bouncy thing in the saddle?"

"You're not actually supposed to bounce," Rory explained. "Those riders have a lot of work to do." She turned her eyes back to the road. "You know, Jane, when I was very young, I'd sneak out to the barn before the sun came up and sit on my pony while she did nothing at all in her stall. When I competed in shows as a teenager, it was the same. Horses were my escape. No—my emancipation—from instability, from my parents' constant warring. Not fighting—warring. The routine and demands of caring for the horses—that was my reprieve from the measured hell of the house. Whatever else in my life was unstable or traumatic, horses were always there for me. They still are. And now, all these delays at the farm . . ." Her voice broke.

"Jane, I may have to sell Titian. . . ." She choked out a sob and squeezed the steering wheel. "Crying again! I'm tired of it."

"Hold on," Jane said with a surprising softness. "I wish I knew what to say. I've never seen this side of you."

"It's not something I share with anyone—except my sister." Rory took a deep breath and exhaled slowly. "And then, that's only if she brings it up. Too painful."

"Do you want to pull over for a few minutes?" Jane asked. "Maybe I should drive."

"I'll be okay. I have to be okay."

"Rory, don't talk about selling your horse. We'll come up with another way to get you through this."

When they arrived at Brook Manor, Jane opted out of accompanying Rory into the building. "I think I'll stay out here and smoke a cigarette if you don't mind. Maybe walk across the street to the water. These places depress me. Besides, this is your gig." She opened her eyes wide for dramatic effect. "I don't want to arouse any unnecessary suspicion."

"All right, but I'll be in there an hour or so."

"Then I'll smoke a whole pack of cigarettes!"

Rory retrieved a small cooler from the back seat and started toward the entrance. The receptionist recognized her from her visit with Dan several weeks earlier.

"Be prepared—she's really failing," the woman whispered. "Been going downhill every day here lately for some reason. This might be your last chance to visit her."

"Thanks for telling me," Rory said, turning in the direction of Julia Whistler's room.

The receptionist gently called her back. "Would you mind opening that cooler? I have to check for, uh, contraband." She saw Rory's surprised look. "Oh, it's not what you think, hon.

Some families try to smuggle in restricted food and drinks. Diabetes and all—just a precaution."

"Really? I never thought of that. Good policy," Rory said, momentarily distracted from her own covert mission by the image of caring but devious visitors being frisked for food on their way into their grandma's or great-uncle's room.

Except for a different patchwork afghan drooping from her shoulders, it appeared at first glance as though nothing about Julia Whistler had changed since Rory's last visit. She was propped up in the same chair, in the same corner, next to her room's single large window. But as Rory moved closer, she noticed that the old woman was significantly thinner and more fragile than during their first meeting. Her eyes had a milky cast. *She's waiting to die*, Rory thought. "Do you remember me from my last visit, Mrs. Whistler?" she asked after knocking on the open door a few times.

"Ronnie . . . isn't it?" Julia mumbled, her breathing labored.

Rory pulled the afghan up around Julia's shoulders. She had to remind herself that the woman was in her seventies, not her nineties. "You're close, Mrs. Whistler—it's Rory Fielding. I brought some camellias from your old farm." She pulled a mason jar full of fuchsia blossoms out of her cooler and placed it on the nightstand. "Last time I was here, I asked you if you knew anything about . . . any old . . . graves or a family cemetery in the back woods of your old farm on Whistler Ridge."

"Pretty pink flowers you brought, but I don't know anything about any graves." Julia sounded weak but agitated. She waved her hand dismissively. "Don't go blaming my boy for any of this. I'm sick of that! He left here ages ago."

"I didn't mention Jimmy—" Rory stopped midsentence and silently tapped her phone's voice recording button, as Dan had done on their last visit. It was a waiting game to determine whether Julia could again engage in a coherent conversation even though she suffered from advanced dementia. Rory sat down on the room's lone spare chair, passing a couple of minutes in silence. "Mrs. Whistler, you did tell me something about Jimmy's relationship with Kerry McCullough, and you brought up a confrontation between Kerry's father and your husband, Herb."

The old woman corrected her slump enough to lean her head back in her seat, as if to take in more air. "That Joe McCullough," she began breathlessly, "he said Kerry was in trouble, and . . . and he said Jimmy was the father."

"Do you know what Joe wanted Herb to do?" Rory asked.

"Joe wanted Herb to make Jimmy admit he was the father—put his name on the baby's birth certificate. Help with the care and all. Can you imagine?"

"Yes, I can. Did Herb agree?"

"No!" she cried. "Herb threw him out and went right after Jimmy. He beat Jimmy so bad—Jimmy stayed hidden in the barn for a week. Then things got quiet for some months."

She directed her dull eyes at Rory, pointing to a green oxygen tank. Rory got up and pulled the wheeled tank over to where Julia was sitting, and opened the valve. "Are you sure you can do this without help? Maybe I should get a nurse."

"No!" Julia insisted. "No nurse." She scratched for the mask with gnarled hands and pulled it to her face. Rory put a hand on her shoulder and waited for the oxygen to take effect, then sat in the chair again.

"Who are you?" Julia said after she dropped the mask, searching Rory's face as she tried to reorient herself.

"Rory, Rory Fielding," she said slowly, carefully enunciating the syllables.

"Where's my son? Are you with my son?"

"No, Mrs. Whistler, Jimmy's not here. I've never met him."

"Who are you, then? What do you want from me?"

Rory wasn't sure she possessed the killer instinct required to pull any more information out of a failing old lady. Julia had to be exhausted—it was time to go. As Rory pulled together her belongings, the old lady reached out a quaking hand. "Wait, Ronnie . . . please."

Rory sat back down. *Okay*, she thought, one last round. "Mrs. Whistler, do you remember telling me about your husband Herb and your son Jimmy? Can you tell me . . . did your husband ever, uh . . . hit—hurt you?"

"If he was sober enough, and things weren't the way he liked, he'd let you know it. But not when I had to be in my chair—he needed a livelier punching bag those times. That's when he'd turn his sites on Jimmy. Many a night, he never got that far. He just passed out—especially if he went in the tub. When that happened, we knew we'd have no trouble till morning."

Rory was incredulous. "The tub?" she asked. Her skin crawled at Julia's description of a day in the life of the Whistler bunch. She wanted some of the sick old woman's story to be the product of a confused mental state, but Dan had already corroborated some of Julia's claims the day he'd delivered the police report on Herb Whistler's death.

"Mrs. Whistler, sometimes, a dream or a thought might be so real to us—"

Julia cut her off. "I've been keeping . . . this inside . . . for too long. Got to . . . finish it." She lowered her head as if to gather strength, and then continued, her gaze locked on the tile floor. "That last spring . . . things got bad with Herb and Jimmy— we didn't see Kerry around anymore. She dropped out of school. Herb said he knew she was up to something. He went to Joe McCullough once more to try to talk sense into him, to see if he would take money . . . to get Kerry to get rid of the baby. Joe told Herb he didn't want our money and that Kerry was havin' that baby."

Rory didn't want to hear any more of the story, but there was an urgency in Julia's voice that kept her in her seat. "Come summer, folks—they started talking about a light-skinned baby they'd seen at Joe McCullough's place. No one knew if it was from family up north or what. Herb pulled Jimmy into the barn many times—'teachin' him a lesson,' he'd say. I was worried for Jimmy's safety. Do you know what it's like to see your boy bruised—hurting—over and over again?" Julia appeared oddly energized by telling the story. "At the end of the summer, just before school started, Herb told me to pack a few of Jimmy's things, some clothes and traveling money. He said Jimmy was to take care of some loose ends and get out of Southern Point that night."

"Did you know where he was going?"

"No. Just that he had to go away and stay away—for good. It would have come to a bad end with him here. I don't know all of the things Herb did in his life, but I know plenty. I thought Jimmy might come back home someday, maybe after Herb was dead and gone. I waited and waited. A sick feeling all the time. Day and night. Then, one day, I gave up waitin' for him. He'd left me. But I didn't blame him. Not one bit. I like to think of him off in California—someplace warm and sweet. His bruises long faded away. Far from here."

That's it? Rory thought. "Mrs. Whistler, your son left and never came back? Never called or wrote?"

"He knew he'd shamed his daddy one too many times. Herb said there was no way that a—that—baby—you know what he called it—was going to grow up and disgrace our family name."

"And you agreed—to him taking care of Kerry?" Rory struggled to stay in the chair and continue the questioning. "You agreed to—to—what Jimmy was going to do?"

"I—I just knew . . . how things were going to be. No way around it. I saw Jimmy take to drinkin', like his dad, when he was only a boy. Caught him with some of Herb's whiskey when he wasn't more than twelve. The boy was better off going away. It was his only chance. Once, he even tried to join the army, but he failed some of the tests. When Herb found the enlistment papers, he locked Jimmy out of the house for days—in February. Jimmy had to make do with staying in the barn and taking what I snuck out to him through the back porch while Herb took his bath. Herb's stomach pain was so bad that every night, unless our water heater was out, he took a bottle of bourbon and a pack of cigarettes into the bathroom and we knew to leave him alone."

Julia reached for her oxygen mask and took several breaths. "Herb's last night on this earth was Jimmy's nineteenth birthday. Jimmy'd been gone near a year. Herb didn't even mention the boy's name, like he'd never existed. Jimmy—he was the only real family I had." She looked at Rory. "He took my boy from me, Herb did. Nothin' mattered to me after that."

Rory tried to put herself in Julia's place. She thought of Ian, and how far she might go to protect him.

Julia stared blankly across the room for a minute or two before speaking again. "All I did," she said firmly, "was make Herb comfortable."

"What did you say?" Rory asked, confused by the statement. "What do you mean by 'comfortable'?"

Julia tucked her shoulders into the afghan as though she were retreating inside herself. "We both deserve to burn in Hell. Herb, for what he did to us. Me, for what I let him do to other people. But not for what I did to him. I—I was trapped too. He'd never let me leave."

"How—how did you make Herb comfortable?" Rory tried to redirect her, to take advantage of her transient lucidity.

"The man liked his liquor and I didn't stop him. I even brought him a second bottle—one I kept on hand for times when things got really bad. You see, Herb always drank as much as he had in front of him—until he fell asleep or passed out. He was already drunk when he got into the empty tub, and he told me to turn the water on."

Rory recalled reading in the police report that when they interviewed Julia following Herb's death, she said that she went to bed that night and found her husband's body in the morning. Rory thought about what Dan would do in this situation, concluded that he would see how far things would go, and then took the same path.

"Mrs. Whistler, I'm not here to do anything but listen—to whatever you want to tell me." She waited.

"I only gave him . . . what he asked me for. I only did what I was told. Herb passed out after he got in the tub. I filled it with water, cleaned up his bottles, and went to my room. Then I went to bed. I let the Lord—make the final decision."

"Final decision?" Rory asked. She remembered Dan telling her that Herb's autopsy listed his cause of death as heart failure secondary to hypothermia. But the investigating police officer noted in his report that it seemed impossible for someone as drunk as Herb was on the night of his death to clean up his booze, get in the tub, and fill it with water, and then turn it off and lie there all night without slipping under the water. The report cited that while the November night was cold, it was questionable that the open bathroom window could have cooled the bathwater fast enough for hypothermia to set in before aspiration could occur. The report also stated there was no water in Herb's lungs.

"Did you check to see if the water temperature was too hot?" Rory had to be sure of Julia's intention that night.

"Hot water? I never turned on the hot water."

"You filled the tub with *cold* water?" she asked, picturing Herb—drunk and nearly unconscious—in the bathtub, while Julia struggled from her wheelchair to turn on the water.

"Yes, I did."

"And he . . . passed away . . . by himself. Or were you there?"

"I left him there and managed to close the bathroom door and to get myself into bed. It was God's will. I found him—still in the tub—in the morning."

"That's why the police photos of the bathroom showed no glasses or liquor bottles—you had already cleaned up," Rory said, barely audible. "Mrs. Whistler, did you know that Herb had advanced liver disease?" Julia didn't respond. Rory tried again. "And what about Kerry?"

"That poor girl and her baby . . . God . . . forgive me," she groaned. Her eyes drifted shut and her head dropped to her chest. The groan turned into a hissing rasp.

Panicked, Rory ran to the bedside table and pumped the nurse's call button with her palm.

The nurse arrived but did nothing. "Ma'am, it's okay. She's just snoring. You must'a wore her out with your nice visit."

Rory raced out of the building, nearly tripping on the edge of the sidewalk.

"Hey, how'd it go in there?" Jane asked, hopping off the truck's tailgate and slamming it shut. "I thought you were never coming out."

"I think I'm going to be—sick," Rory moaned, holding her stomach. "I—I need to sit for a minute." She slid into the truck and slumped over the steering wheel. Jane smashed an unsmoked cigarette on the pavement and walked around to her side of the truck. "You're starting to worry me, honey."

"I feel like I've been to Hell and back," Rory said, clinging to the steering wheel, still shaken by Julia's story and its implications. "This was a totally dysfunctional family. The husband was racist, sadistic—a criminal. The wife was disabled and repressed. And it sounds like the son was an abused alcoholic—before he even hit puberty."

"Hold on, Rory. You said Mrs. Whistler was senile. Maybe not all of what she told you is true. . . ."

"That's just it. Now I think it is true, that's what's so incredible."

"Did you record it like the last time? Can I hear it?"

"Yes, but not here. I don't want to stay here another minute. I feel like I'm suffocating."

They pulled out of the parking lot and onto the road. Rory put the recorder on the center console and pressed the play button. They crossed the state line just as Mrs. Whistler's voice questioned whether God would forgive her for what she'd done to Herb, and whether the McCulloughs could forgive Herb for what he'd done to them.

"Holy shit," Jane said. "The mom and dad kick the son out—"

Rory corrected her. "The father kicked him out, not the mother."

"Okay, the father kicks him out, after he's ordered to do away with his girlfriend and baby? And then the mom drowns her husband in retaliation? That's better than a fucking movie."

"Except that it's a not a movie, Jane. If Julia Whistler's story is true, there may be another, smaller set of bones back there too, and the police are going to find them. A teenage girl and her baby died back there, for Christ's sake. Killed by a teenage boy. What horror did she and the baby go through? It's monstrous—criminal! I wish I'd never bought the place."

"Let's pull over," Jane said. "I'll drive for a while."

Rory ground the truck to a dusty stop at a wooded roadside rest area, where she and Jane sat together on top of a weathered picnic table half-covered in bird droppings. Months of unrelenting stress had finally made its way across Rory's face.

The faintest purple cast crept downward from her lower eyelids to her cheekbones. With much of her property off-limits in the past months, she had spent more time than usual indoors during the day, giving her already fair complexion a stark pallor, and her dark eyebrows the appearance of perpetual crossness. She hadn't had a haircut in three months; the hiatus produced unruly brown curls reaching down her back that overpowered her small, oval face. She started to cry. "God, I think I'm done."

Jane inched closer to her on the picnic bench. "I've never seen you cry this much, Rory. No—until this month, I've never seen you cry—period. That's how I know things are tough. Don't worry. I'm not going to tell anyone that you're going crazy." Jane put an arm around her and patted her shoulder. "Seriously, anyone would be overwhelmed with what you're going through right now, with the divorce and Ian. Add in that bone, these whacko people. Rory, that's what's fucking crazy! We all read and hear about things like this, and from a safe distance, it's fascinating, I guess. But this must be what happens to the people involved, behind the scenes. Families, lives wrenched apart. You know that all the secrets, all this stuff is safe with me—I'll never tell anyone any of it—ever. But what are *you* going to do with all the information—this bedside confession of the murderer's mother—who's also a murderer?"

Rory wiped at her eyes with her hand. "I just don't know right now."

"Here." Jane yanked a tissue out of her purse and handed it to Rory.

"That's okay," Rory said, pulling her gray linen handkerchief, folded and pressed knife sharp, from her jacket pocket.

"And you talk about my obsessive behavior?" Jane said, trying to combat the gravity of the situation with a little humor. "You could cut yourself on that thing."

"It's . . . special to me."

"I get it. That's sweet. Kinda weird, but sweet."

"There's more to it. I was with my dad when he died. He'd just come out of recovery from surgery—something routine with his gallbladder. My mother was somewhere else, as always. They let me and Mad sit with him in his room. We were underage—she was fourteen, I was twelve—but it was a professional courtesy because he was on staff at the hospital. I was sitting next to his bed, telling him about some inane incident at school, and all at once, his vital sign monitors starting beeping and wailing. Nurses flew into the room, yanking us out of there. I pulled this handkerchief out of dad's hand—it was still warm from him holding it. It was the last thing he touched—our last connection. We found out later that he'd been bleeding internally since the operation. He was dying the whole time. This . . . piece of cloth, in a small way, it keeps his memory alive." Rory managed to force out a smile before erupting into full-on sobs.

"I'm such an idiot!" Jane said, tearing up. "Give me that damned handkerchief."

"It's okay," Rory said, and sniffled. "I've kept this stuff buried for so long—I've got to deal with it—get out ahead of it."

"Honey, I think you need some more of what Dan's been giving you and less past tense in your life, if you know what I mean. I think—maybe—he's part of your future. And you need the police to go away and leave you alone so you can get your life back."

Rory rubbed at her eyes with the handkerchief once more. "The problem is, Jane," she said, "if I ever do wade through this mess, I know I don't want the life that I had before. But the way I've lived all these years—I'm not sure I know how to go after the kind of life I do want."

CHAPTER TWENTY-FOUR

"Gum?" Sergeant Adderson stood with Rory in her front yard, an open pack of Big Red the size of a deck of cards in his extended hand. The gesture reeked of either a bribe or a consolation prize. "Uh, it looks like we have to stop our work and remove a few trees, Mrs. Fielding." He sounded apologetic as he spoke. "Shelly King is having trouble accessing an area she thinks may yield something eventually."

"What do you mean, 'eventually,' Sergeant?" Rory asked, frustrated. She had just reconciled herself to Shelly's thorny presence. Now she had to agree to let the woman kill off some of her trees.

"Mrs. Fielding, I know this is inconvenient, and I'm sorry . . . about your trees. All can say is, I try to think about how

I'd feel if it was my family member out there in those woods. I'd want to find out what happened."

She couldn't disagree with him on that point.

"Now, I know Shelly—Ms. King—is pretty rough around the edges," he continued. "Too much time working—and most likely livin'—alone, I think." He adjusted the waist of his pants and tucked his thumbs into his gun belt. "I can't guarantee anything, but there is a way to try to preserve the trees you want to save the most."

"Just tell me what to do," Rory said resignedly.

"I can't technically allow you inside the restricted area, but how about if you tried to mark some of the trees from outside the fenced-off area, and I'll do everything I can to try to save them?"

"How do you suggest I mark the trees if I can't get inside the area?" she said through clenched teeth.

Always the diplomat, Sergeant Adderson forged ahead. "I know it sounds kinda strange, and it's more work for you, but I suggest you attach a paintbrush to the end of a broomstick with duct tape, dip that end in fluorescent paint, reach over the fence, and put a mark on those trees you want us to save. That's how I do it."

"Trust me, Sergeant, I've developed a whole new definition of *strange*. I'll take you up on your suggestion for painting the trees. How long do I have until they come down?"

"Well"—he turned the omnipresent wad of red gum in his mouth several times—"how does this weekend sound?"

She bit her tongue in a new spot. "Oh, that's three days from now. I'd better head to the hardware store for some paint."

When Rory entered the woods with her paint can and paintbrush on Sunday morning, the ground was as soft as biscuit dough from another full night of rain. It gave way and pulled at the soles of her boots with each step she took toward the fenced-off crime scene. After a few tries, she figured out how to balance on one leg at the fence's outside edge while extending both arms out from her chest with the broomstick. She marked as many trees as she could reach and hoped for the best. After plastering an X on one last tree—located a fair distance from the dig site—she lost her footing and began a backward slide in the mud. She grabbed at the orange plastic snow fence and dropped to her knees, pulling it down with her. "Shit," she hissed, her jeans now glazed with gritty muck. Pushing herself back up with her hands, she felt something sharp squish between her fingers where one of her palms had hit the ground. It was inside the cordoned-off section of the dig site, but something made her pluck it out of the brown sludge. It was the red Ritchie Blackmore guitar pick she had given Ian one week ago.

CHAPTER TWENTY-FIVE

"You went back there, didn't you, Ian?" Rory bellowed as she stood in the hallway next to the kitchen. "What were you thinking! It's a crime scene, for God's sake!"

"What do you mean? I wasn't back there!" Ian yelled. "Besides, you said it was probably just an old grave!"

She held the guitar pick inches from his face. "I found this back there."

He turned bright red as his eyes darted around the hall, avoiding contact with hers. "I—I—just wanted to—you know—take some pictures. Show the guys at school."

"Ian that area is off-limits, by order of the police. And you lied to me—again."

"I was . . . looking around, that's all." His voice trembled as he swallowed the words.

"Rocket found the bone, Ian. Nothing's changed since then. If it had, Sergeant Adderson would have told us."

"Mom, you're wrong. There's something else—" He turned away from her and started down the back hall.

"Ian, I'm talking to you!" Rory threw up her hands in frustration. "Do not walk away from me!"

She heard the alarm system for the garage door sound and decided to take a minute and cool down. A few seconds later the alarm sounded again, and Ian was back in the house. He walked to the dining room and dropped a brown paper bag on the table.

"What is this, Ian?" she asked, exasperated. "What have you done?"

"Mom, I promise, I didn't use any of this," he said, sitting down at the table. "I saw what you did with the bone—putting it in a bag—I did the same thing."

"What do you mean, Ian? What's in that bag?"

"I found something in the woods. I put in here to keep it dry. Honestly, Mom, I didn't take any of it."

Rory sat across from him at the table and unrolled the top of the bag. Her first impulse after opening it was to call the police, but she stopped herself, unsure of the ramifications of tampering with a crime scene and removing evidence. She ran through her options and kept coming back to the same one. She forced herself to pick up the phone and dial Dan's number. Their fledgling relationship had crashed to the ground, they hadn't spoken in two weeks, but he had told her to call him if she was in trouble. She had to trust that he meant it.

When Dan answered the phone, he sounded like he had been asleep. "Hello, Aurora."

She figured bothering with an attempt at an icebreaker was pointless. "Dan, I'm sorry to bother you, but I don't know who else to turn to with this." She wouldn't have blamed him if he hung up. She would have hung up on her, too. "I wouldn't ask you, if there was anyone else I could trust. . . ."

"Okay, that really built me up," he mumbled, his stinger full-on.

"I didn't mean it that way," she said, clearing her throat. "Dan, I'm desperate. Ian went back to the woods and removed evidence."

He exhaled into the phone. "Do not move or touch anything. I'll be over in five minutes."

"Dan . . . I . . . appreciate this," she said.

He hung up without saying goodbye.

She stood at the front door, one hand on the doorknob, waiting for Dan. Somehow it seemed to make the time to pass faster.

Ian paced the living floor back and forth in a line, fidgeting with his hands. "Mom, why does he have to get involved in this? Can't you call someone else? What about Dad?"

"Dan's the best person—no, he's the only person—who can help us with this. If we're lucky, he'll be able to figure out how to handle it, without anyone going to jail."

At the word *jail*, Ian's resentment turned to fear, and his eyes welled up. "*Jail?* Mom, what's gonna happen to me? I was gonna tell you about the money."

His remorse failed to move Rory. She opted to let him worry for a few minutes. "Be quiet and wait."

Dan arrived in a pair of new jeans and a crisp white shirt, both in sharp contrast to what looked like a one- or two-day-old beard. And he looked drained. Rory had never seen him look that tired. She took the jacket he was carrying, passed him a cup of coffee, and sat down at the table. They said nothing, instead feeding each other a seconds-long glance that somehow embodied the mutual anguish of the past weeks.

"Okay, Ian. Let's hear it," Rory said, waiting for her son to speak.

Ian stared at the wall.

Rory pressed on. "Ian, tell Mr. Deal what happened—now."

Ian squirmed in his seat. "I just wanted to back there."

"Just like you wanted to get away for a few days when you ran off with your crazy friend last fall, and we had half of Southern Point driving around looking for you?" Rory couldn't stop herself. "Do you have any idea what it was like when Sergeant Adderson asked us if you had good dental records?"

"Yes, *Mom*, in case they found me dead. I told you and Dad I was sorry, and it wouldn't happen again."

Dan looked from Rory to Ian and back at Rory, shrugging. "Are you sure you need me here—for this?"

"Sorry about that," she said. "That kitchen sink stuff just came out of nowhere."

Dan sipped his coffee.

"Okay, Ian, back to your trip to the woods," Rory demanded. Ian looked terrified, but Rory didn't budge. "Go ahead, Ian."

"What's going on, Ian? Why the hangdog expression?" Dan asked, bewildered.

Ian cleared his throat. "Well, I wanted to see it—see what they were doing—you know, the police."

Ian nervously relayed to Rory and Dan how he thought his friends would love to see pictures of the crime scene. And how, while he was looking around, he saw something in the dirt. He kicked at the muck until he saw the corner of a soggy, green duffle bag, it fell away to mush. Left behind were several white plastic rectangles secured with plastic-coated wire. He tried jamming an unopened package in his jean pocket, but discovered it was too big and pulled it back out. "That must have been when the guitar pick fell out of my pocket," Ian said. He cleared his throat again and finished his story.

Since the money wouldn't fit in his jean pockets, he had tucked his hoodie into his jeans, unzipped it halfway, and stuffed the packages inside. After pushing the ragged duffle bag back down into the ground, he sprinkled leaves on top of it with his gloved hands. Canvassing the dusk in all directions for potential witnesses, and seeing none, he ran back to the garage, pulled down the attic stairs, climbed up, and stationed himself cross-legged on the plywood floor. When he pulled off his hoodie, ten plastic packages fell into his lap. He ripped at the plastic and wire. It had taken Ian a minute to realize he wasn't holding play money. "I heard it start to rain, so I left it up there in the attic and went back into the house. After that, I went up to the attic a few times—just to, you know, to look at it."

"How much is it?" Dan took a sip of coffee.

Ian looked at Rory before answering. "Mom and I counted it. It's, um, fifty thousand dollars."

"Jesus Christ," Dan said, choking on his coffee. "You cannot make this stuff up."

"Dan, what should we do?" Rory asked. "We disturbed the crime scene—we tampered with evidence."

"Hold on. It's not like you robbed a bank—although by the looks of this pile of cash, someone else may have. Ian, did you notice anything else lying around the area where you found this money?"

"No, sir. Just the duffle bag it was in. It was kinda dark out."

Dan picked up a pack of bills. "It must be connected to the body. I can check to see if there are any unsolved robberies or drug busts out there, but I think I'd already know about anything like that, between Sergeant Adderson and local chitchat. Since I'm not technically a cop anymore, I'll tell you this strictly as a layperson: if I don't come up with anything, do what you want with it. It's been there for decades; no one's looking for it. Whatever happened in those woods happened a long time ago, and obviously the money's forgotten. If it weren't, someone would have come forward by now. There'd be holes dug all over your back woods. There's most likely a statute of limitations on whatever act landed it there—long run out. And, it's on your property, so I say that makes the money your property. If you can't fathom holding on to it, donate it to charity—some worthy cause. But keep it quiet. Don't get your name in the paper or anything like that, or this investigation is going to drag on for years."

"But what if it's not legal tender anymore?"

"To be legal, the currency numbers just have to be legible—readable. That's it."

Rory took the pack of bills Dan was holding. "It looks to me like it came directly from a bank, freshly minted. . . ."

"Well, there's your answer," he said.

"But it's dirty money, right?"

"You know, it's probably best if you don't tell me any more about it. That way, if I'm ever questioned, I won't have to lie." He put down his coffee cup and got up from the table. "I'd better take off," he said, and as he pulled his arms through the sleeves of his tan Carhart jacket, his familiar scent drifted Rory's way. She thought her heart would break right then and there.

"Okay," he said, looking at Ian. "I hope I helped you out."

She struggled to keep her composure. "Dan, I'm sorry again that I bothered you with this. I'm grateful for your help."

"If you don't hear from me in a week, that means I didn't come up with anything." He walked to the door and left without saying anything more, drained of advice and the unconditional affection he had freely given for months.

Alone in the house again, Ian asked Rory about the money. "Mom, what are we going to do with all of it? Can we buy something?"

"Are you joking?" she snapped, bruised by yet another of his betrayals. "That's all this means to you? Every time I build up a little trust in you—in our relationship—you knock it down with lies and disrespect. Go to bed, Ian. We'll talk about it tomorrow."

Later, while she stood at her bathroom mirror brushing her teeth, the reflected paper bag full of money stared back at her from her closet shelf. Two months of listening to Sandy's stories, reading Dan's pilfered police files, and bearing witnessing to Julia Whistler's rambling testimony had erased any doubts Rory had harbored early on that the bone in the woods belonged to Kerry McCullough.

Tonight changed that. The money put a new spin on things, suggesting a drug deal gone bad, or some kind of botched robbery—scenarios that were, while unfortunate, less sinister and tragic than the premeditated, cold-blooded murder of a teenage mother and her child.

CHAPTER TWENTY-SIX

Spring break was Ian's opportunity to catch up on some much-needed time with his father. Rory dropped him off at the Rock Creek house, wishing a respite from the farm's turmoil for him and some time to work toward a resolution for herself. She'd talked with him about the money before driving over to Tom's house.

"Mom, I want to leave all that stuff here, if you know what I mean. Dad will ask questions—I don't know. Do I have to tell him?"

"You can keep it to yourself for now," Rory agreed. Tom was on the outside of the situation, and she wasn't sure how much of it she wanted him to know, if anything. If she was making Ian choose sides, being a bad parent, she would have to live with that.

Rory didn't want to slip and say anything to Sandy about her visit with Julia Whistler. The smallest suggestion or hypothesis would burn through the local grapevine like a summer brush fire and make its way smack into the middle of the police investigation. Initially Sandy protested Rory's offer of a week off with pay, but ultimately agreed to take a staycation, using the time to volunteer at the senior center.

Dan had given Rory every sign that it was over between them. She knew he wouldn't expose any of the secrets they shared; he had too much integrity for that. She questioned whether their relationship was just a by-product of the turmoil surrounding the discovery of the bone, or if the two of them could have had a future together. She was sure of one thing—Dan was the first person she'd met who was unwaveringly true to himself, motivated more by his beliefs and values than by fear of how he was perceived by others. "I don't care what anyone thinks of me," he had told her the day they'd gone fishing on his boat, "except for God—and the Deal family." His example had taught her to strive for a deeper knowledge of herself, and she loathed most of what she'd learned from the process. Self-recrimination tore into her, but she accepted the accompanying pain, knowing that, at its end, she would somehow be better, stronger, because of it.

Her opportunity for reflection that weekend was brief. The tree crew arrived early on Saturday, along with Sergeant Adderson. She braced herself for a chaotic day involving bulldozers and crashing timber, resulting in a yawning crater in the middle of the woods. In the end, they took out only three trees, two of them less than fifteen feet high, none of them were among those she had marked.

Shelly King came out to the farm to observe the work, shuffling around in her rubber clogs, telling the workers to slow down, to stay to one side or the other of her tarped area, or to stay clear of her worksite altogether. Rory watched for the first hour and then looked in on Olga, who passed her waking hours dangling her head out of her stall door, living for an occasional glimpse of the other horses as they rotated around the pasture in pursuit of the sun and the grass's new growth, or came near the barn to visit the water trough.

Before he left, Sergeant Adderson stopped by the house and explained that some material Shelly deemed significant to the investigation was entangled in the roots of some standing trees, and that exposing them to get to it might very well kill the tree later on. He warned Rory, "We're leavin' them alone for now, tryin' to save 'em, but I don't need to tell ya, they might weaken and die, and a falling tree could seriously injure someone." His tone turned ominous. "We really can't afford to have anything else happen back in those woods of yours, Mrs. Fielding. So just keep on with staying out of there." He tipped his hat. "Good day to ya."

Before Rory had moved out, Tom had recommended that he review her business plan. She declined, predicting that he would return to her a glut of cons and few, if any, pros since he found her idea of a horse-boarding operation "silly." He would have undoubtedly advised against the purchase and forecasted financial doom once she chose to go through with it. The farm had cost Rory significantly more than she'd originally budgeted, taking a chunk out of her household budget before she'd even crossed the threshold and moved in. Now she found herself looking for expenses to cut, including letting Sandy go if the pasture project didn't commence in the next few days.

No calls from Dan by Monday meant that he'd found nothing tying the money to any known crimes, so she was back where she'd started. The fifty thousand dollars that was stuffed in the bag in her closet was tempting. Keeping it could buy her some time if the farm didn't get up and running. It could mean she wouldn't have to sell Titian. But she was certain it was dirty money of some kind. The only way to repurpose it was for some absolute good. That would wash it clean.

CHAPTER TWENTY-SEVEN

"I think we may be able to solve this thing after all," Shelly King said with pure delight in her voice. Her face flushed red with excitement.

"What's the latest, then?" Sergeant Adderson sounded patient but tired. Rory was in her bedroom when she heard them talking in the driveway.

"Well, Sergeant, with the trees gone," Shelly gushed, wringing her hands in greedy delight, "I've put my hands on a jaw partial! A jaw! Who knows how much more might be down there? Could be the rest of the body, or enough for an ID."

"Guess you scientific types like this sort of thing, eh?"

"Oh, we live for it, Sergeant."

"Any idea how old it is?"

"We've got some root infiltration, but I don't know if the body was originally placed there. I've got no teeth, not even one, and I should if where we found the bone is the actual death scene. It's hard to say. The arm could have been dragged here from anywhere."

"Well, keep up the good work."

"I can't work but so much longer, Sergeant. The county's running out of money for my paycheck." She pointed to her large midsection. "Obviously, I've got to eat." She chuckled. "I'll keep you posted."

"Good day, then." Sergeant Adderson got in his car and drove toward the road; Shelly scrambled into her SUV and aimed it at the woods.

Anxiety or anticipation. Rory wasn't sure which she was fighting harder against at the prospect of the police identifying the body. Every day it grew more difficult to differentiate between the two emotions. *At least they're moving on something*, she told herself.

To fend off ulcer-inducing apprehension regarding the future of her farm, she focused on constructive planning. If she managed to pull off a minor miracle and get the farm construction back on schedule, her new barn would include two stalls dedicated to fostering rescue horses, most likely thoroughbreds.

Each year a staggering number of racehorses were put down or slaughtered for pet food because they couldn't run quite fast enough, or they had sacrificed their soundness for their owner's two minutes of glory on the racetrack. It was strictly business; if it cost more to feed and stable them than they brought in for their owner's coffers, they were expendable inventory. Rory wanted to prevent that horrific end for at least two of them. But first she had to gain approval by the rescue foundations; most were strict about fencing materials, barn specifications, and turnout areas.

Online research yielded mixed results regarding local regulations and resources for Rory's horse-fostering project. With all of the agricultural activities and commercial barns in the area, she was sure the library had some reference materials on the subject. Library hours were nine to six on Monday. If she left her house by four, she would have about an hour to browse and check out books before closing.

Once Rory and Titian successfully negotiated their way around police vans, crime tape, and the uniformed strangers who now seemed an integral part of the farm's landscape, they had three miles of dirt roads to cover before reaching the back entrance of the library. It was a therapeutic ride for Rory, reminding her of why she'd fallen in love with Southern Point in the first place. Except for the occasional faint roar of a fighter jet or the hum of a diesel truck in the distance, she supposed the countryside had changed little in the last couple of centuries. Although countless generations had witnessed the same seasonal cycle she was riding through—vast crop fields in various stages of growth, hawks and vultures sweeping the sky, quail and squirrels picking through the underbrush, searching for seeds and insects—the scene remained a pleasant novelty to her. When she'd lived in the house on Rock Creek Road, she couldn't access the immense network of trails and lanes crisscrossing the heart of Whistler Ridge.

The old Whistler house came into view, a phantom topiary cloaked in thick, leafy Virginia creeper vines. Rory stopped for a minute, circled the house at a safe distance, and then rode on, wishing that the ground would swallow up the homestead along with all of its sordid secrets.

After arriving at the library, she secured Titian's bridle reins to a bike rack, estimating that it would take about fifteen minutes for him to liberate himself from his tether and sample the grass on the lawn. She put her helmet in a large saddlebag intended for any books she checked out, dusted off her breeches, and went inside.

The librarian was typing intently at a computer on the information desk, one letter at a time, using her forefinger. Her sole companion was an old man reclining in a light blue reading chair, half-asleep, thumbing his way through a short stack of news periodicals resting on his round belly. Rory guessed this was one of the man's routine weekly outings.

She made her way to the information desk. "Hi," she said, smiling, "I'm looking for some books on equine rescue. Do you have anything covering that topic?"

"Well . . . yes," the librarian answered. "We have one or two books, and some on dog and cat rescue as well. Are y'all thinking of opening one of those places?"

"Yes," Rory said. "I live over on Whistler Ridge Road. I bought the Barnetts' house."

"Oh!" The librarian's eyes widened. "The place with the body! Have the police figured out who it is yet? Ya know, it could be that girl of Joe McCullough's—that's something that's always been floatin' around."

"It's not exactly a body," Rory said. "Some bones—they found some bones. And they're still working on it. I'm sure they'll come up with something to report soon."

"Listen, dear, years ago my grandmother had my two uncles bury my grandpa under her bedroom window, so she'd have him right next to her. He was there for years, until she died. Then we had to move him with her to a regular cemetery, so they could stay together." She leaned over the desk and dropped her voice to a whisper. "Out here you can get away with near anythin'—or could, anyway." She put her hand to her mouth, her face turning ashen. "Lord, I guess I shouldn't have said anything. . . ."

Rory scanned the woman's name tag. "Ms. Allen, don't worry about it."

"Oh, y'all can call me Rhea, please. I never did go in for that 'Ms.' business, anyhow."

"Rhea, while I'm here . . . someone mentioned that you have information about the slaves who used to live in Sothern Point."

"Oh yes, of course. We have a slave journal listing the slaveholding family's name, number of slaves owned, and the slaves' names. The real thing. All handwritten entries. Beautiful handwriting. The listing is divided into under ten and over ten."

"Under ten?"

"Under ten slaves per household. Most families, like mine, had ten and under."

Rory baulked at Rhea's cheerful delivery of the family slave count.

"We also have the journal on . . . oh, what's it now?" She measured out the words carefully, "Oh, uh, on flash point—no, flash drive—if you prefer."

"The hardcopy journal is fine," Rory said. "Where is it?"

"In the children's section."

"The children's section?"

"It's just—we have more room in there. Put on the white gloves that are tied to the desk so ya don't get oil on the pages. Let me know if you need any help reading it. Ya know, that McCullough family's in it. After the war, their master—Sally's grandmother's master—gifted them twenty-five acres of prime land. That's why they're still here. The only Neg—eh—the only African Americans down here to own their own place. Some say that's why Herb Whistler hated 'em so much, on account of the fact they 'acted like white people,' he said."

Rory thanked the librarian and then entered the children's reading room, where she found the *Southern Point Slave Journal* in a shadow box frame above a chest-high bookshelf. Reading it reminded her of when she'd first seen a cotton field, a slave cabin. Foreign and repulsive to her Yankee upbringing and beliefs, its ugliness an inherent part of the beautiful place she now called home. The journal listed owners' names and addresses, property descriptions including acreage, and then name, sex, and age of slaves.

The names of slaves who died while the journal was active were lined out; those who escaped had details scribbled next to their names indicating whether they were found dead or alive, reward paid out for their capture, punishment imposed and whether they were sold to another owner. The majority of slaveholder families in the book had descendants presently living in Southern Point—she passed their mailboxes and farms every day. She didn't look for Joe's family in the journal. She had seen enough.

CHAPTER TWENTY-EIGHT

As Rory reined Titian around the edge of the back woods of Whistler Ridge, the bright headlights of a police van, idling a few hundred feet ahead, blinded her through the trees. A cloudy, light drizzle began to fall. It was dusk, late for the forensics team to be working—unless they had made a discovery too important to risk delayed retrieval.

    A county police helicopter chopped overhead, the beam from its attached strobe light following three silhouetted figures working in the woods. The intense light and noise generated from the chaotic activity tested every ounce of Titian's training and mettle, but Rory was safe. He had never thrown her, never bucked, never even bolted. Feeling like a traitor at the prospect of giving him up for money, she forced back tears. Through a break in the trees she saw a strand of white lights lining the road in front of her house. Media vehicles, she guessed, working a tip about some new development with the bone, whatever was going on in the woods. The two miles separating her farm from Tom's house now seemed like a world apart, and she was glad Ian was at the other end of the visitation globe.

Approaching the back of the barns, she heard an intermittent thumping sound coming from one of the buildings. At first, she thought it was the top of an unlatched stall door hitting the side of the barn, but it wasn't a windy night. The sound was baffling. She jumped down from Titian and tracked it to its source—Olga's stall. Something or someone had set off the mare, who was now covered in frothy white sweat and kicking her stall's back wall repeatedly with her bad leg. Her frenzy was contagious, prompting Mystic to snort and prance in front of the injured horse's stall.

Think fast, Rory told herself. She knew that the sight and nearness of Titian, if only through the iron bars of his neighboring stall, always calmed Olga, so she led him in, tack and all, and latched his Dutch door. She threw a pad of hay in Mystic's open stall and turned on the wall fan to distract her from Olga's panic. The next step for Olga would be at best colic, or worse, irreparable injury to her leg. For the mare's own safety, Rory had no choice but to tranquilize her. She ran to the storage room and threw open the first-aid cabinet, grabbing an alcohol prep pad and a syringe packet, then pulled a bottle of acepromazine from her mini-refrigerator. Her hands trembled as she felt for a good neck muscle mass in Olga's thick winter coat. The smell of the prep pad caught Titian's attention, and she heard him stomping in his stall, in fearful anticipation of being next in line. Luckily, the intravenous injection was fast acting, assaulting Olga's central nervous system within a minute, leaving her just conscious enough to stand, her head hanging inches from the ground. Rory tossed a pad of hay in Titian's stall and removed his saddle and bridle before moving back into Olga's stall to rub her down and blanket her. She left all of the barn lights burning so she could monitor the situation from the house. As she slid the barn windows closed, she saw headlights from the large police van still shining on the entrance to the back woods. She strained to see more across the pitch-blackness. Two figures cut through the headlight beams, carrying an empty stretcher into the woods and then returning with something under a blanket. She watched, incredulous, as they carried the stretcher out a second time, now with a smaller, blanketed mass in its center.

That sight gave credibility to the media swarm.

Rory entered the house to a ringing phone but missed the call and checked her voicemail. There was one message from Jason Grimes, informing her that he couldn't hold off on other jobs to wait for her project to start. He suggested she call him next year. Next year? He was her last chance for planting the pastures in time to open her business. Without his help, there wouldn't be a next year.

Exhausted, grief-stricken for virtual strangers, and in too deep to come clean with the police, she saw no option other than confronting the only living person she was convinced knew more of the truth than anyone else. Steeling herself for the bottleneck of cars at the foot of the driveway, she started up her truck.

CHAPTER TWENTY-NINE

Joe McCullough met Rory at the foot of his front porch steps. He straightened up to his full height, folded his enormous arms across his chest, and shook his head at her, like an adult ready to chastise a disobedient child for some major household infraction. She had seen him lumber through the screen door when the beam of her headlights passed across the front porch.

"Mrs. Fielding, what are ya doin' back at my place?" he scolded, making no effort to hide his aggravation at her arrival.

This time she was undeterred by his attempt to intimidate her. "We have to talk, Mr. McCullough," she said firmly.

"I told ya last time, I got nothing to tell. Go on. Leave now."

Rory held herself squarely in front on him. "Mr. McCullough, I've got media blocking my driveway, the police just removed what looks like two bodies from my woods, an old woman told me she's sorry about the bad things *she* let happen to your daughter, and more than one credible person has told me that your daughter and Jimmy Whistler had a—a—child together." She took a breath. "Now, you're either lying about where your daughter is now, or she and her baby disappeared, and you didn't report it. Do I go to the police tonight, or do you have something to tell me?"

He looked like he was about to strike her. "How dare you talk about me and my family like that!" he yelled. "You don't know nothin'—nothin'—about what she and little James went through."

Rory guessed that little James was Joe's grandchild. The porch light came on, and Sally emerged and stopped at the top of the steps, grasping a pillar for support.

"The police just found Kerry and James buried in my woods, didn't they?" Rory demanded, looking over at Sally and then back at Joe. "Joe, what did Herb Whistler do to Kerry?"

"It ain't them, Miss," Sally said softly.

"You think I'd let him touch her—my only child?" Joe asked angrily. "I'd have killed that man if he even put one foot on my land. It was that fool son of his did it—it was Jimmy."

"Jimmy? What did Jimmy do?"

Joe walked up onto the porch and sat down in a weathered rocking chair. Sally motioned silently for Rory to follow him, and then went into the house, leaving them alone. Rory sat next to Joe, waiting for him to speak.

The rage he had displayed a few minutes earlier gave way to battered resignation. "My daughter always cared too much for people, even those who didn't deserve it," he said, shaking his head. "She and that Whistler boy walked home together almost every day from the time they'd started first grade. The bus could have let Kerry off before Jimmy, right in front of our place, but his family was white and owned most of the land around here. My daughter had to backtrack a half mile home from the Whistler's farm lane because the bus driver wouldn't make a separate stop for our house. Most days, Jimmy would walk Kerry to the edge of the trees bordering our land, and then go home."

"The two of them were childhood friends?"

"Yeah, but not around others—whites, that is. Herb wouldn't have allowed it. When they got older, Jimmy . . . I gotta say . . . he never talked bad about Kerry or called her names, even stood up for her sometimes when the other kids treated her bad. She was the only black girl in the whole school. I wanted to move her out of there, but she wanted to stay because the teachers were so good. She wanted to go to college. She was smart. She could have been a doctor. Anyway, folks knew that Herb was no good. Like his father before him, he was just mean. No, he was evil. My mama caught Kerry takin' some of her salves, you know, medicines. It turned out she was using 'em on Jimmy's cigarette burns and welts. Herb did that to his own boy. I warned her not to mess with Jimmy—that there'd be trouble comin' out of it."

Sally came out to the porch again, this time carrying two blue-speckled enamel mugs. She said nothing, but behind her glasses, her eyes were filled with tears. Once she delivered a cup of black coffee to each of them, she vanished, the hinge on the screen door squeaking and then slamming behind her.

"Maybe it was all the beatings, I don't know, but Jimmy took to drinkin' and he changed—quick. He got in trouble at school, stole things. The worse he got, the worse Herb beat him."

"Joe, are you saying you really don't know whose bones are on my property?" she asked, feeling the same sense of relief she'd felt confessing to Dan about the money Ian had found. It appeared that another of her worst-case scenarios had been just that and nothing more. Joe stared into his coffee cup for a minute, and then turned to her. His expression said he had more to tell.

"Well, now . . . don't know that I'm sayin' exactly that."

"Joe?"

"I wanted Kerry to go up to Baltimore to have the baby. She wouldn't do it. She wanted to have him here. See, my mama can midwife. In her day, some of the white hospitals wouldn't take a black woman, so we had our children at home and cared for most ailments here, too."

"Mrs. Whistler said that you and Herb argued about the baby and that things turned violent," Rory said.

"Mrs. Whistler? She still livin'?" He shook his head. "Never mind about her. Herb . . . he . . . tried to pay Kerry to get rid of my grandson, and then he threatened us because she wouldn't do it. After that, Kerry shut herself in at home till the baby came."

"And after she had the baby?"

"Things were all right at first. We didn't mean nothin' around here. No one around here knew or cared what we did as long as it didn't involve them. In early summer of 1985, Kerry had her baby—with my mama's help. A beautiful boy. Yep. She named him James. She stayed to herself here at the house, only went out to shop for the baby—all the way across the border in North Carolina—to keep the local folks out of our business with the baby, but somehow someone must'a seen little James outside, because it wasn't too long after that when Jimmy Whistler came sniffin' around our place."

"And then there was trouble?" She braced herself for his answer.

"That boy always carried trouble with him," he said, shaking his head. "One night, come the end of the summer, Kerry had James out in a little play yard I'd made for him. No one could see it from the road—our houses and the trees blocked it—I'd made damn sure of that when I built it. The night it happened, I was sleepin'—just back from a long haul to New York. My mama was making supper. I woke outta a dead sleep to hear Kerry screamin'. I ran outta the house and Jimmy was standin' over Kerry and my grandson. Kerry screamed that Jimmy had hurt the baby, but the baby wasn't cryin' or anything. I couldn't tell how bad he was. Jimmy was drunk like always. He saw me coming and took off on his motorcycle. I ran back in the house for my shotgun and got in my pickup."

"What were you going to do?"

"I didn't know. He'd hurt my grandson. I still didn't know how bad."

"You chased him?"

"He was drivin' all crazy. I couldn't keep up with him. He was all over the back farm lanes. Then he turned down toward the woods behind your place. Maybe he was tryin' to take a shortcut to the main road through Whistler Ridge Road. I lost sight of him for a minute; he must'a thought he knew the way better than I did. But he was wrong. I'd hunted those woods, all on foot, my whole life. No one knew their way around these parts better than me. Anyhow, I almost caught up with him—I could near touch the back of his motorcycle with my front bumper. Just then he turned his head around and looked right at me—laughin'. He was plain crazy drunk. But when he did that—turned like that—he swerved . . . more like he slid sideways and went hard left straight into your woods. I knew it was on accident, 'cause no one ever went in there. Those woods, they were a swampy mess, crawlin' with snakes, most of the year."

"He jumped the ditch?"

"Back then, there was no ditch along the back line of the woods, so it was a straight shot in."

"Did you continue to follow him?"

"I couldn't get in with my truck and it was getting dark. I grabbed my gun, three shells, a little flashlight, and my swampers—on account of the snakes—and took off after where he'd gone. I could see the tire marks. . . ."

"You were going to shoot him?"

"Shoot him? No! I was thinkin' he'd probably come back out the way he went in, and when he did, I'd be waitin'. I'd shoot out his tires if I had to, to stop him, and make him go with me to the police and tell what he'd done to little James. I knew that sheriff would never believe me against whatever lies Herb came up with, unless Jimmy confessed, in his own words, in person. Ya see, Herb had me arrested once, sayin' I threatened to harm his family. I knew what had happened to Jimmy that night—knew I didn't do it—but Herb would say I did it on purpose. With that dirty sheriff in on it, I'd be in jail or worse. But I didn't do it. I swear it was on accident."

Joe wasn't lying about the sheriff. Rory had seen the old police report for Joe's arrest. Without any more prompting from her, he went on with his story.

"This whole time I'm thinkin', *Is my grandson alive or dead? Did Jimmy murder his own kin, his own baby?* Then it hit me: I couldn't hear the motorcycle engine. It was dead quiet. I figured he'd try to come at me in the dark, but I was ready for him. I was gonna wait for that crazy boy to come for me."

Joe looked down at the porch floorboards, his face tormented by the memory of an image only he could see. "I waited and waited. Nothin'. Then I figured I might as well have it out with him in the woods. I started into the trees—calling his name." He took a breath. "It was bad . . . so bad. I—I—almost stepped on the boy. When I turned on my light, there was blood everywhere. I never seen so much blood. And his face—his face was like—I—I couldn't make even make out his eyes or nose. And for a few minutes, he—he . . . was still . . . movin'."

Joe put his head in his hands, releasing a muffled, agonizing groan. He tried to suppress his sobs.

"There was nothin' I could do for him." He wiped his face on his shirt sleeve. "Nothing at all. God or the devil, one or the other, they caught up with 'im first."

"You left him there?"

"My people, we don't disrespect the dead—no matter what they done in life. When he passed on a few minutes later, I said a prayer for him and then wrapped him in a blanket I had in my pickup. I took his wallet, and some things that had fallen off his bike—stuff was scattered everywhere—so no one would know it was him. I never found his duffle bag—the one he always strapped to the back of his seat. That must've fallen off his bike somewhere else along the way from my place. It was wrong. I know it. I grabbed a shovel and buried him right there. Then I covered the grave and dragged out as much'a the wrecked motorcycle as I could. It was in pieces, all twisted. I piled what it could carry in the bed of my truck. But I swear to the Lord, I didn't kill Jimmy Whistler."

"I believe you, Joe. What about the baby? Did he—"

"I got back home, and he seemed all right, just real sleepy and quiet. Kerry saw me, covered in blood—I told her what happened—the accident—and that she had to leave Southern Point right then—that night—and let Herb think Jimmy'd taken care of things. As long as Herb and that sheriff were alive, I was marked. My family, too."

"So you drove to Baltimore."

"Yeah. That's when things started goin' real wrong with little James. He wasn't registered with the state yet, since Kerry had him at home, so we took him to a hospital in the northwest side of Baltimore where they're used to hookers, homeless, and poor folks, and don't ask many questions. Kerry, she lied and said she birthed him in Baltimore and that she didn't know who the father was. They must'a thought she was just another hooker or addict, and let it be. I hated her havin' to do that."

"Didn't they involve the police or social services in the case?"

"There are people who don't count in this world, and no one at that hospital was real concerned about us. They said James probably had a virus and to make sure he was drinking his milk and that he rested. They had a hundred other folks in that emergency room, cut up, drugged up, waitin' for help they couldn't pay for. They moved us through right quick. If only we'd known that the baby's quietness was his brain in trouble. A few days after we were in the hospital, he stopped nursin' and Kerry said she could tell he didn't recognize her face anymore. We took him to a friend's doctor who ran a small clinic. It was then that we found out . . . he . . . was . . . you know . . . retarded. That's what they called it then. It was all on account'a Jimmy shakin' him so hard that night."

"God, Joe, I'm sorry."

"We were so scared'a Herb coming after us, we didn't help James in time . . . at home. . . . We waited too long. It was all my doin'. It was my fault. I made Kerry go to Baltimore."

"Where is James now?"

"He lives with Kerry in Baltimore. She had to give up her dream of bein' a doctor to take care of James by workin' in a nursing home. She gets some free things for James there. They have some handicapped residents and a real good program, but she can't afford to send James. If she could, she might be able to go to night school—get her nursin' license, at least. That's why I still drive my rig. I send her money when I can—helpin' out. Yep, I try to help out."

Joe stood up and took a shuffling step in the direction of the front door, his intimidating demeanor now gone, replaced by a tired, broken old man. "I guess I better get some things together, get 'um straight, before we go to the police."

By the middle of her last visit to Julia Whistler, Rory had moved beyond the point of being shocked by the bizarre confessions of total strangers. If the last few months had taught her anything, it was that no relationship was without multiple layers, and that pain and complexity seemed to run like thread through even the simplest of lives—at least in Southern Point.

"Joe, is there anything you haven't told me?" she asked him as he stood at the door, his hand on the old glass doorknob.

He turned to her, fear in his eyes and in his voice, as he waited for her to mete out his fate. "I told you everything I remember. Are you calling Sergeant John now?"

"He and the rest of the police will finish their work, and I can't lie if they question me specifically about this," Rory said as she started down the steps. "But I'm not offering up anything about your story to anyone, if that's what you mean."

"Then what's going to happen?" he asked.

"I don't have that answer for you, Joe, or for me," she said as she walked away. "I really don't know."

CHAPTER THIRTY

A knot of anxiety sloshed around Rory's stomach as she listened to the phone ring on the other end, waiting to find out if she would get voicemail or a live voice.

Dan skipped the hello. "Here you are, calling again." His tone was harsh. Rory credited herself for bringing that quality out in him.

"Yes," she said, "again. I know how things are between us now, but I'm in trouble. Please, don't hang up." He didn't respond. Her impulse was to end the call, but instead she waited out the agonizing silence.

"Yes, I did tell you I was here if you needed me," he finally said. "If you're asking me for help, telling me now that you need me, I'll be home all night, Rory. You do know where I live, don't you?" He was testing her now.

"Yeah, I . . . think so," she said, then gave up the ruse. "Actually, no. I don't."

"That's because you never asked. I'm on Heron Point Road. Last house on the right. On the waterway."

A moonless night set in as Rory pulled into Dan's cedar-lined driveway, less than five minutes by car from her farm. She barely missed hitting a state historical register plaque, bolted to a gray boulder on the side of the drive. Iridescent oyster shells led the way to a well-lit front porch, which was shaded by a red tin roof. She guessed that the immaculate white farmhouse looked now much as it had when it was built in 1825.

A sudden rustling made its way toward Rory from somewhere in the darkness along the left side of the house. She braced herself, terrified. Her heart skipped and bounced. "Not here," she whispered, taking a slow breath and holding it, willing her heart to stay in rhythm. There had been several recent sightings of black bears in the area, and she wasn't prepared to meet one tonight. More rustling—louder this time. She reeled toward the sound as a black-and-white spotted hog the size of a bathtub ambled into the light stream from the porch, stopping in its tracks when it saw her. She focused hard on the mass of spots to be sure of what she'd seen.

"I see you've met Jewel." Dan was at the screen door in jeans, boots, and a pea-green T-shirt. Rory never thought that color could look good on anyone—until now. "I bought her from the livestock auction ten years ago," he explained. "I couldn't let her end up on someone's dinner table." He stepped past Rory. "Jewel, go to your pen, please!" he called, clapping his hands. The pig trotted back into the darkness. "Good girl!" he called after her.

Rory stepped through the front door of the farmhouse—the home had no central hall—and landed directly in its large parlor, which was filled with rustic antiques. Well-worn braided rugs of various sizes and shapes were scattered over rough-hewn pine floors. A fire blazed bright orange in a brick fireplace fronted by a stone hearth. The whole place smelled of old wood, and reminded her of her church, when the morning sun's rays crept through its transom windows and warmed its antique pews.

"This is beautiful," she said with some embarrassment. Her relationship with Dan had been one-sided, she realized, mostly about her.

He watched her scan the room. "What did you think—that I lived at the store?" he asked. "I have a life of my own, too."

"I was selfish not to ask you more about yourself, the times we were . . . together."

"Right on. You won't get any argument from me on that point." His voice softened a bit, both encouraging and distracting her. She longed for another chance with him, but now wasn't the time for that.

"You must be here for a good reason. What's the latest?" he asked. "Status change on the investigation? Another discovery?" He sounded as though he were shifting into police mode, as he had done for countless interviews and interrogations over the years.

Rory sat down on the fireplace hearth. "Dan, you're right—with the way you—we left things. I wouldn't bother you—I wouldn't be here—if it wasn't important, critical."

"Okay, we've established that you're definitely not here to beg my forgiveness," he said, hands on his hips, staring down at her. "Go on."

"I—I—feel like I'm going out of my mind. All of these people—I'm trying to make peace with myself about coming forward—not coming forward." The words came rushing out. "I know what happened back there. And I'm saying nothing. And then there's the money. I don't know if I can carry this secret—all the things I know now. If the police make progress with this new lead, everything is going to come out. If they don't, it's because I'm standing in their way—"

"Hold on, let's take one thing at a time," Dan cut in as he sat down next to her. "Mrs. Whistler's story—that's just an incoherent old woman's ramblings. I don't know why I suggested we visit her anyway. What's this new lead you're talking about?"

"That's just it, Dan. I went to see Mrs. Whistler again—on my own."

"Why the hell did you do that? To hear the same story a second time?"

"I'm not sure why I went back, but when I did, it wasn't the same story. She told me everything—everything she knew or could remember. Unbelievable—the things she described. You were right about her husband. The circumstances of his death described in the police report didn't make sense, Dan. They could never make sense because the police missed it—missed that she helped it along."

"What do you mean, 'helped it along'? Are you suggesting she had a part in Herb's death?"

"Not a part in his death." Now she felt like the cop. "The whole thing. She killed him!"

He jumped up off the hearth. "Jesus Christ, Rory! How?"

"Right now, I need to tell you about Joe McCullough."

"Joe McCullough?"

"Dan, he told me what happened in the woods on my property. And it was an accident—and connected to Julia's story. It all fits."

"You mean what happened to his daughter?"

"Dan, it's not Kerry. It's Jimmy Whistler. It's *his* body that's back in the woods—not hers."

Dan walked the floor. "What the hell happened? What about the money? Where did that come from?"

"Dan, I think Herb paid Jimmy off to get rid of his own child and then leave town."

"Wait. Is that what Joe told you?"

"No! He doesn't know anything about the money."

"Then how'd you come up with that theory?"

"Julia told me she sent Jimmy off with some clothes and money the night he and Kerry disappeared. I assumed it was some traveling money—nothing much—until Joe McCullough told me how Jimmy had died. Joe said Jimmy had a duffle bag with him when he took off from Joe's house. A bag that Joe couldn't find after he found Jimmy. The duffle bag filled with cash that Ian brought out of the woods. It was the one Jimmy'd had when he was thrown from his bike. It has to be."

"I am trying to follow this ping pong match of a story of yours, but I may need some help. Stay put. I'll be right back." He went into the kitchen.

Left alone for a few minutes, she took in more of her surroundings, starting with the dozens of photographs lining the walls of the room: Dan alone on a beach somewhere in what looked like the South Pacific; Dan with women, obviously lovers, hanging on to him in adoration; in a canoe out West; on horseback in what looked like Africa; at a black-tie fundraiser with a former United States President. He was a complete contradiction, presenting himself to her humbly, and all the while far worldlier than she was.

He returned to the parlor carrying two glasses and an open bottle of wine. He poured hers first and handed it to her. The wine was deep purple, pungent, and as thick as blood. A drop of it trickled down the side of the glass and stained her finger. She thought of Joe finding Jimmy Whistler, and the blood he said was everywhere.

"Are you sure you want to hear this after everything that's happened—everything I've done?" she asked.

"Bring it on," he answered, lifting his glass to hers.

She fought the wine's bitterness and gulped it down like Kool-Aid before recounting Joe's story.

"Joe did what he had to do," Dan said, as he stoked the waning fire.

His non-reaction stunned Rory. "I understand his circumstances now, his panic," she said, "but, here I am talking to a homicide detective, contemplating withholding the truth—lying—as a way to ensure some kind of . . . sideways justice. Is that how it works down here in Southern Point?"

"First of all, I'm a retired homicide detective. And there just aren't a lot of absolutes in this situation, Rory. We both know what it was like here back then. Remember Joe's arrest for his run-in with Herb? The sheriff and Herb fabricated that as a scare tactic, and Joe has a permanent police record because of it. I'll bet that man's lived in fear every day for thirty years, wondering if someone saw something the night Jimmy died and might come forward about it. With his history, why would he assume he'd be treated fairly by any member of law enforcement?"

"Dan, I understand what you're saying—"

His brow was knitted. "Who'll mourn Jimmy Whistler? His mother? I think telling his mother what really happened to him would probably kill her. But the McCulloughs—they still have a chance, a future. The way I see it, Joe did the only thing he could do to protect his family."

"Dan, I don't know if I can take responsibility for other people's lives—people I don't even know—strangers."

"We all take some responsibility for other people's lives when we enter into a relationship with them. You took on that responsibility with Joe McCullough when you went to see him the second time. When he told you his story—when you forced his confession. Now you have a relationship of with him and with his family. You're not strangers."

Rory put herself in Joe's place, imagining him and Sally—and Kerry—wondering each day if their family would be destroyed by the discovery of a past mistake.

"Dan, even if I don't come forward with what I know, this whole thing might come out—now—tonight—"

"What do you mean?"

"I saw the police take two stretchers out of the woods, before I went to Joe's. I was certain they had found Kerry and her baby. Now I'm sure that it's Jimmy—and God knows what or who else—that they found back there with him."

"You said you believed Joe McCullough's version of what happened to Jimmy."

"I do believe him. But that doesn't explain the second stretcher. Maybe he forgot something—missed something. He's older now, something might have slipped his mind, I don't know."

"Wait and see what they've found. With all of the digging back there, it could be another old grave, something related to Native Americans or the Civil War for all you know."

"There's something else, Dan. Sergeant Adderson lives among us, here in this community, and he's been busting his butt to be thorough about the investigation. If people start talking and someone remembers something, he can reopen it, start the whole thing over."

"I know John. He's done everything within his power to run this investigation right, but I can guarantee you that with his personal history, the last thing he would do is slant things unfairly in favor of the Whistler family."

"How can you know that, Dan?"

"I'm certain that Sandy Cross told you about Herb's bullying and threats against locals."

"Yes, she did."

"Well, one of those families owned a hog farm, and when they didn't give into Herb's demands, he poisoned their whole sounder of hogs."

"Sandy said there was a family here who lost their farm over it."

"Yeah, they did. It was Adderson Farm—Sergeant Adderson's family. They never let on to anyone what had happened—John's dad was too proud. John told me one of the reasons he joined the police force was because of what had happened to his family. He wanted to make up for some of the sons of bitches working in law enforcement."

"God, Dan, I wonder—how many people does this involve? How deep does it run?"

"Deep as the dirt. Maybe as deep as the part of yourself you keep hidden from everyone, Rory," he said. "Especially me."

She took his dig without flinching. "I deserved that."

"Sorry," he mumbled. "I don't usually indulge in recrimination. As far as who around here knows what happened, God only knows—you and I probably never will. What we do know is that one person's actions can destroy countless others, and just the same, one person can make a difference—start the healing process. I guess in this situation, that's you."

"So, I don't really have a choice."

"That's the tough part: you have to choose, Rory, for yourself, and for Joe and everyone else involved. That decision has to be one you can live with."

She felt the weight of the choice she would have to make. "And I've got to make the decision alone, not knowing if I've done the right thing until after the fact."

She looked at the clock above the fireplace mantel, her inhibitions softened by the wine and the heat of the fire. "I wish . . . about what happened to us . . ." The words came out before she could consider their consequences. "You kept exceeding my expectations. I know I fell short of yours."

"You hurt me, Rory," he cut in, "more than anyone else ever has, and I let you do it."

"For what it's worth, you were right about me. I am damaged—and afraid. I've spent a lifetime trying to shield myself from pain. What have I accomplished? I've robbed myself of real happiness. I blamed *you* for the way I felt about myself. I do know how much I hurt you, and I'd give anything to take it back. It's pathetic. I'm forty-eight, my life's more than half over, and I can't admit that I've fallen in love." At first, saying the words to him out loud freed her. Seconds later she fought back tears.

He looked surprised at her admission.

"Yes, Dan, you were right about that, too. I've been fighting with myself over it for too long."

Dan put his hands on her shoulders. "Right now, Rory, you have to focus on getting to the other side of this whole Whistler thing."

They got up and walked the few steps to the door together. "I know. You're right." She wanted to go back in the house, hide in his arms, and stay there with him, but she knew she couldn't. "I'm afraid," she said quietly as she walked down the steps, "of everything."

He caught her arm and pulled her to him. "Aurora—Rory—you were named for the beautiful Northern Lights, dear. Up there." he motioned to the sky. "And, you are—beautiful. And, you are . . . often beyond reach. But the truth is, you're an earthbound creature, Rory. Mired in gravity. Come on down here where you belong, down here with the rest of us. Crawl around a little. Feel the weight of things. Get messy—get in the muck. You're going to have to claw your way out of it sometimes, find your bearings. Then, you go back down again. It's the only way. The only way to really get through it."

He leaned toward her, his lips nearly brushing hers, but stopped short, wiped the tears from her cheeks, and let her go.

"Wait for me, Dan," she whispered, walking into the dark. She looked back at the house. The front door was closed.

Reverend Chris Webb stood in the narthex of Atlantic Episcopal Church, readying programs for the Wednesday Eucharist services. Tom had opted out of attending church shorty after Ian's baptism. For years after that, Rory and Ian had attended one of the Wednesday services when she knew they wouldn't be able to make the drive from Southern Point on Sunday.

"Hi, Rory, we won't get started until nine thirty," Chris said cheerfully as he straightened his plastic nametag. "It's only ten of nine now. You want to wait in the parish hall?"

"I'm not here for church. But, I'd like to go in alone for a while—if that's okay."

"No problem. You'll have it to yourself for half an hour. I'll knock on the door five minutes before the service starts."

Rory slid across a pew in the center of the church and leaned her elbows on the back of the pew ahead. She pulled out the kneeler and squeezed her eyes shut. The silence and darkness formed her chalkboard, host to a scrolling list of Herb Whistler's victims.

Joe McCullough. A good man in an impossible situation. His offense? A victim's response to a heinous act. He and his family would never see justice for that crime. Yet, somehow, they had patched their lives together and gone on. What if she turned Joe in? Would the memory of his provoked threat from decades past be construed as a forewarning of violence against the Whistlers? Could Jimmy's accidental death look like homicide, with Joe facing serious charges and jail time? Was she ready to take responsibility for destroying a family who had already suffered a terrible loss at the hands of Herb Whistler—a dead man—a man beyond the reach of the law, to wave the banner of righteousness? Jimmy Whistler. In his own way, another victim of Herb, his fate sealed before he was old enough to fight against it. And the money. No one missed it. No one, still walking this earth at least, was the better or worse for it—yet. She couldn't find a line to draw, a center point to divide right from wrong. The only way forward was to start the crawl—back up—against gravity.

Three loud knocks on the church's double doors jolted Rory's eyes open. Her knees throbbed from kneeling on the hard bench for what she was surprised to learn was half an hour.

"Is everything okay?" Chris called out from behind the double doors.

She rubbed her knees and stood up. "Fine, Chris. Just fine."

"Are you sure you don't want to stay for the service?" he asked as she passed back through the narthex, where he was putting flyers on a tabletop bulletin board.

"I can't today. There's somewhere I have to be. Please don't think I just used the space—disrespectfully."

"Did you use it to try to solve a problem, or to create one?" he asked.

"The latter," she answered.

"Glad to hear it. No worries."

She hobbled out of the church.

CHAPTER THIRTY-ONE

April 1 delivered another clear, dry morning to Southern Point. It was barely past nine when the front gate beeped and Sergeant Adderson's cruiser crept up the drive. Only after he cut the engine did it occur to Rory that she hadn't seen any other police personnel drive back to the site the entire morning.

He was pleasant as usual. "Good mornin' to ya, Mrs. Fielding."

Rory's heart was racing. "I ought to give you a reserved parking space, Sergeant," she said, working hard to sound calm and detached. "What's going on here today?"

"Is there somewhere we can talk?" He sounded as though he was either restrained or tired. She couldn't tell which.

"Let's go to my office," she said. *Office.* Her wishful thinking at work again. Would she ever have a business, a legitimate reason for the space? They walked to the garage and sat at her desk. "Any updates for me?" she asked.

He rubbed his face with one hand. Short sideburns, leveled to military precision, gave away a fresh haircut. His ever-present gum, which he chewed with the quiet, rhythmic desperation of an ex-smoker, rolled back and forth between his teeth and the right side of his mouth. Today's color was neon green. She didn't think it mattered much to him what flavor it was.

"First off, Mrs. Fielding, let me say how badly I feel about all the delays we've caused you," he said. "I know you planned to have your business underway by this date."

"I appreciate that," she said. "Where are you now—with the investigation?"

He leaned back in his chair, inhaled deeply through his nose, and resumed churning the gum in his mouth. "Well, that's just it."

"What do you mean, Sergeant?" Rory waited for the bomb to drop.

"When we're dealing with skeletal remains, dental records or identifying fractures are the best way to determine identity. Short of that, the skull and pelvis can determine gender and ethnic origin. We don't have either. We do know that it was a tall individual, probably a young adult. And based on estimated height and some fabric scraps nearby, most likely a male."

"Didn't you know all that back in February?"

"Well, mostly yes." He shifted in his chair. "The medical examiner believes that the deceased sustained an injury to the jaw—maybe a fall or a blow. He may have died on your property, or he could have died elsewhere and been transported here. Most buried bodies are victims of homicides, and shallow graves are typically associated with homicides because they were unplanned and dug quickly.

"Ms. Fielding, we've investigated missing person reports and unsolved murders as far back as the late sixties, and we've come up empty. He may have been transient, homeless; we have nothing to follow up on. We've been digging around your woods for three months now. What've we got? An arm bone, a piece of shattered jaw, and a seashell with a hole drilled in it. The community and the county have spent a lot of time and money out here, and no one's come up with anything solid."

"No one?" She felt her entire body loosen up with relief.

"We thought we were close the other day."

"Really? What did you find?"

"Well, at the eleventh hour, we got a new lead from a viewer who saw one of the news reports. Someone's grandfather remembered that years ago—decades back—a local boy rode around on a motorcycle on the farm lanes. You know, we thought the fender you saw might be connected to the body."

"Right. Whose body did you think it was?" she asked.

"Whistler. Jimmy Whistler. I'm sure you know that the Whistler family owned most of the land down here once, including yours." His jaw was locked in place as he said the Whistler name. "It was a stretch anyway; there was no way to be sure. But the medical examiner said she was willing to try to identify the remains through a DNA test if we found a maternal relative."

"What happened?"

"When we investigated, we found out that his last living relative, his mother, passed away a week or so ago in a nursing home in North Carolina. We called down there, and they said her ashes were scattered on Edenton Bay a few days ago. If we had found out in time, the medical examiner could have used the ashes to run the test."

"I guess it wasn't meant to be." Rory forced a neutral expression as she took in the news about Julia Whistler.

"Jimmy's mother had evidently been down there for a long time. People around here had forgotten about her. To be honest, I'd kinda forgotten about her too." He paused for a moment and then stood up and walked to the window. "Anyway, we don't think that would have panned out. The anthropologist and the medical examiner think that our minimal evidence points in another direction."

"What direction is that?"

"Remember that crazy girl who got drunk and drove her convertible under a tractor-trailer a couple of years ago? Her younger sister was decapitated, but she walked away. They think it might have been something like that—this person may have died in an accident and whoever was with him got scared and took him back there and buried him. They might not have had a license, or they were intoxicated, something along those lines. We'll never know. The man may have been undocumented, homeless, or a runaway, so he was never reported missing or dead."

"Why would a seashell be there?" she asked.

"Now, that's interesting. It's unlikely that it got there any other way but on purpose. It's actually from a mollusk found in Florida, not here, so we think it was also placed with the body. Dr. Kelsey told us that there was a slave tradition of burying shells with the dead; it was symbolic of returning to their homeland across the sea. But again, the skeleton isn't that old, and the shell was treated with sealant, a fairly recent practice. It could have been a necklace or bracelet, something like that, with that small hole in it. And we don't have any proof the bone is of African American descent, but the practice may be something adopted by another group of people. We're thinking maybe some migrant workers who came into the area from Florida. . . ."

"So, the fender wasn't important after all?"

"Well, it is a motorcycle fender. But we also found a washing machine, a roll of wire fencing, a baby blanket, scraps of an empty backpack or duffle bag, some car tires, and part of a rusted car door back there, so they were probably all dumped at different times over the years—meaning they're most likely unrelated to any past events out here."

"I'm sure that I saw two stretchers."

"The officers didn't want to risk leaving anything at the scene that might be of significance or take a chance on any of the items falling apart on the way out of the woods, in case they held evidence. Everything was so rotten—deteriorated. They used stretchers to keep it all together, and when the rain moved in, they covered the stretchers. Those damned news people nagged us for two days about it."

"I suspect they thought there was something—or someone—else on the stretchers." *Like I did*, she thought.

"I guess. Anyway, we've come to the end of all the leads we've been following, and as of now, the case, if there is one, is cold. The manner of death is still uncertain. Technically, it was homicide . . . accidental death . . . or suicide. In other words, we don't know the manner of death."

"What happens now?" she asked carefully.

"I have an official release for you to resume your farming activities. Of course, if you find any additional evidence—and it could come up in the course of working your land—notify me. My advice? If you want to keep us out of your woods, maybe you keep that area off limits to that Lab pup of yours." He laughed and shook his head. "Who knows what the little devil might dig up the next time?"

Rory searched his face for the slightest betrayal of his words, any indication that he knew more than he was saying about Jimmy Whistler. She came up dry. "Does that mean you're finished here?" she asked, and then held her breath, waiting for him to answer. She felt her heart begin to race.

"Unless you have something for me—some new lead, a piece of information you've been keepin' to yourself that's gonna blow the lid off this investigation."

Her pulse pounded in her ears. "Well, I—"

He talked over her. "You know, something to bring a violent criminal face-to-face with their long-overdue date with justice. Make things better for everyone involved. Anything like that."

"I do have something to tell you," she said slowly. "I want to tell you how much I appreciate your handling of this . . . investigation. Your consideration of me and my family."

"Well, families, they're what's most important in life. Got to do whatever it takes—to keep the good ones together, right? To protect them from heartache and harm from the bad ones."

"Absolutely," she said.

"Well then, Mrs. Fielding. Me and my people—we're finished here."

She wanted to scream with joy, and then remembered her problems were far from over.

The sergeant continued what she assumed was required police rhetoric. "I appreciate all you've done to cooperate during all of this, and again, I'm sorry about the delays."

Then he threw her off. "Now, let's just allow the dead to finally rest in peace, if that's what they deserve." He tipped his hat and adjusted his gun belt. "Good day to you, Ms. Fielding."

Of course he knows about Jimmy, she decided. He had probably known all along.

CHAPTER THIRTY-TWO

Rory watched from just outside the pasture as Tom's new white Suburban made a full revolution in the parking circle, and Ian climbed out, lugging a large backpack. He looked like he'd grown in the week he'd been gone, and he actually looked happy to see her. Tom stuck an arm out of the window and waved it absently a few times as he headed back down the drive, exiting Rory's life for another week.

"Mom?" Ian's voice was barely audible over an airborne flock of snow geese, ready to move on to colder climates. There were so many of them, flying so low to the ground, that Rory could hear the muffled pulses of their individual wingbeats. While their impending departure was a welcome harbinger of full spring, it also marked the end of any planning or construction extensions she could grant her business. Ian walked to the front pasture fence, where Olga trotted back and forth for the first time after weeks of stall confinement.

"How's she doing?" he asked quietly.

Rory was surprised at his question. As much as she'd hoped for it over the years, he'd never showed any interest in horses. "I think she's going to be fine, but we have to watch her for a while, just to be sure she's healed."

Ian let out a heavy sigh.

"You want to tell me what's going on?" she asked.

"Mom . . . ," he started, his voice free of expected rancor. "I think I'm tired of being a jackass."

Rory thought she'd misheard him. "Okay . . . do you want to explain a little bit more?"

"Well . . ." He swallowed hard. "I think I blamed you—I did blame you—for, you know, the divorce."

"I know it's been tough at times—"

"Mom, you always say I never talk, so let me talk now."

She smiled and nodded. "Touché."

"When I was at Dad's last week, I heard him talking on the phone with Kathie, the woman I met when he took me to DC." He twisted his hands and then clasped them together. "Remember—last March—before we moved?"

"Yes, Ian, I do remember last March," Rory answered. "But back to your dad. He and I are divorcing. He's allowed to date. So am I."

"I know that, Mom. But Dad was talking to Kathie about going to some resort or hotel place for the weekend."

"Honey, I know it's hard to hear about other people in our lives."

"No!" he insisted. "Dad was talking to her about going away to a resort, the same resort they visited last spring. Mom, that was a year ago. You weren't planning to separate a year ago, were you?"

"No, we . . . hadn't talked about it," she mumbled.

"Um, that means Dad was definitely fooling around on you," Ian said, looking as though he'd just solved a difficult puzzle.

"Yes, it does." She didn't have to incriminate Tom after all. He'd already done that himself.

"Were you fooling around on Dad too?"

"No, Ian."

"I didn't think so." He straightened up. "Well, then I guess I'm okay with you hanging out with that Dan guy. You're not gonna marry him, right? I'm not gonna have to call him Dad or anything, am I?"

She laughed. "Ian, I can't say that I'll never marry again. But I won't lie to you about any changes like that in my life. I know it hurts when you trust someone to be honest and they let you down. Honey, I promise I'll do my best."

Ian nodded. "I'm cool with that." Rory could tell that he had more on his mind. "Mom, after Dad finishes his trips up to DC for the sale of the agency, and he's home more. . . ."

She pushed the lump in her throat back down toward her stomach. "It's okay if you want to live with him—"

"I still want to live with you if that's okay."

She almost broke down in front of him. "Of course, it's okay. We can talk more about it after my trip to Baltimore."

"Your trip? I'm gonna go with you. We can talk about it *during*."

"Ian, I don't know if that's a good idea. I can't predict what's going to happen on this trip."

"That's why you shouldn't go by yourself," he said. "I should go with you—as long as you let me bring some good music along. Deal?"

"Deal," she answered back.

Classic rock blew out of the windows of Rory's truck all the way up north on Interstate 95 as she trailed Joe McCullough's rig into Baltimore. He led them through the outskirts of the city, ending the drive on a quiet street in an older neighborhood, north of the city.

"Mom, why didn't you tell Joe why we're really here?" Ian asked.

"Because I know if I did, he wouldn't have agreed to it," Rory answered matter-of-factly.

Joe pulled his tractor-trailer to a squealing stop in front of a freshly painted pink turn-of-the-century row house. Orange and yellow daylilies spilled out from a round brick garden in the center of the home's small front yard. Three white rocking chairs lined the front porch. Rory pulled up behind Joe's truck and waited for him to approach their car.

He walked over to her door and pushed his hat up on his head. "I know ya mean well, but I gotta say, I don't like this."

"We had an agreement, Joe. Remember?"

"Yes, I remember."

Rory and Ian followed Joe up a wheelchair ramp covered in AstroTurf leading to the front door. Joe knocked twice and looked through a window while they waited. The door was opened by a pretty woman about Rory's age and height, her dark hair pulled tight in a low ponytail with a red bow. She was wearing bright green scrubs and white orthopedic clogs. She smiled at Rory and Ian, and then hugged Joe. "Glad you made it here okay, Dad. You wore your seat belt, didn't you?"

She stepped backward into the house and they followed.

"Yes, child, I did. Now, I think I'll go out back for a minute." He tucked his broad shoulders inward and negotiated the narrow hallway, leaving the three of them in the entry.

"Kerry, I'm Rory Fielding, and this is my son, Ian. Thank you for letting me—us—come to see you." She smiled at Ian.

Kerry led them into the living room. Ian made his way to an overstuffed recliner, while Rory sat next to Kerry on a sofa under the front picture window.

"Rory, I know my dad told you our story...."

"He did, and I just want to say how sorry I am for what you've been through. Honestly, some of it was hard to believe the first time I heard it."

"Whatever my dad told you—it's the truth."

"I know it is."

"If he told you everything, I'm not sure I understand why you ... wanted to see me."

"Kerry, before your dad told me about the night Jimmy died, I visited Jimmy's mother, Julia Whistler."

"I didn't know she was still alive."

"She was—until a week ago—down in North Carolina. When I visited her, she told me about Herb, how he tried to pressure you into an abortion, and how he threatened your family."

Sadness from the memory passed over Kerry's face, oddly countered by loud giggling emanating from the back of the house.

"Kerry, Mrs. Whistler regretted her part in not stopping Herb from hurting your family. She believed she was as guilty as he was. I'm certain she wanted you to know that. It was as though she hung on long enough to try to make some sort of peace for what happened."

"Well, she lost her son. And I know she suffered, living with that evil man."

"She asked for your forgiveness."

"You came all the way here to tell me this?"

Rory put her hand on Kerry's. "So much has happened to your family, and to mine, since this started. I needed to meet you, and to tell you in person about Mrs. Whistler. I don't know. ... I may be here as much for me as I am for you."

"Excuse me. Can I use the bathroom?" Ian asked.

"Yes, of course," Kerry said, pointing to a door across the hall from the living room. "Through there."

He got up and left them alone.

Kerry leaned in and half-whispered, "I've never told my dad this, but when Jimmy, when we—when James was conceived—it was only the one time we were together. Jimmy had asked if I would meet him out in the woods. I was only fifteen and he was seventeen. We were friends—we were so close. He was upset because he couldn't get into the army and leave his dad. He'd failed one of the tests. He knew I'd always listen to him." She halted a stream of tears from her eyes with a tissue. "When he got there—to our secret place—he was drunk. I tried to talk to him, but he started—doing things to me. I told him to stop, but he wouldn't. It was too soon for me—I didn't want to." The last words came choking out of her. "After, he said he was sorry, and told me he didn't know what made him do it. I never told my dad how it happened. He still thinks we were carrying on like that the whole time, but we weren't. That was the first—and only—time for me with Jimmy. I loved him—trusted him. And then he did that to me." She cried into her cupped hands. "Then that night, a year later, what he tried to do to James, his own child—our child . . ."

Rory put her arm around Kerry's shoulders. "I would never tell you what to do, but I believe your dad would understand—would want to know the truth. Would want to know that you trusted enough him to tell him the whole story."

The bathroom door opened, and Ian emerged. "Is something wrong?" he asked.

Kerry ran out of the room, returning moments later with another tissue in her hand. She leaned in the doorway and wiped her eyes. "You know, my dad and I only see each other once or twice a month, and I miss home. . . ." She took a deep breath and held it, as if to calm herself.

"Kerry, I think your family's days of hiding are over. As long as I live on Whistler Ridge, those woods will remain undisturbed. I don't want you to lose any more time. No good can be gained by resurrecting the ghost of Herb Whistler. He ruined enough lives the first time around." As Rory said the words, a wave of peace passed through her. She felt unburdened for the first time in months, washed clean, as though she'd stepped out of a heavy, tattered skin. Things were beginning to make sense again.

Kerry's eyes lit up. "Would you like to meet my son? I'll be right back." She left to walk down the hall. "Dad?" she called out. "Some help?"

Ian looked at Rory. "It's going to be okay, isn't it?"

"Yeah, it's going to be fine."

Joe came down the hall first. Behind him, Kerry pushed a young man with a full Afro. He was wearing blue sweats that matched his wheelchair. He looked about thirty, the age James would be. He smiled at Ian.

"This is my son, James," Kerry said. "James, say hi to Rory and Ian."

"Hi, Rory-dean." His smile crashed into a frown with the sudden lurching of his arms and legs. Seconds later, the spasm stopped. He smiled again.

Ian waved his hand. "Hey, James. Nice hair." He pointed to his own mop of curls.

"It's nice to meet you, James," Rory said. She saw Joe's unease with her presence in the house and pulled out her keys. "Ian, we'd better go. Traffic's crazy and we need to be home by tonight."

"Wait," Kerry said. "Can you stay for a quick minute? We'll fix some lunch before you get on the road again." She threw Joe a stern look. "Right, Dad?"

They sat around the table in Kerry's kitchen, eating sandwiches and coleslaw. Kerry talked about her dream of completing nursing school, or maybe even medical school, while Joe carefully fed James, never losing patience with him as he struggled to bring a spoon or cup to his mouth.

"It was just a young girl's dream," Kerry said. "I'm afraid I wouldn't be able to do that now. I think I'm too old to start over—take that risk."

"Kerry, it's never too late for a dream—to start over," Rory said. She wanted it to be true for herself, too. "Don't let fear hold you back." She turned to Joe. "I have a question for you."

"All right." He was like a different man here with his daughter and grandson; the years he'd worn on his face for months now gone.

"There was a seashell found with Jimmy's remains," Rory said. "The police thought it might be significant—tied to an old funeral tradition."

"Oh, I don't know 'bout that funeral idea. But there was a shell I left behind. Did I forget to tell you about that?" Joe asked. "Kerry gave that to me when she was a little girl, when I took her with me on a trip to Florida. It was a vacation, even though I had to make a side trip and deliver a load of produce on our way home. She bought the shell with her own money." He looked lovingly at his daughter. "Had it polished up and strung on a piece of leather, just for me. I always carried the shell in my pocket for luck. When Jimmy died, I thought about Kerry. 'Bout how she would want me to put somethin' of hers—with him."

"The drinking is really what killed him," Kerry said. "He wasn't always that way. It changed him into someone else, someone I didn't know. That last night, when he hurt James . . . when I looked into his eyes—I saw. I saw that he was already dead." She pressed a hand to her chest, over her heart, and held it there. "Dead—in here."

James was restless, signaling the end of lunch. For the second time that day, Rory and Ian got up to leave Kerry's house.

"Thank you—bless you," Kerry called after them as they walked out the front door to the sidewalk. She wheeled James to the front porch, where he managed a goodbye wave.

Joe came out of the house after them. "Miss—Rory—wait. Your son forgot his backpack."

"No, he didn't," Rory said as they walked to her truck. "You missed something in the woods the night Jimmy died. Nothing can replace what he took from your family all those years ago, but what's in this bag rightfully belongs to you, Kerry, and to James. I know you'll find a good use for it. See you around, Joe."

Rory and Ian climbed into the truck and watched through their rearview mirrors as Joe handed Kerry the backpack. As Rory's truck cleared the stop sign at the end of the street, Kerry's pink house disappeared from view.

"What do you think she'll do with the fifty thousand dollars, Mom?" Ian asked.

"Start over, I hope."

CHAPTER THIRTY-THREE

On April 3, Rory woke up a little later than usual. She decided to let Ian sleep in, too; she could drive him to school if he missed the bus, or maybe let him take the day off.

The final deadline for spring planting had passed, and that meant not opening her boarding business in September. Getting the job done in time would have required a small army of workers and equipment; she had access to neither. The pasture grass seed mix was a special-order brand out of Kentucky and took a week or more to ship. She had a respect for the farming way of life. A family's livelihood and its traditions rested on a few short weeks, some seeds, and equipment most people would never see or think about.

Her decision was made. She would sell Titian to Rebecca Kent, owner of Kent Farm, for twenty thousand dollars.

That way she might catch a glimpse of him when she passed by Rebecca's farm—when Rebecca wasn't trailering him to statewide and East Coast shows. Or keeping him in his stall to prevent him from rolling in the mud or kicking up his heels or otherwise acting like . . . a horse. She would dig out her black pumps and suits and go back into the business world part-time, as a consultant. That would tide her over until fall, and then she'd have another go at establishing her pastures, or she'd sell the farm. She'd run through most of her settlement money. And she'd run through Dan, the only man she had ever really loved, and the only man who had figured out how to love her. But she had Ian again, and the McCullough family had their future back. It didn't seem worth the risk, worth what Tom called her silly dream, to get to where she was now, but she had made her choices and she had to live with them.

Al and Rocket dozed in the morning sun on the living room floor. No sound came from Ian's room. It was strange to have a quiet house after months of turmoil. The clock said seven forty, and she knew the horses were anxious to get outside. It looked to be a beautiful day, so she opened the windows in the front of the house and was greeted by red-winged blackbirds and house finches warring over their last free meal up for grabs at the bird feeder. She fed them in the fall and winter but tapered off in the spring when their natural food was in ample supply. The larger birds clung to the base of the feeder, flapping their wings and picking at the seed. The smaller ones hopped on the ground, waiting for cast-off seeds to drop like manna from above.

Without warning, the dogs were up, a frenzy of growls, barks, and claws and paws on windowsills, all in response to a line of tractors and trucks, led by Dan's red pickup, hauling various implements across the front lawn. The chain of vehicles swung wide around the side yard, heading straight to the first pasture. Behind them was Joe McCullough's flatbed tractor-trailer, loaded with tightly bound green-and-black bags. While she couldn't make out the writing on the bags, they were ringers for the special-order grass seed she'd needed for the horse pastures. She threw on a jacket and headed outside.

"Dan, who are all these people?" Rory asked, out of breath from running to catch up with his truck, which was now parked in the pasture.

"Months back I promised to help you. I keep my promises."

"But what are they doing *here*?"

"Nothing much. Just planting a little grass seed."

"I—I never placed an order for seed. I don't have any money for a palette of grass seed. How did it get here?"

"I ordered it for you," he answered. "My treat. A farm-warming gift. Kind of like a covered dish—but different." Then he pointed at Joe McCullough. "Joe made the haul all the way to Kentucky and brought it back on his own dime. Said his family came into a little money recently."

"Isn't it too late to start this now—to chance that the grass will come in on time?"

"You managed to convince Joe McCullough and his daughter that it was never too late to start again, to take a chance. I think you should take your own advice."

"Do you think this can work?"

"I wouldn't be here if I didn't. Now, I think you need to make a phone call to what's-her-name Kent about not selling Titian to her, so she'll stop blabbing about it to me and everyone else. I need to get back to work so we can meet that deadline."

CHAPTER THIRTY-FOUR

Another weekday morning and Sandy was due any minute. Rory gathered together cleaning supplies and lined them up on the kitchen counter.

"Mom!" Ian yelled from the front hallway. "The mail is here. You got a package."

"Would you take Rocket and go get it?" Rory asked. "It's probably some tax forms. Tomorrow's April fifteenth."

"All right." He called Rocket to the door. She had doubled in size since they'd moved in and had learned a few simple commands.

Rory went to the back of the house to check the status of the pastures. In two weeks, fine razor-sharp blades of new grass had cut through the dark soil, thanks to unusually high levels of rain. Because Sandy's cousin had pushed through a line of credit for Rory at Southern Point Farmer's Bank, oak-board fencing was up in two pastures, with three left to complete. The barn kit, wrapped in black plastic and stacked in fifteen-foot-high mounds, sat on large palettes in the first pasture, waiting for a few days of dry weather to permit the pouring of its concrete footings.

The front door slammed, and Rocket skated across the floor, startling Rory back to the unknown delivery.

"Mom!" Ian shouted. "It's from someone in North Carolina. What's the Brook Manor Rehabilitation Center?" He handed her a package the size of a shoebox.

She pulled off the mailing wrapper. A note was taped to the top of a plain cardboard carton:

Dear Ms. Fielding, please call my office upon receipt. Thank you for your time.
  —Joan Beyer, Administrator
  Brook Manor Rehabilitation Center

Thinking the delivery was made in error—some assumed family ties from her recent visits to Julia—she bypassed opening the carton, tucked it under her arm, and called the number on the return address.

"Joan Beyer."

"Ms. Beyer. I'm Rory Fielding. You sent me a package—"

"Yes. Thank you for calling me. I know this may sound strange, but I found your card among one of our resident's personal effects."

"Whose personal effects?" she asked, already knowing the answer.

"Mrs. Julia Whistler left us—passed away a few weeks ago. When my staff was cleaning out her room, they found your card and told me you had been to visit, that you were from her hometown."

"I live in the community where she spent most of her adult life, where she raised her family."

As Joan spoke, Rory opened the cardboard carton, revealing a black fabric-covered box.

"I'm sure this is a strange request," Joan said slowly. "Yes, I'm sure it is. And—well, I—could lose my license for this, or worse. Really hoping you're not recording this call."

"What do you mean?" Rory asked.

"Well, that box you have—it's her ashes."

The hair on Rory's neck stood up, and she almost dropped the box. "Her—you mean Julia—Julia Whistler? But the police told me that her ashes were scattered in the bay two weeks ago."

Joan sighed into the phone. "That's just it. She'd been with us for almost twenty-five years, and we all thought a lot of her. We always felt that she was a tortured, troubled soul."

"I can understand that, but what does this have to do with me?"

"Well, a few days before she died, Mrs. Whistler asked our head nurse to give her ashes to 'that tall lady with the curly hair.' No one knew what that meant until a nurse found your business card in Julia's nightstand and remembered that you had visited her."

"Yes, I did visit—twice."

"Anyway, Julia said she wanted you to have her ashes in case you ever saw her son, Jimmy. She wanted you to give them to him. You know, she'd always held out hope that she'd see him again someday. Her will stated that she wanted my staff to scatter her ashes in the bay, and I just assumed they had taken care of it. We were the closest thing she had to family, I guess. When the police up your way called me to impound her remains, I said that we'd already scattered them. When I found out later that we still had them, I decided it was best to send them to you. Perhaps you might know of an appropriate way to disperse them. A good place for them to rest. And we don't ever have to talk about this again, if you know what I mean...."

"Yes, I know what you mean." She said goodbye to Joan and then cut the seal on the box without opening it. Next, she called Dan and waited as his phone rang.

"Hello?"

"Hi, Dan."

"Yes, Aurora." He called her Aurora. She had missed that.

"Is there any way you could come over here this morning—help me with something? There's no one else I can ask."

"Building me up again, I see. Like a matchstick house next to a bonfire. What's going on? I haven't heard from you in more than a week."

"I know—I'm sorry. No—I'm not. I mean, I did what I should have done months ago. I sorted things out."

"Me too. Give me ten minutes." He hung up.

It was a little past eight o'clock by the time Dan arrived. Rory was out by the barn, waiting for him with a cup of coffee. Titian and Olga stood quietly by the gate, tacked up and ready to go.

"Good morning and thank you," she said to him, depositing both sets of reins into his open hand.

"So . . . what's going on here?" He looked at the horses, his brow pensive and a little troubled, and rubbed his beard stubble. "You're gifting me your horses? I thought we solved the whole 'horse selling' dilemma a couple of weeks back."

"We did. Just need you to hold them still for a moment, please."

Should I have shaved?" he asked. "Are we jousting?"

She smiled. "You're fine as you are."

Ian clomped down the deck steps in a pair of red Vans, his backpack fully loaded. "Mom, I'm leaving for the bus." He eyed Dan a bit critically, but managed to utter out of the side of his mouth, "How's it going, Mr. Deal?"

"Pretty damned good," Dan said. "Thanks for asking."

Rory walked partway down the driveway with Ian. "I'll see you when you get home," she told him before turning back to the barn. Dan looked bewildered when she returned to him with the black box under her arm.

"Are you taking Olga out to see how she goes on that leg of hers?" he asked.

"Yes and no. She's been good on the lunge and at a walk carrying a rider the past week."

He took a few gulps from his coffee cup before setting it on the fence post. "Are you going to tell me what this is all about, Rory?"

She took Olga's set of bridle reins. "You ride Titian."

"Okay, I'm in," he said. "No camera today?"

"No camera," she confirmed. "This is definitely one of those no-camera, face-life-head-on situations you warned me about."

Dan held the black box while Rory mounted her horse, handing it back to her once she had settled in her saddle. Then he carefully hoisted himself into place atop Titian and patted his neck, respectful of the burden he was asking the horse to carry. Rory slid the box into a large saddlebag attached to Olga's cantle.

As they made their way past pyramids of lumber and building supplies, the fragrance of honeysuckle, draped between the evergreen and gum trees lining the inside of the property border, hit them like a thick curtain. Red-winged blackbirds babbled and whistled back and forth to one another from the safety of pine saplings and fence rails. The sky was a pale, cloudless blue with a lone bald eagle circling overhead, gliding so high in the atmosphere that its features were reduced to a brown bar with white spots on either end. The horses snorted off pollen and dust as they paced together along the tire tracks left by four months of steady traffic. Despite the solemn circumstances, for Rory, it was the boat ride on Redhead Bay all over again. She wanted to freeze the moment right where they were and live inside it.

They came to a stop at the edge of the woods. Gum and maple trees stripped bare by the frosts and ice storms of the previous winter now presented a wall of bright green leaves that danced and snapped against the breeze, shielding Rory's farm from the degenerated Whistler homestead beyond. The dense canopy was alive with the trilling and chipping of warblers, chickadees, and squirrels, fervently driven by the instinct to find food and stake claim to nesting sites.

The police had painstakingly restored Jimmy Whistler's exhumation site to nearly its original condition: the dig site reburied, the soil neatly raked and tamped. All traces of Shelly King's plastic tepee and forensic tools and gadgets were gone.

Dan stepped his horse closer to Rory's. "You know, if you had moved here in the spring, with the woods dense like they are now—hiding the ground—I'd venture a guess that most of the chaos of the last four months wouldn't have happened. Your new barn would block your view from the house. No 'shiny object' to start the wheels of the investigation—no digging up the past."

She turned to him. "People talk about destiny. Growing up the way I did, I used to pray every day for things to change. They didn't, so I stopped believing in any of that. But look at what's happened. The chain of events, the past, the present, all melding together, bringing us here—to this place—today. I believe it was destined. For the Whistlers, the McCulloughs—and for me." She reached into her saddlebag for the package. "I even learned how to cry again. Now, I just have to learn how to stop!"

"Maybe so," he said, staring at the box in her hands. "Are you going to tell me what's in that thing you've been shepherding so vigilantly?"

"It's Julia Whistler."

He looked as though he'd been tased into silence.

"It's her ashes. "You know she died only recently," Rory continued. "The nursing home sent them to me. They arrived this morning. Before she died, Julia said she wanted her ashes to be given to Jimmy. This is the closest thing—the best way I know of—to fulfill that request."

"You're sure you want the ashes here—on your property—knowing the Whistler's whole story?"

"Julia told me that all she wanted was to see Jimmy again someday. I'm certain this wasn't what she hoped for. In her way, Julia Whistler loved her son . . . and all they really had was each other. Where better to end things than here?" she asked, searching his face for some show of affirmation.

"Agreed."

She took a deep breath. The top of the heavy box slid open easily, pouring a stream of fine gray powder onto the leaves below. "Oh God, I thought they would—"

"They're heavy, Rory, with all the sins and pain from life." Dan leaned toward her in his saddle. "Let me help you with that."

Rory laid her reins down on Olga's neck and stretched out her arms, cradling the box. He covered her hands with his for a moment. Her pulse surged at the warmth of his touch.

"You said it, Dan. Gravity. Back to the earth." She forced her eyes to meet his. "We belong here. All of us. We . . . earthbound creatures. This—today—is the end of the Whistler's journey. What about ours? Do we end here, too?"

Dan smiled softly and took the box. "I think we've got a distance to go on this journey of ours."

Rory put a hand to her cheek to brush away a tear, but instead let it fall, watching Dan guide Titian to the edge of the wood line. As Dan shook the open box from side to side, a sudden breath of wind picked up, ferrying a final plume of ashes into the woods until they disappeared.

EARTHBOUND CREATURES

Thoroughbred Retirement Foundation
https://www.trfinc.org
The Thoroughbred Retirement Foundation is the largest equine sanctuary in the world devoted to the rescue, retirement, and retraining of Thoroughbreds.

Love EARTHBOUND CREATURES?
Read Volumes I and II of Jennifer Olmstead's
VIRGINIA SOUTHERN POINT COLLECTION
"Fiction you wish was reality."©

Available in soft cover and e-reader/Kindle versions worldwide
Visit: www.jenniferolmstead.net
FB: Jennifer Olmstead, Author   Twitter: jolmsteadwrites
AMAZON.COM and other retailers

Made in the USA
Middletown, DE
14 October 2023

40579041R00156